MIDSHIPMAN GRAHAM

AND

THE

BATTLE OF ABUKIR

Midshipman Graham

and

the

Battle of Abukir

by

James Boschert

www.penmorepress.com

Midshipman Graham and the Battle of Abukir by James Boschert

Copyright © 2017 James Boschert

ISBN-13: 978-1-946409-22-5(Paperback)
ISBN :13: 978-1-946409-23-2 (e-book)

BISAC Subject Headings:
FIC014000FICTION / Historical
FIC032000FICTION / War & Military
FIC031020FICTION / Thrillers / Historical
Editing: Terri Carter, Chris Wozney
Editing: Danielle Boschert
Cover Illustration by Christine Horner

Address all correspondence to:

Penmore Press LLC
920 N Javelina Pl
Tucson AZ 85748

DEDICATION

To Danielle and Markus my islands of support

ACKNOWLEDGEMENTS

Bonaparte in Egypt by Christopher Herold
Wikipedia

Awards

When the Grand Seignior of Constantinople, who was still suffering from the shock of the great defeat inflicted upon his armies at Mount Thabor, learned of the retreat of the French from Acre, he was overcome with joy and presented the messenger who bore the tidings with seven purses of gold containing 3,000 florins. He despatched a special Tartar courier to Sir, Sidney Smith with an aigrette and sable furs (similar to those presented to Lord Nelson, for the victory of the Nile) worth 25,000 piastres and afterwards conferred upon him the insignia of the Ottoman Order of the Crescent.

In England, once news of the event had arrived there was tremendous enthusiasm and Parliament passed a formal note of thanks on behalf of the nation to Commodore Sir Sidney Smith and the officers and men under his command.

A pension of One thousand pounds per annum was also voted to the gallant commodore as a further testimonial to his great services. The City of London presented him with its freedom and a sword valued at 100 guineas. From the Turkey Company he received another valued at 300 guineas.

Eastern Mediterranean Theater of Operation for Sir Sidney Smith

CHAPTER 1

AN ARMY IN RETREAT

Two large war ships were about a mile off shore; with their white sails full set, including top gallants and top sails, they looked beautiful against the azure blue of the sky and the green-blue of the sea. The two broad, dark lines running from bow to stern denoted that the ships were Third Rate war ships of the British Navy. They had been brought as close to the shoreline as it was safely possible and their guns run out, showing their teeth to an enemy who knew that these otherwise beautiful vessels represented imminent and terrible danger.

To the exhausted men trudging along the coast road, it was yet another example of the long reach of the British Navy. They knew what was about to happen, yet despite the clear menace discipline held, and the long column continued to march.

The ships announced their intentions with rippling smoke along their sides. This was quickly followed by the distant boom of the 32-pounder guns, then the terrifying howl of iron balls hurtling overhead, hammering into the beach or smashing into the ranks, and the screaming began.

Aboard the leading ship, *HMS Tigre*, Midshipman Duncan Graham was perched uncomfortably high on the crosstrees of the main mast. The light offshore wind was ruffling his reddish blond hair but it did little to cool him despite the height above the decks. He wiped away the sweat which was trickling down his forehead into his eyes with the sleeve of his jacket wishing he could take it off. The merciless sun almost directly overhead was burning his lightly freckled face. His hat, which had almost blown off his head twice now was wedged in a secure junction of the mast and beam.

He lifted the borrowed glass and stared towards the long blue and white column of marching men to the east. They were moving along the only road to Egypt along the Sinai desert coast, and he marveled at their discipline. They could have, even should have, dispersed by now, but they barely seemed to notice the two ships preparing to send death and dismemberment in among their ranks.

The crash of guns shook the ship but Duncan rode out the bucking motion with practiced ease. He had been sent up here to observe the effect of the shot. It was a long moment before he finally did see what happened. 32-pounder balls ploughed into the beaches ahead of the marching column, throwing up large sprays of sand; others ricocheted off rocks and then smashed into the French ranks, throwing the bloody and torn victims about like rag dolls. To his astonishment the column seemed to reassert itself, shrug off the destruction and continued marching.

"By God, I dinna ken how they do it!" Duncan marveled, his Scottish accent always stronger when excited.

"Them's brave men, those Froggies are, Sorr," commented one of the sailors sharing the top mast with Duncan. "Ah would hate to be them right now. Remember how they just kept on comin' at Acre?"

Midshipman Graham did remember. He had been on the walls from time to time with the Commodore, as the Turkish garrison and British ships repulsed attack after attack by the French, who had come like a blue tide to wash up against the high stone walls of the city and then had drained back again, leaving their dead and wounded behind. He could still hear the screams of the wounded and dying at the base of the walls.

Now this same army was in retreat, but Commodore Sir Sidney Smith was not about to let Napoléon off with a nod. His intent was to harry the French all the way back to Egypt.

"Call down the shot, Midshipman Graham! If I have to come up there and show you what to do there will be trouble!" The voice of Lt Bowles roared from the quarterdeck below where a group of officers were gathered. The Commodore himself was standing with several other officers on the poop deck port side with their glasses to their eyes, staring at the distant shoreline. Lest he forget who was on board, the blue pennant of Sir Sidney Smith snapped in the breeze directly above his head.

"On target, Sir!" he called down quickly, with a glance at the sailor next to him, whose expression was wooden. "Or as near to dammit as we are likely to be at this range," he muttered under his breath. The sailor grinned.

He heard a shouted command, there was a pause, and then the ship shook again to the roar of fifteen heavy guns firing at almost the same time. Acrid smoke billowed high in the air, obscuring for a brief moment even the view from the top mast.

"On target, Sir!"

He heard the voice of Lieutenant Bowles but this time it was directed at some other luckless person. "That was very badly done! I want the names of the gun captains who were late!"

Duncan exchanged glances with the sailor again. Someone was going to get hell down in the stinking, crowded, smoke-filled gun deck. They both heard the answering bellow from HMS Alliance, the frigate that had been following in their wake, as she let loose her broadside, and they witnessed even more destruction.

"Poor bastards," Duncan commented to himself. "They don't stand a chance."

He noted that the column was turning inland behind the cover of sand dunes, gradually disappearing from view.

He looked forward along the shore to where he could see the dark line of some rocky teeth protruding from the beach well out to sea. His attention immediately switched to the danger the ship faced should they continue to sail this close to shore.

"Deck below there! Rocks dead ahead, half a league!" he yelled at the top of his lungs.

His shout generated a lot of activity on the deck below. Orders were bellowed, bosun's mates herded men to their places, and men came running up the shrouds to take in sail, while the angle of the main sails was shifted to allow the vessel to turn more speedily. In only a few minutes the ship heeled gently as she was set upon a new course that would take her out to sea. Signal flags were run up and the ship behind them altered course to follow *HMS Tigre* out of harm's way. Obstacles at sea took precedence over a defeated army.

The French army, after several weeks of forced marching from Acre, harried constantly by the Bedouin on land and by Sir Sidney Smith's ships wherever the road came close to the shore, finally reached Katya on June 5th. At this point the army was so strung out that it was just one long thin line covering many kilometers, trailing back into the desert of Sinai. Many of the soldiers had drifted off the roads and become lost because they could no longer see where they were going, many were half mad with thirst and could barely walk. Others just wandered off into the desert to die or to be tortured to death by the ever-present Arabs who lurked on the outskirts of the army all along its path, preying on luckless men.

That evening the commanders at Katya fired a field gun at regular intervals to help the men at the rear or wandering off the road to find where the main army had encamped. The enticement was that here they could find sweet fresh water and rest before the final push on to Cairo: a land that was verdant and where food and water could be found aplenty. Many arrived long after nightfall, but still more did not arrive at all.

The army was in total disarray and morale was at rock bottom.

Captain Clément of the Carabiniere d'Infantrie and his men were no exception. They were staggering with exhaustion, their lips were parched and cracked with thirst, and their eyes burned red with the grit and sand blown into their faces by the fierce desert wind, which scoured the skin to raw bleeding sores. It took four men to carry the captain's comrade who had been wounded in the thigh from one of the scraps with the Bedouin. They staggered under the weight of the officer and often stumbled. When they fell it was usually without warning, and Captain Horace Jean Baptiste would often cry out with pain, even though he tried very hard not to. It would take long minutes for them all to scramble back onto their feet and then Captain Clément would order another four from his company to pick up the makeshift stretcher. On they would go for another league.

Clément admired his friend for his forbearance but knew that there was a fine line between his men continuing to carry Horace and defying his orders. His men were demoralized and exhausted. The defeat at Acre, and they all knew it had been a defeat, even if Napoléon said otherwise, had hurt the morale of this army to its core. Only an ingrained discipline held his tiny group together, determined to reach Katya and safety.

Horace himself knew other men had been abandoned in the desert to the tender mercies of the Bedouin, so he held his peace when they grumbled, knowing that his life depended on these men. As darkness approached they grew apprehensive. They were the rear-end stragglers, and there was no safety in being last. Still Clément urged them on, even taking his turn at carrying Horace.

"Corporal, make sure that you cover our rear. It cannot be too long now before we are at Katya, where we can rest and obtain water," he tried to reassure them. No one responded; they were too tired.

They all heard the dull thud of a distant gun. The men stopped to listen. Over the otherwise eerily silent desert came another distant thump.

"A gun! There is where we must be tonight!" Captain Clément croaked. "The van is either engaged or they are telling us where they are. I hope it is Katya," he finished through his cracked lips and swollen tongue. He unwound the cotton scarf he had about his lower face and wiped his forehead, and it came away dusty. He had almost ceased to sweat.

"I think they are telling us where Katya is so that we don't get lost in the dark, Sir," Corporal Émile grunted through his parched lips, as he and Gérard, another of the men, scanned the darkening desert behind them.

"Then let's make haste, as I don't want to be caught out here with the Bedouin. They have a nasty habit of cutting people up into pieces," Private Poupard grunted.

"If you mean for your meat, they would have to stew you in a large pot to soften you, and for all their trouble they'd only get a thin, stringy soup," Hugo, his companion in arms, commented. Corporal Émile waved an empty water bottle; he had not thrown his away, although many others had. "I am going to put Champagne in this when we get there!" he joked. It got a few grunts of amusement from others in the squad, but then they were silent again. They continued to stagger on.

"Captain! Captain! They are over there!" Corporal Émile warned. His voice took on an urgency when his captain failed to respond. "I can see horses to our left on that rise, Captain!"

Captain Clément shook his head to clear it. "Check your weapons!" he called to his company. The twenty men left under his command immediately glanced down at their flints and the pans. They had done this a hundred times and did it instinctively. Even though they were young, these were hard-bitten veterans who knew their lives depended upon being prepared.

"They will come in a rush," Corporal Émile muttered.

"Be ready to form ranks," the captain croaked. "Place Captain Horace next to me." When his men had complied he handed Horace a loaded pistol. "One shot, Horace."

"Thank you, my friend, I know what to do," Horace murmured with a weak smile. Clément drew his sword.

"Come on, you bastards. Come and feel my bayonet!" Hugo murmured.

Thirty or so horsemen had appeared on the rise to the left of the troops. They spurred their mounts and charged recklessly towards the French soldiers. Their light horses, bedecked in colored cloths and tassels, kicked up sand to waist height as they galloped down the sandy rise. Their masters, wearing loose turbans and clad in wide flowing robes, shouted battle cries and brandished muskets and swords. A few impulsive horsemen discharged their muskets in the general direction of the French, the bullets humming harmlessly overhead.

"They think they are dealing with finished men! We will have to teach them a lesson," Captain Clément called out to his men. "Form two ranks!" he shouted. "Front rank, kneel and prepare to fire!"

With almost clockwork precision the formerly ragged line of men quickly formed two straight lines of ten men with the front rank kneeling, their muskets pointed at the charging enemy, who continued to disturb the evening air with war cries as they rode headlong at their hated enemy.

"Come to papa," Claude, by far the largest man in the company, murmured as he sighted on an approaching horseman.

The very stillness and silence of the French soldiers should have alerted the Bedouin that these men were not easy prey, but greed for plunder blinded them and drove them forward.

The sun had already set, leaving a red glow in the western sky, and a light breeze sprang up out of the south. There was still sufficient light for the soldiers to see by, and now they waited calmly while Clément estimated the closing distance between the riders and his thin blue lines.

When the Bedouin were forty yards away he dropped his sword arm. "Front rank, fire!" he shouted, his voice hoarse.

The sharp crash and echo of the muskets in the evening air drowned out the yells of the Arabs. The muskets spouted smoke into the space between the French and the Bedouin, which the breeze wafted back over the soldiers, allowing them to observe their handiwork. The soldiers had aimed well, as a half-dozen men tumbled off their mounts into the sand.

"Rear rank, prepare to fire. Front rank reload!" Clément shouted. He was pleased with the shooting, but the impetus of the riders, while broken, had not been halted.

"Fire!" he called, and again the muskets spewed fire and death as his second line of muskets took their toll. When the smoke cleared they could see that many more of the Bedouin had fallen; their war cries changed to cries of pain and alarm. This time they dragged their horses to a stop, and the ones at the rear, seeing the destruction wrought by the French, spun their agile mounts and lashed and spurred their horses back up the slope to disappear into the gloom, leaving their luckless companions lying where they had fallen. Several of the horses quickly chased after the fleeing Bedouin, leaving a couple to stand looking lost near their former riders.

One rider had been thrown forward so far that he landed almost at the feet of the French soldiers. He was stunned by his fall and evidently wounded because he groaned, nevertheless he began to crawl, reaching for his musket, which had fallen with him.

"Sir?" Corporal Émile asked.

"Deal with it, Corporal," Clément said.

Émile took two steps forward, kicked the Bedouin onto his back and plunged a bayonet into his chest. The rest of the company watched with utter indifference as the Bedouin's arms and legs flailed, then he choked and fell back dead. In one smart motion Émile gave a sharp twist to his rifle, tugged out his long bayonet and stepped back into line, leaving the inert and bloody body of the Bedouin in the sand.

Clément didn't waste any time. "Get any water he had and then form up, men. Reload on the march and don't forget to take Captain Horace with us."

"The other enemy wounded, Captain?" Émile asked as a formality.

"We won't waste time on them. Their 'companions' will come back soon enough to loot their own. They don't have anything we want, other than water perhaps," Clément responded.

The men were grinning as they did as they were ordered and resumed their march. They liked their captain, he had started his career as one of them, so if Horace was his friend they would take him with them no matter how tired they were.

"That shook the bastards up!" Hugo muttered to Gérard as they plodded on.

"Hum," his companion muttered back. "I could do with a good horse right now, my legs are complaining."

"Your legs never stop complaining," Hugo grunted.

"Close up there," Corporal Émile called. "You, Hugo, have you reloaded yet?" he demanded.

"Done, Corporal," Hugo replied.

The whole company picked up the pace. No one wanted to be out here in the dark. The Bedouin would surely return.

Their breathing was labored as they staggered the last kilometer towards the picket lines and into the scattered encampment where the rest of the army had settled in for the night. Most of the men were too tired to go any further and collapsed where they were halted within the picket lines. Captain Clément and Corporal Émile detailed a couple of the men who could still stand to come with them and obtain water. No one cared about food at that moment, just water to slake their burning thirst.

Clément, exhausted though he was, saw that his men were given water and chivied them to find a place near to a fire, where he negotiated with the men already there to share some of their meagre rations with his own men. After this, he made sure Horace was taken to a makeshift medical tent where the doctors were doing their best to save the lives of those wounded who had made it thus far. He made sure that an orderly had begun to attend to his friend before leaving.

He then searched out and reported to his commander, Colonel Estagne, who greeted him with a wan smile. "If you keep this up, Captain, you will soon outrank the others because they will all be dead!" He laughed at his own wit. "You have a knack for survival. I see, though you have been wounded." His voice held some concern.

Captain Clément gave him a tired salute. "This, Sir?" He touched his bandaged head. "It is nothing." He grimaced. "My men are indifferent to hardship, so I must pretend to be so, too."

His colonel grunted. He was well aware of how tough his captain was. Clément went on to describe the final engagement and then the condition of the men.

"My comrade Horace, who has a thigh wound, was saved by my men's care and by the twenty men charged with carrying him in turns on a stretcher. Five of our unit died crossing the desert. An hour ago we held off a charge by the Bedouin, back about two kilometers."

"There was mention of a brisk firefight back up the road an hour or so ago. That must have been you, Captain. I suspect it was a last effort to cut us up. Pity any of those still out there." His colonel sighed and scratched his five days' growth of beard.

"You did well to bring in that many men. I shall mention you in my report when we get back. With any luck we might have made it through the worst of it."

He indicated a leather cup and a small bottle on the collapsible table nearby. "Join me for a cup of brandy?"

Clément nearly shook his head. All he wanted to do was obtain another long drink of water and put his head down for a week, but he nodded and stayed. His gray-haired colonel was a decent man, brave beyond doubt, yet somewhat aloof, an aristocrat. He didn't mingle with his men, leaving that to his company commanders. He did, however, have the ear of Général Bonaparte, and Clément was curious to know how things had gone at the top end of the army.

"You know that Captain Francis du Pont died of exhaustion? This is a true test of our men. It is a soldier's lot to endure, even more than to just survive a battle. Some men have it and others do not," the colonel remarked as he began to pour the clear liquid.

Clément nodded as he took a swig of the plum brandy. It burned its way down his dry throat and settled like fire in his empty stomach. The colonel listed the names of the officers who had not appeared, most having perished along the way. It was depressing news. His colonel went on to describe the gossip from the headquarters.

"Bonaparte is set on getting back to Cairo as soon as possible, but I suspect it will not be with us looking like a band of gypsies," he remarked. "Headquarters is still seething at the debacle at Acre, and that damned English Commodore, Sir Sidney Smith, is being cursed by everyone. We'll just have to get over it and hope that we can get back to France before too long."

"You will have to submit some names of your men for a promotion," he continued. "We have lost so many NCOs. Bring their names to me and I'll sign off on them immediately. We can't have great gaps in our ranks because of a lack of sergeants."

Clément agreed. He was prepared for this and had already marked out several men for promotion to Corporal; Émile was going to get the rank of Sergeant.

The stragglers limped in all that night and some even arrived at dawn. It became clear to those who had survived that they had lost a great number of men on that last leg of the march, and not all of them due to wounds or the heat. The Arabs had picked off every man they could. The stories told by those who had heard the screams as they were tortured to death were chilling.

The arrival of dawn revealed a disconsolate army. The men were revived somewhat by the plentiful and clean water available, also there was fresh food to be had. Even though they were still on the edge of real safety, Napoléon ordered the army to rest and recuperate while he thought about his next move. Those who understood the urgency began to work on reviving the morale of the men. Inspections were called and promotions in the ranks were made. Painfully the army collected itself and regrouped, so that within a week, although ragged and patched, it was once again a force to reckon with.

Chapter 2

Strategy

Along the way back from Acre, Napoléon had been thinking. This was not at all what he had envisioned for his army upon their return to Egypt. Indeed, he had imagined taking Constantinople before he even considered coming back to the Nile. Had it not been for that damned English admiral, Sir Sydney Smith, he might well have taken Acre, and from there he could easily have taken Cyprus and then gone on to the fabled city of Constantinople.

He paced slowly up and down the narrow confines of his tent, barely aware of the bustle of the camp all around as men re-organized themselves into their former companies and regiments. Even he had to acknowledge that his army was not in any shape to sound or look victorious. It was an army of men who resembled beggars and an army in retreat, although it was not part of his make-up to admit that they were a defeated army.

He paused and looked out of the tent opening at the bright sunlit sand. During his relatively short time in Egypt he had learned that it was the strong the Fellaheen looked up to. Not the vanquished. He could not possibly arrive at the gates of Cairo with his men in this condition. He shook his head vehemently.

"Call Colonel Estagne at once. I need to talk to him," he called out to the sentries. One of them immediately snapped to attention and ran off to comply with the order.

While he waited, Napoléon formulated a plan.

Colonel Estagne hurried into the tent, clicked to attention then snapped a salute. "Mon Général?" he queried his leader's back.

Napoléon turned from his thoughtful stance and said, "Ah, there you are, Estagne. Inform the generals that I have decided to spend some time in Katya resting the men. I will meet them this evening at dinner to discuss the overall plan, but for the time being I want them to separate the wounded from the fit men to send them to recuperate on the coast."

Colonel Estagne breathed a silent sigh of relief. He had not known how they could have marched much farther without some rest.

"You are to send an equerry, someone able like Ensign Andre perhaps, who will take a letter from me posthaste to Cairo and deliver it to Général Dugua. He is to observe complete discretion but he is to send food and plenty of it, as quickly as possible, along with clean new uniforms and boots to our army. Is that understood?"

"Yes, Mon Général."

"Find Général Murat and ask him to come and see me."

"Yes, Mon Général. Immediately."

Estagne saluted and left hurriedly.

Later that evening, Napoléon and his generals picked at their stringy boiled food. The only consolation was that there was still plenty of wine, albeit somewhat vinegary, to wash down the horrible concoction the cooks had valiantly tried to produce.

Sipping his wine and trying not to grimace at the sour taste, Napoléon enlarged upon his plan.

"You all know by now the kind of people we are dealing with here in Egypt. The Fellaheen are simple people, and although we have treated them fairly they are easily led by their treacherous sheiks. If they get the idea that we are an army in retreat, their leaders, ever on the look out for weakness, will cause problems. I want to at least give the illusion our men are well-fed and in high morale when we arrive back in Cairo."

He said to Murat, "You will have to provide an escort for the messenger who leaves at dawn. I must have that letter get through. We have no way of knowing how dangerous the road is between here and Cairo. I need to prepare the way for our victorious army, with its great success in the Syrian campaign, to make a triumphant entry into the city."

Général Murat smiled in wry agreement. "I shall make sure that the messenger gets to Cairo, Mon Général."

It was while the army was resting at Katya that Général Menou appeared. Napoléon had appointed him governor of Palestine almost three months previously. Menou had been so reluctant to leave Rosetta, and his new wife, that he had only made it this far in his journey to Syria.

When the general was shown to his tent, Napoléon had his back to him and kept him waiting for some very long moments. Finally he turned and looked the corpulent officer up and down with contempt. Menou, wearing the loose clothing of the Arabs, was definitely not dressed as a French officer should be. He looked more like a gaudy sheik. This served only to incense Napoléon, who had not been in a good frame of mind towards his wayward general to begin with. He strode up to his officer, his face suffused with rage.

"Good of you to come," he said, his tone dripping with sarcasm. "I was under the impression that you were to go to Palestine and be my governor!" Napoléon almost shouted this last sentence. Bonaparte barely came up to the shoulder of his errant general, his uniform was stained and dusty and his knee boots were scuffed, but there was no doubt whatsoever as to who was the dominant presence in the tent. Menou, sweating in the afternoon heat but even more from the ire of his leader, quailed under the fierce glare but even so attempted to defend himself. Napoléon, seething with anger at what he considered desertion by a senior officer, was not in the mood for excuses. He cut him off before he could speak.

"Be quiet! I am still talking. I should have you arrested and sent back to Cairo for court martial and then shot!" He turned his back on the frightened man.

"You are dismissed from the position, it no longer exists for you, and it remains to be seen if I shall pursue the charges of desertion and dereliction of duty. In the meantime, you will take yourself off with your entourage, Abdullah Menou, as I hear you call yourself now, and stay in Rosetta on pain of death. You are dismissed."

Menou knew better than to argue with this diminutive man facing him like an angry cockerel. Napoléon's erstwhile general saluted, then slunk out of the tent and made his way past the hostile officers gathered outside waiting to talk to Bonaparte. Having suffered the rigors and hardships of the siege of Acre and the long trek across the desert, these men despised Général Menou and wished him gone. They had hear the angry words of their general and such was their anger that many were the muttered threats of reprisal, should he show his face anywhere near them again.

Clément, who had been in attendance upon his colonel, was there to witness the scene. Once again he marveled at the power of Napoléon over his men. One would never know, he reflected to himself, that we are a defeated army.

His general might well have carried out his threat to Menou but he had much more pressing issues to deal with. It was important, however, that Menou stay in Rosetta and not go to Cairo, where he might have let it be known how depleted was the French army. He ordered one of his generals to provide an escort with explicit instructions to make sure Menou remained in exile.

Not very long after their arrival at Katya, and feeling somewhat more rested, Captain Clément walked over to the tent where his friend Horace lay on a crude pallet. The casualties were to be taken up towards the coast to recover from their injuries, or to be repatriated to France if their wounds were too severe. Horace's wound might just be severe enough to get him a trip home.

"At least you will have rest and good food, while we will have to go and parade in Cairo looking like a lot of popinjays with those ridiculous palm fronds he wants us to wear on our shakos," he told his friend.

"Ah, but after the parade you will doubtless avail yourself of the women and the wine, so I don't think I am getting the best of the bargain," Horace said with a grin. "My, my, but those surgeons are a rough crowd and no mistake," he winced as he shifted on his bed. "They just dump whoever is unfortunate enough to be next on the surgery table, already so covered in blood it resembles a butcher's block, and get to work without even saying good morning."

His friend looked alarmed. "Will you be all right?"

"Oh yes, they are competent, that isn't in doubt, and the orderlies are experienced. I suspect it's because they have seen so much that just another person lying on the table has become meaningless."

"We now you can loll about in one of the new carriages they have designed for the likes of you and enjoy a ride to the seaside," Clément told him. He was referring to the light carriages designed to carry wounded men rapidly and in relative comfort to and from the Surgeons.

"No women there, I fear," Horace said, pretending gloom.

Clément laughed, "Perhaps you are right, but cheer up Horace, my old friend. You might have ended up as so many others did in the hands of the Bedu. You will be well out of this, though. I can just imagine the beaches and the calming sound of the sea, with a horizon empty of those cursed English ships. Take good care, Horace, and see if you can't get onto a ship and back to France. This fly-infested country is no place for any of us."

They shook hands, and Clément turned away to see to his men, who were forming up for inspection in the remnants of their uniforms: their once white trousers and green jackets (which distinguished them from the Grenadiers), the red epaulettes with white cross bands torn and stained, or simply worn out. Some of the men didn't even have hats anymore; those that did wore them at all angles, and the distinctive red pom-poms were, for the most part, missing. To his professional eye however, the things that mattered were the muskets, bayonets and cutlasses, which were clean and polished and ready for use.

"We can't possibly go into Cairo like this," he thought to himself as he looked at the remains of his company. "As for victory...what victory?"

Captain Clément, who had once himself been a private soldier, looked his men over with critical eyes and pretended disgust. "I have no idea why I should have been put in charge of a bunch of brigands like you. Just look at you!" he joked.

"Do not fear, Mon Capitaine," the irrepressible Hugo said. "We will take on anyone you like and still beat the merde out of them."

The other ragamuffins facing the captain grinned their agreement. Morale was as high as ever, it would seem.

Clément had to turn aside. Though he stifled a laugh, there were tears in his eyes.

Chapter 3

An Incident in Cyprus

Sir Sidney Smith, having harassed the French all he could, proceeded by way of Beruta road to Larnaca road, Cyprus, in order to refit his little squadron.

The tiny fleet of ships sailed into Larnaca on the south coast of Cyprus in the first week of June. Most of the ships were badly in need of maintenance and this was the only port where they could affect meaningful repairs. *HMS Theseus*, although so damaged from an explosion it could hardly be called an effective war ship, was able to hold station while Sir Sidney took his other ships for re-victualing and re-supply. He brought with him the Alliance and the bomb ketches, all of which needed fresh supplies.

Midshipman Duncan Graham found himself once again up on the fore topmast yard, but this time he was on punishment. He had been involved in a squabble with his arch-enemy Tewksby, another midshipman. Nothing unusual about quarreling young men, but this had been too public for Lt Bowles to tolerate. Now they were perched on the cross trees of the main mast and the mizzen mast respectively.

Duncan still seethed at the unfairness of the punishment. He had ably demonstrated his familiarity with the sextant—he'd had a hard task master in his uncle and knew how to take the sun—such that he had calculated and predicted their point of arrival far more accurately than Tewksby, who, although his senior, was not a good hand at navigation. Duncan had spent many a long month at sea with his uncles on the Banks, where navigation without very much sun was a crucial part of their survival.

Tewksby had made the mistake of sneering at Duncan's figures. The ship's master had opened his mouth to correct Tewksby, but an incensed Duncan had opened his first and sworn at his tormentor. Lt Bowles had been on the quarterdeck at the time and had overheard.

He'd summoned the master and they'd held a short conversation, whereupon the two midshipmen had been ordered up the masts for the next two hours.

"In order that you will contemplate your impetuous words, Mr Graham. I shall not tolerate foul language on my deck. And you, Mr Tewksby, may contemplate your inability to navigate with any accuracy," he had told them and sent them aloft.

Duncan gloomily scanned the wide bay where they were anchored. Larnaca was a small town of only about five thousand souls, located towards the south side of the wide bay. It was an ugly jumble of mud-walled, flat-roofed mud brick houses with the occasional cypress tree or palm to break the brown monotony. He could see the tall tower of the Church of Saint Lazarus, an old Byzantine church, and the minarets of the mosque. The town had the only functioning dock yard in the entire island, so it was at the pier of this port that barges and the gun boats were tied, being repaired or re-supplied. The land around the bay was relatively flat, but somewhat greener than the desert countryside he had observed in eastern Egypt.

With the arrival of the British ships the ancient port had come alive. The Greeks, being ardent merchants, were not about to let this opportunity pass them by. There were dozens of lighters and small boats plying between the ships, carrying all manner of supplies, from iron balls and powder, to barrels of beef and great sacks of biscuit. Fresh vegetables were being hauled aboard in huge baskets, along with cages of hens and even several goats. Where they were going to put the live animals, Duncan had no idea. The already crowded main deck had little room, the quarterdeck was off limits, and the gun decks barely had room for the men, let alone a herd of bleating goats and noisy chickens.

He noted with wry disappointment that Larnaca would not be supplying women, as could be found in Spithead and other ports of England. The behavior he had witnessed by the boat women in those ports had been entertainment in of itself, without the need to explore their presence any further. Duncan had a shyness of women that was common enough among his mess mates. He was not unused to girls, but they represented an opaque and mysterious species of whom he had not had much experience. The Greek women, it would seem, were not inclined to mix with foreigners of any ilk.

He noticed idly that a small cutter was making its way deliberately and speedily between the traffic towards his ship. Peering down towards the deck he noted that an alert midshipman, Standforth he thought it might be had notified the quarterdeck. There was some bustling about as the marines lined the opening to the starboard side and the two bosun's mates, in white ducks, stood ready to pipe an officer aboard.

Soon the boat had pulled alongside, dropping its sail in one smooth motion that allowed it to bump gently against the gangplank hanging off the side of the ship. A man dressed in some kind of military uniform, Duncan could not tell what, jumped off the boat and clambered up the side of the ship to the shrill pipes of the bosun's mates and the crash of Royal Marines presenting arms. The man was met by Lt Bowles and immediately led below. Duncan wondered what was going on.

He looked about him. Off to his left in the distance he could see the foothills and the high rising mountain of Trudos, a green jumble of foothills that clung to the side of a significant peak, hazy in the heat of the summer day. He was sweating despite a light sea breeze and wondered if he had spoiled any chances of going ashore to enjoy the few taverns that lined the harbor front.

While he seethed another hour went by. Then he heard a noise from directly below his perch and a young face, surmounted by a mop of dirty blond hair stuffed under a naval hat, poked itself over the edge of the crosstrees. "Hello, Graham," said Standforth, the youngest of the midshipmen on the war ship.

"Hello, Minnow. How are ye?"

"Mr Fowler said you can come down now, as he wants to see you," Standforth said, as he settled himself next to Duncan.

"He does, does he? What's going on down there?" Duncan pointed at the abrupt activity below. Marines were assembling on deck and the boats were being prepared for launching.

"I have no idea, and if you don't hurry you might be spending the night up here," Standforth stated. "Come on, I'll race you down!" he called out cheerfully as he seized a line and began to descend to the deck, disdaining the shrouds. Duncan jumped for another line and, at the risk of burning his hands, sped down to the deck behind him.

They arrived almost together, whereupon Duncan checked his coat and hat, which had fallen askew, and then reported smartly to Lt Fowler.

"Ah, there you are Graham. You are late. You are coming with me in the jolly boat. Sir Sidney is going ashore."

Duncan glanced around at the assembled marines and armed seamen.

"May I ask respectfully why we are going ashore with so many men, Sir?"

"You might well ask. Sir Sidney, in his capacity as the commander of the Sultan's land and sea forces on the coast of Syria and Egypt, is responsible for representing the authority of the Sultan in that region and maintaining order. There appears to have been a mutiny."

"Does that mean," Duncan was excited, "that we are going into action, Sir?"

"Yes, quite possibly, now stop asking questions and get in the boat. The seamen have pistols and a cutlass for you there. Hurry up, now. You are holding us back."

"Yes, Sir!" Graham almost shouted. He cast a glance upward at the mizzen mast to check if Tewksby was still there but couldn't see him. "Pity that. I'd enjoy seeing him eating his heart out," he muttered to himself as he rushed over to the port side and the waiting crewmen, one of whom, Bosun's Mate Chauncey, grinned at him and tossed him a pistol and a cutlass in a sheath.

"Glad to see you're comin' with us, Sorr," he growled with a gap-toothed smile.

"Very glad to be going along, Chan." Graham grinned back as he checked the priming of the pistol.

The flotilla of boats crossed the water and the passengers made haste to disembark on the narrow wharf of the town. Lt Fowler, with Midshipman Graham and about twenty crewmen, represented the Navy. The men men formed up and waited for the officers to decide where they had to march. Sir Sidney Smith and his Royal Marine officers, Colonel Douglas of Marines, Major Bromley off the *Tigre* and two other junior marine officers from the Alliance huddled around a small, well polished bronze field gun that men were hitching it to some horses. Several saddled horses were being held in waiting off to the side.

Once the field gun was secured, Sir Sidney addressed the assembled men.

"We have been informed that there has been a mutiny by a certain number of Janissaries who have turned on their officers and are running wild. The information we have is that they are in the area of the villages of Aradhipou, and just beyond that the village of Alampra and Lympia. In other words, Gentlemen, they have cut off the town of Larnaca from Nicosia and are looting and pillaging the countryside."

He looked around at the officers. "In my capacity of Commander of the Land and Sea forces for the Sultan in this region, I am responsible for the good order and lawful behavior of the Sultan's forces. We are going to march to Aradhipou and persuade these men to surrender, then we will decide what to do with them."

"How far away is this village, Sir? Do we know?" Colonel Douglas asked.

"Only a couple of leagues and furthermore we have a guide in the presence of Captain Williams here, who has recently returned from there. Captain Williams is well known to myself and several of you here." Sir Sidney motioned Captain Williams to speak. The officer stepped forward and addressed the gathering.

"Gentlemen, just as Sir Sidney stated these are disaffected Janissaries. For the most part they are from Albania. The Turks have a law that takes the eldest child from each family for service in the ranks of the Janissaries. It is not a popular law, however, it is generally highly effective. In this case it would seem that the officers were too high-handed and indifferent to their grievances, so the men butchered them and are now running loose in the aforementioned villages." He paused to let this sink in. "It is important that we contain these men before they run wild all over the island and cause incalculable trouble. If they get among the foothills of Mount Trudos we will never winkle them out of the villages there and we cannot have that, as then they will threaten the entire island."

"We must make haste and nip this in the bud," Sir Sidney stated. "Gentlemen, to your places. We march at once!"

The column of Redcoats wound its way out of the port and along the single main street of Larnaca, which was lined with nervous but curious Greek inhabitants who cheered the men in a desultory manner as they passed, even throwing a few flowers in their path. Some shouted what seemed to be encouragement to the passing troops.

"It's somewhat ironic that we are marching to help these people against their own occupiers when we would prefer that they were independent of the Sultan," remarked Lt Fowler in an undertone, as he led the Naval contingent at the rear of the column.

Assuming his remark was directed at him, Duncan asked, "So all these people are Greek? Not Turks, Sir?" His voice was muffled. They had wrapped cloths over their noses to ward off the dust raised by the marching marines ahead of them.

"Yes indeed, Graham. The vast majority are Greek. They have been occupied since the Ottomans arrived, back in the fifteenth century. I doubt very much that there is any love lost on either side, and this situation doesn't help at all."

Duncan began to notice that there were native people traveling in the opposite direction. Laden donkeys led by very poor-looking men and their families trudged by, heading for the relative safety of Larnaca. Some women were carrying wailing children; older women clung to the backs of the over-loaded donkeys and hand carts being pushed by boys. They looked frightened.

It was less than an hour later when word moved along the line to halt. Leaving the sailors and the gun in Graham's charge, Lt Fowler made his way forward to where the officers were grouped. They had been marching through cultivated land almost all the way; but the road, if it could be called that, was simply a track wide enough for a small carriage.

Sir Sidney, now wearing the badge of a Commander for the Sultan of Ottoman on his hat, was staring at the low buildings of a village through his glass. A column of black smoke was billowing slowly into the sky, lending a desolate look to the place. The flat-roofed outlying hovels indicated it was a poor village.

"Not a very prepossessing place is it? We shall parley," Sir Sidney stated, wiping his neck with a handkerchief. "Ugh, it's hot!" He peered up at the remorseless, pale blue sky from which the sun burned down. "Wish it would rain," he muttered. "I don't see much activity, but there are some of the Janissaries if I am not mistaken. If they do not wish to surrender then we shall take the place and move along. I shall go with Captain Williams here; we'll need a white flag. I suppose they should respect a white flag, eh, Captain?"

"One might hope so. I would much prefer it if you did not go forward, Sir. I can go myself and take one man with me."

"No, I shall accompany you. They will see my badges of rank and there might be some hope that they will respect that."

Reluctantly, Captain Williams shook out a white handkerchief and tied it to his sword, then led the way forward towards the village.

They had not gone more than sixty yards when there was a puff of smoke, a report, and a ball hummed by, followed by a shout from one of the houses.

Captain Williams halted his horse and indicated to Sir Sidney that he should, too.

There followed a voluble exchange of words that only Captain Williams, who spoke Greek, French and several other languages, understood; but within a minute he turned to Sir Sidney and said, "They are not interested in surrender, Sir. They know only too well the penalty for mutiny. It is impalement. They told us to go away or they would shoot us."

"Bother. Do they understand that they will be under my protection if they do surrender?"

"I pointed that out to the man I was talking to, Sir. He sounded belligerent and not interested in anything we might have to offer."

Sir Sidney stared at the village for a long moment, then he lifted his reins and turned his horse. "Very well then, we shall assault the village and move on to the next one. We will have to be as careful as we can not to cause injury to any civilians who might still be left inside the village."

After a short conference, the orders came for the sailors with the field gun to come forward while the Royal Marines were formed up and marched to the flank. There the marines were divided up into two companies and formed up on either side of the gun, which was unlimbered from its horses and prepared for firing, while the animals were led to the rear. There were a brief few minutes of feverish activity, then the gunner turned to the colonel and raised his arm.

"Ready to fire, Sir!"

Lt Fowler came running back to the small group of sailors standing with Duncan, who was wondering what they were going to do.

"We follow the marines in and help with prisoners and wounded," he told his men. "Check your arms and prime weapons," he ordered.

The men saw to their arms while Duncan stood alongside Lt Fowler and stared at the impassive houses to their front. "Our job is to protect Sir Sidney and also to deal with any of the enemy who try to slip by," Fowler said. His excitement at the impending fight communicated itself to Duncan. He took a deep breath to still his rapidly beating heart and followed Fowler to stand near to Sir Sidney Smith and Colonel Douglas. Major Bromley was going to lead the marines into the village with the first wave of men.

Duncan heard the command, "Fix Bayonets!" followed by the sinister snick as the long bright blades were affixed to the barrels of the muskets. "Prepare to march!"

On a signal from Sir Sidney, the small field cannon boomed. A house wall disintegrated as the ball smashed into it, leaving a small landslide of rubble and a cloud of dust. When the smoke cleared Duncan could see some of the enemy moving into the opening and preparing to fire.

"Forward march!" Major Bromley called out, and started forward. The marines began to march in line abreast towards the houses, only about seventy yards away, their muskets at the ready with the bayonets glittering in the sun.

There was a spattering of shots, but the Janissaries aim was poor and the shots simply buzzed overhead.

Major Bromley shouted an order and the marines closed ranks, then the NCOs called out another order. There was a crash of musketry and some of the brightly-dressed insurgents fell, while others, seeing the firepower directed at them, turned and fled for better cover.

In response to Major Bromley's next command, the marines gave a cheer and ran forward. By now they were among the outlying hovels of the village. Major Bromley ordered the men to take advantage of cover but to keep moving forward. A general firefight ensued, where red-coated marines in small groups ran from house to house kicking in doors, yelling as they did so. The insurgents put up a stiff fight. Their backs were against the wall and they had nothing to lose, so they fought as hard as they could, but the discipline of the marines and their inexorable forward momentum made it very hard for the Janissaries to respond in kind. Casualties mounted on both sides, but before long the marines had gained the middle of the village and could pause.

"What a miserable place to fight over," remarked Lt Fowler as he and his sailors crouched on the corner of a dirt street. Musket balls smacked into the wall and chipped the corner nearby or hummed overhead.

"They do not impress me with their musketry," he remarked dryly.

They had been left behind by the marines who had galloped ahead in their enthusiasm to take the village. Sir Sydney had finally dismounted, due to the pleading of Lt Fowler, and was peering around the corner of the mud brick wall with the lieutenant.

"Wonder where they've gone?" he mused.

The first indication that they were in trouble came when one of the sailors uttered a yelp of pain and collapsed with nasty-looking knife sticking out of his leg. There followed a bloodthirsty yell and five insurgents charged out of the sun-dried wooden gates of a nearby house.

Within moments it was hand-to-hand fighting, but there were more of the sailors and they were protecting their Commodore who, not to be outdone by his men, was fighting alongside them, his sword flashing in the sunlight. Men hacked and stabbed at one another, screaming and yelling; the sailors were armed with pistols, which they used at close quarters then using them as clubs because there was no time to reload. Despite the fog of smoke that sometimes obscured targets, they were used to close quarter fighting so it was not long before they began to gain the upper hand.

His adrenaline pumping, Duncan stepped aside to dodge a flailing scimitar, then fired his pistol straight into the chest of a man who was about to stab Sir Sidney in the side. The man gave a cry and vanished underfoot. "Well done, Graham!" exclaimed Sir Sidney, when he realized what had happened.

Then Duncan had to fend off a savage swing from yet another huge dark man wearing a white turban who towered over him. He thought it had broken his wrist, the blow was so hard. But then came a volley from behind Duncan and the man, with a look of surprise on his face, fell over backwards to join his comrades lying in the dust.

Duncan whirled and saw that a small contingent of marines were standing behind his group, their muskets still smoking. "Reload!" bellowed their Sergeant.

"Thank you, Sergeant!" Sir Sidney nodded in approval to the marines. His youthful features were alight with the excitement of the engagement. "Come along, men. I fear we will be tardy and Colonel Douglas is expecting us," he said, with a grin at his men as he cleaned and sheathed his sword, then moved to reclaim and mounted his animal, which had drifted away while the men fought for their lives.

It fell to the sailors to tend to the wounded on both sides. Duncan had a chance to observe the enemy who were being looked after. For the most part they were dark-featured men with huge mustaches and black hostile eyes who regarded their captors with wariness. The fight had gone out of them, however, so it was not difficult to bind their wounds and start them on their way back to Larnaca under an escort. The walking wounded helping to carry their more seriously injured friends.

The Janissaries who'd surrendered were herded into a small group and told to squat on the ground under guard, while the marines and sailors checked the rest of the village for more holdouts. They noticed that some were fleeing down the road towards the other villages.

"Let's hope they are passing along the bad news," commented Lt Fowler as they watched them running away.

Duncan wiped the sweat from around his neck with a handkerchief. He was hot and dusty but still exhilarated from the encounter. "They don't appear to be very disciplined, Sir," he remarked.

"No, they are not; but then they are used to charging madly in among their enemies and creating fear and despondency. They certainly don't know how to fight in the manner we employ," the lieutenant replied. "But one must not underestimate the enemy, Graham. They do not lack courage."

Possibly because the fleeing men told the other insurgents what their fate would be, further resistance crumbled. Again a message was sent in advance to assure them that they would not be punished in the traditional sense—which would be a ghastly form of execution by impalement—but would instead be under the protection of Sir Sidney Smith.

As the column of Redcoats approached Alampra, three men dressed in the bright, baggy pants and red fez of the Janissaries were waiting for them outside the village, holding aloft a large white rag on a stick. Sir Sidney, with Captain Williams and Colonel Douglas and an escort of armed sailors, approached them warily.

Captain Williams listened to the men as they talked volubly for several minutes. He then turned to Sir Sidney and said, "They want to surrender to you personally, Sir. They will not surrender to anyone else, as they do not trust the officers of the Turkish Army."

Sir Sidney nodded acceptance. "Very well, I accept their surrender. We will escort them all back to Larnaca and there I shall decide what to do with them. Tell them they are to put down their arms and they are to go with us back to Larnaca."

There followed a lively exchange between Captain Williams and the men, who reluctantly agreed to the terms; amid much gesticulation, they hurried off to tell their companions.

Apparently, the terms were agreeable to the rest of the insurgents, not just at Alampra but at Lympia as well, so under a white flag and the supervision of the marines, they began the march back to the town of Larnaca. Because of concerns about reprisals from the angry Greek populace, the prisoners were marched around the town to the beaches to the north, where the disconsolate group of former Janissaries settled on the sand to await their fate.

"We have some old ships lying in the bay, do we not?" Sir Sidney asked Lt Fowler.

"Yes, Sir. I believe there are some. I'm not sure what condition they are in."

"That doesn't matter. Tomorrow we will pull the ships together, ferry the insurgents out to them, and then tell them to leave Cyprus. That way I will have kept my word and they will be free to go wherever they please, as long as the ships don't sink beneath them. They'll probably become pirates."

Lt Fowler laughed. "It's certainly better than what would happen if the Turks catch up with them, Sir."

Late that evening Sir Sidney Smith, Lt Fowler, Duncan and the seamen were taken out to the ships while the majority of the marines remained to stand guard over the former Janissaries.

As they stepped onto the deck, to the shrill whistles of the bosun's mates, Sir Sidney beckoned Lt Fowler over. "A word, Mr Fowler?"

"Yes, Sir." They walked a little distance along the main deck, talking quietly together, then Sir Sidney smiled and went below.

Lt Fowler strode back to the waiting midshipman, who was waiting to be dismissed.

"You appear to have made your mark with the Commodore, young man," he told Duncan. "He gave you a nod of approval for today's work. No small thing," he told the awed boy. "That does not mean you can grin at me like a Cheshire cat. Nor does it mean a swelled head. Dismissed."

"Thank you, Sir!"

Lt Fowler watched the boy scurry away and shook his head. He glanced at Chauncey, the bosun's mate, who also shook his head and grinned.

"There's trouble and that's a fact, Sorr," he offered. "But e' knows how to fight an' no mistake."

Fowler nodded his agreement. "Dismissed, Chauncey. Sir Sidney said a tot for each man."

"Thank ee, Sorr!" Chauncey beamed. "That'll please the lads. Good night, Sorr."

"Good night."

Chapter 4

Awards

It was late in the second day that another small boat sailed up to the *Tigre* and delivered mail. The sack of letters and newspapers was taken immediately below to the steward's cabin for sorting. Almost every man on the ship looked forward with keen anticipation to the arrival of some letter or other. Not least Duncan but as was so often the case there was nothing for him this time. He watched moodily as Standforth gleefully opened a letter and went up on deck to read it, the light in their crowded quarters next to the orlop being almost non-existent.

Duncan found him an hour later in the bows looking pale and shaken.

"What's the matter, Minnow?" he asked the distraught-looking boy. Standforth turned towards him and it was clear that he had been crying. Duncan was taken aback. He knew that the boy on occasion had come close to tears from the hardship and bullying that was meted out by the likes of Tewksby, but Standforth had courage and refused to cry no matter how much he was pinched and bullied. He had earned Duncan's respect by this, but now the boy was almost sobbing.

"Och, lad, what is it? Can ye no talk about it?" he offered, his Scottish accent coming out in response to the distress of his young friend.

"It's ... it's my youngest sister, Charlotte. She's ... she's dead!" the boy almost wailed.

Duncan glanced around the deck. They were being given a wide berth by the sailors on duty, who sensed that something was wrong, for which he was grateful. Duncan knew all about losing members of his family. His middle brother Jamie had died of consumption when he had only been eight years old. His mother had taken it hard, and so had he. But not long after she too was gone. The boys had been close, getting up to all sorts of mischief— and getting strapped for their pains often enough. The loss of his mother had been devastating.

"What did she die of?" he asked Standforth, who was trying hard to bring himself under control, well aware that it was not seemly for a midshipman to be weeping on deck.

"Jaqueline, my other sister, thinks it was the measles. She was only six years old!" Standforth gave a low wail of misery.

"What have we here? A pair of crybabies?" a high-pitched voice sneered from nearby.

Duncan whirled and found Tewksby standing with Midshipman Brown a few paces away. They were on watch so they had every right to be on deck, whereas he and Standforth were spare bodies, 'Idlers' as it were.

Standforth sniffed and wiped his nose, then turned away to look out to sea. "Go away, Tewk," he said in a cold undertone.

"It's none of your damn business, so why don't ye bugger off, eh?" Duncan snarled at the two boys.

Brown, more sensitive to the situation, turned away. "Come on, Tewksby. Leave them alone." He nodded to Duncan and walked off towards the quarterdeck.

Tewksby lingered. "Tell his little nibs that crying on the deck is for babies, not for men."

His anger rising rapidly and threatening to get him into trouble yet again, Duncan took a step towards Tewksby with his fist clenched. "Go away or I'll..."

One look at Duncan's face, suffused with blood and very set, and Tewksby finally got the message. With a sneer on his lips he turned around and sauntered away, heading for the quarterdeck.

Standforth, having heard the exchange, turned to watch with Duncan as the other boy left.

"Thanks, Graham, but you didn't have to do that," he sniffed. "I'll be all right."

"Aye ye might, Minnow, but I don't like that bastard to begin with, so it was a pleasure," Duncan growled. There was a world of difference between a fourteen-year-old-boy and a boy heading into manhood at sixteen, and bullies took advantage of it all too often for his liking.

"I'm sorry for your loss, Minnow. A've lost family too. It's very hard," Duncan said briefly.

"I ... I appreciate your concern, Graham. One day perhaps I can introduce you to my family," Standforth said with a smile. "They would like you, I am sure."

"I'd like that," said Duncan, sure in his mind that it wouldn't happen. He had already grasped the fact that most midshipmen moved up the promotion ladder by virtue of their family's rank and his lacked all of that.

He fully expected that Tewksby and even Standforth would rise to lieutenant before he. Tewksby rarely let him forget this either. It was one of the reasons he disliked him so much. To his mind the other boy was useless. Their feud went back some time now. He was equally sure that meeting Standforth's family was a very remote possibility.

"I've got to go and write a letter myself or I'll lose the chance to get it taken on the mail boat," Graham said and turned away, wondering why he had said that. He didn't have anyone to write to. His father could barely read and his mother was dead. He envied Standforth, who appeared to have an extended family. The lad received letters almost every time a packet boat arrived with the mail, whereas Duncan had not received one the entire time they had been on station.

However, he didn't have time to brood because the word came down that Sir Sidney was disembarking and Graham was required by Lt Fowler to be in attendance. Seizing his chance, Duncan walked hurriedly up to the lieutenant and asked very politely, "May it please you, Sir, but could we take Midshipman Standforth with us?"

Lt Fowler looked put out. "Why him in particular, Graham?"

"Er... well, Sir. He's just received some bad news and it might take his mind off things."

Lt Fowler stared at him for a long moment as though reevaluating Duncan.

"Very well, tell him to get ready. We leave in ten minutes. Don't delay."

"Thank you, Sir!" Duncan rushed off to tell Standforth the good news. The two delighted boys ran below to pick up their swords, hastily brush their hats, and hurry back on deck to join the crew of the jolly boat which was to accompany Sir Sidney Smith on his new venture ashore.

Just as Duncan clambered aboard the jolly boat he looked up and saw Tewksby peering over the side. He waved cheekily, but the wave was not returned and the thin face was withdrawn. "Eat yer heart, ye Sassenach bogger," Duncan muttered under his breath, with a grin at Standforth, who was almost jumping up and down with excitement at the adventure about to take place.

"Are we going into action, Sir?" he squeaked at Lt Fowler to the barely suppressed amusement of the rowers and Chauncey.

"Not this time, Mr Standforth, and please sit still. Sir Sidney has business in Nicosia and we are to accompany him for his protection. Chauncey, do we have enough arms for all of us?"

"Certainly do, Sorr, no problem. I can provide the young gentlemen with a pistol each."

Lt Fowler nodded. "Good. Then we need to hurry, as Sir Sidney is some way ahead already."

"Put yer backs into it boys!" Chauncey roared. "We need to be landed before the Commodore arrives."

As the men labored at the oars Duncan had a chance to look around. The small group of ships that had been idling at anchor in the bay had been brought closer to the shore and the former insurgents were being ferried out to them with marines in attendance.

"Where will they sail to, Sir?" he asked Lt Fowler, pointing at the ships.

Lt Fowler snorted. "I have no idea, Mr Graham. Not very far, if what I heard about those ships is true. They are leaky and poorly maintained. Those poor souls will have to make land as fast as possible or the first storm will sink them all. Still, it's better than what they could have expected from their former masters."

Lt Fowler seemed to be in a chatty mood today. "The Commodore has been awarded great honors by the Sultan in Istanbul and by the British Parliament, but now we are going into the town of Larnaca at the invitation of the Archbishop of Cyprus."

"What about these honors for Sir Sidney, Sir?" Standforth asked curiously.

"Ah!" The lieutenant went on impressively. "The Grand Seignior at Constantinople himself, feeling no doubt the weight of his heavy obligation to our Commodore for relieving Acre of the unwelcome attentions of the French Army, lightened his purse and his conscience by sending seven purses of gold to Sir Sidney." He hefted an imaginary purse of florins in his right hand and raised his eyebrows at the midshipman, who looked suitably awed.

"Not only that, he was sent some fancy furs, the kind royalty wears, and the insignia of the Ottoman Order of the Crescent. Remember that gaudy Turk who visited when we arrived?"

"What about the Parliament, Sir? You mentioned them earlier," asked Standforth, who considered awards by Eastern potentates to be trivial compared to the substance of his own King and Parliament.

"I hear that Parliament passed a formal vote of thanks on behalf of the nation to Sir Sidney, and to the officers and men under his command. I presume that means all of us," Lt Fowler replied, and some of the sailors grinned appreciation.

"He is also to receive a pension of one thousand pounds per annum. The City of London, in a letter, has presented him with its freedom, and a sword valued at 100 guineas. And from the Turkey Company he received another, valued at 300 guineas." Lieutenant sounded somewhat envious. Sir Sidney would be well-off for life.

They landed at the wooden pier instead of the stone one. Standforth commented on an aside to Graham, "Looks rotten to me."

"Probably is," Duncan grinned back. "Watch where you put your feet."

They walked along its green and shaky boards to the firm shore with some care.

The people of Larnaca must have heard something of the impending visit to Nicosia by the now famous Sir Sidney. They cheered him all the way out of the town as he rode in an old carriage pulled by four horses that had been commandeered for the purpose, while his entourage of sailors and officers rode whatever horses they could scrounge. Since there were not enough horses for the ten sailors and two midshipmen, some of them had to settle for mules. Bosun's mate Chauncey remained behind with two men to guard the boat.

Lt Fowler rode in the carriage with Sir Sidney and Colonel Douglas. Standforth took to his horse well, riding as though he had done this kind of thing since early childhood.

"It is more of a pony but it will do," he told Duncan disparagingly, whereas Duncan, who was no rider, clung to his mount with the desperation of a drowning man.

"You need to relax more and don't tug so hard on its mouth," Standforth admonished Duncan as his horse, objecting to the treatment, skittered about waving its head in the air.

Duncan let his death grip on the reins relax a little and the horse became less upset. It tossed its head as though it had won a small victory, but Duncan's legs were still locked to its sides and his heels were digging into its flanks. Taking this to be a command, it broke into a trot and then a canter. If Standforth had not seized the reins it is probable that the animal would have bolted and equally unlikely that Duncan could have remained on its back for very long thereafter.

"You do not appear to have ridden very much, Duncan!" Standforth laughed as he sat back comfortably in his own saddle, still holding the reins of Duncan's horse. Duncan could not have been more mortified. He glanced back at the smirking sailors, perched on mules which were stolidly plodding along the track.

"Noo, I've not, but I shall master this bogger before we get there," Duncan swore under his breath.

"Well ... the first thing you need to do is to loosen your legs and sit on your bum instead of clinging to him like a frog. Sit up, and then to keep him going, move your hips on the saddle and he will understand that he needs to walk on, but not to run off."

"Like this?" Duncan asked as he warily moved his legs away from the agitated animal, which immediately reduced its pace to a slow walk. Duncan was surprised, but then the animal walked so slowly that the sailors who had been a little ways back, just where he wanted them, began to catch up.

"Use your hips, Duncan. Hmm ... just like you are having it off with a girl," Standforth said with a mischievous gleam in his eye.

"So ye ken how it's done, ye randy little bugger!" Duncan had to laugh. "Like this, is it?" he asked with a cackle, as he waggled his hips on the saddle. The animal seemed to pick up speed, so he repeated the same motion, his feet now sticking out at a wide angle from the sides of the surprised horse. Duncan gave a vulgar guffaw of glee, while Standforth nearly fell off his own animal, he laughed so hard.

"What is all that mirth about back there?" Sir Sidney called from the carriage ahead of them.

"Er ... nothing, Sir. Graham has a spirited mount," Standforth called back, wiping the tears from his eyes.

"Then hurry up and master the beast, Mr Graham. I do not wish to be late for the ceremony."

"Indeed, Sir. I'll be right there in a moment," Duncan called back, stifling a laugh of his own while warily settling in on the back of his animal.

"If those two midshipmen are playing the fool I shall have to discipline them," Lt Fowler said, sounding cross.

"They are boys, Lieutenant. I dare say that you were one once, too." Sir Sidney chuckled. "Let them be. That Graham did very well the other day, and young Standforth will come to no harm by being with him."

Lt Fowler sat back looking skeptical, but he held his peace.

The journey to Nicosia took several hours along a dirt track that passed for a road in these parts. The dust thrown up by the carriage and the four horses had layered the men at the rear in a light coat of white by the time the city gates came into view.

Word seemed to have gone ahead by some invisible means of communication, because they were clearly expected. A group of Orthodox priests greeted the carriage at the gates. Their tall black hats and robes stood out from the crowd of curious onlookers and monks who had gathered to greet the hero of the island.

One monk, younger than the rest, came to open the door of the carriage and said in English, "A very great honor to meet you Sir Sidney. I shall act as your interpreter, as the dignitaries here do not speak very much English."

"Your men will be given refreshments in the shade by the gates, Sir Sidney, but I would like to escort you along with the worshipful priests to the cathedral where you will meet with his eminence the Archbishop of Cyprus."

Sir Sidney smiled and said, "Lead on. We will be honored to follow." He motioned for his two officers and the two midshipmen to join him. Hastening to obey, Duncan and Standforth dismounted and handed off the reins of their mounts to some servants who hurried to take them.

The young monk led the way into the city towards the huge Orthodox cathedral. Duncan followed the senior officers, and behind them came the gaggle of priests and the crowd of onlookers. He had time to look around as they walked.

The city of Nicosia was larger than Larnaca, but to his eyes it still didn't measure up to what he considered to be a real city. Duncan had been to London and since that time he measured all 'cities' against this formidable example.

For the most part, the houses here were made of mud baked brick walls. The cathedral, as it was called, was constructed of stone and towered over the other dwellings, matched only by the tall minarets of the mosque nearby which by law had to be taller than any other building.

"Now that is a truly beautiful pile of stones," remarked Standforth in an undertone to his companion. Graham, who knew almost nothing about buildings or their history, asked, "What is so beautiful about that? It's just a large church, isn't it?"

"Ignoramus!" scoffed Standforth. "It is Byzantine and was probably built when our ancestors, most certainly yours, were running about in skins."

"Where did ye learn all about these places then, Minnow?" Duncan demanded, bridling at the remark.

"My Greek tutor. He didn't manage to teach me much about the language, but he used to hold forth on their civilization at great length. I am looking forward to seeing what is inside."

"Stop muttering away over there and be quiet," Lt Fowler said in a loud whisper. "Pay attention and do not speak."

They were quiet and watched as Sir Sidney Smith was presented to a man decked out in black robes who wore a high black hat with a rim, similar to those worn by the other priests. The difference lay with three large iconic devices hanging down to his midriff, suspended on thick gold chains around his neck. He also wore a bright red stole over his shoulders that was lined with gold thread, with a large embroidered cross on either side. The priest held an ivory staff, wound about with silver and studded with precious stones, atop of which was a gold cross.

Sir Sidney was facing the Archbishop of Cyprus of the Orthodox Church of Christ, who gave him a warm smile through his long white beard.

"Welcome to our island, Sir Sidney Smith," he said in clear but careful English. "My name is Father Chrysanthos and I am the leader of the church of Christ on this island."

He reverted back to Greek for the remainder of his speech, allowing time at intervals for the translator to catch up.

Father Chrysanthos continued, "We, people of the island, are honored to meet the man who not only defeated the anti-Christ at Acre, but who has saved the island from a dreadful fate at the hands of the renegade soldiers of the Turk. Your speedy action has ensured that the island is to be safe once again, and we thank you from our hearts."

Duncan found his attention wandering during this address, but Standforth nudged him when the speech came to an end. The Archbishop embraced their Commodore and kissed him on both cheeks.

Everyone thought the ceremony was over at this point, but the archbishop had something to present to Sir Sidney.

He held out with both hands a long gold chain; suspended at its end was a cross shaped like the two crosses on the clergyman's stole.

He motioned Sir Sidney closer and slipped the chain over his bowed head, then stood back. Sir Sidney lifted his head and fingered the ancient device. "This is a great honor, Sir. From where does this cross come?" he asked.

"Commodore, this cross once belonged to an Englishman, and I now restore it to an Englishman. It belonged to the man you call Richard I, otherwise known as Richard Coeur de Lion whom we call Agio Ricardo, Saint Richard. He left it in this church when he departed in 1191 for Acre, and it has been preserved in our treasury ever since. Eighteen archbishops in succession have signed for the receipt of this cross. I now give it over to you, in token of our gratitude."

Smiling at the surprise on Sir Sidney's face he continued, "You are now a Knight of the Temple, Sir Sidney."

"I don't understand, Sir," Sidney said in surprise.

"I have just made you a knight of the Temple. You do know of them?"

"Er yes, of course. But they were destroyed, were they not, by Phillip IV and Pope Clement V?"

"Indeed, those two evil men took it upon themselves to dissolve and outlaw the order. Clement's henchman Phillip captured many of the Templars and seized their wealth, burning to death Jacques de Molay, the final known Grand Master. They did this because they coveted the enormous wealth of the Templars. It is not good to be richer than a pope and a bad king. It is said that, as he was being taken to the pyre, Jacques de Molay cursed both men, predicting that they would follow him within the year. The prediction came true: and the king and the Pope both died within a year of de Molay. However, some Templars did escape, and they took much of the treasure with them. No one knows to this day where it is buried."

"I was right then. They were destroyed," Sidney remarked.

"No, not entirely, and Cyprus remained on the Templar books as a property that neither the Pope nor the King of France could confiscate. King Richard sold it to Guy Lusignan. There have been subsequent Grand Masters and most assuredly there are Knights Templar to be found today, Sir Sidney. One of whom is now yourself."

Chapter 5

A Victorious Army Returns

The return of Bonaparte's army to Cairo was to be a spectacle unlike any that had ever been seen before in the city.

The entire population came to watch the victorious soldiers marching through the gates and on to the very heart of the city. Although it was stifling and the sun beat down mercilessly, no one wanted to miss this occasion. The garrison commander had dictated that all the musicians far and wide were to appear to participate in the massive parade. All those of rank and importance, near and far, from land owners to Sheikhs in the outlying villages, were ordered to be present with gifts and congratulations. Failure to attend could mean imprisonment.

To the snap of flags and captured banners flying in the wind, with drums pounding out a tattoo and music wailing from stringed instruments, reedy pipes and blaring trumpets, the expectant crowd gathered to watch their new emperor enter the city. Napoléon rode a magnificent white stallion and was the first to appear through the Bab el-Nasr gate, the Gate of Victory. Behind him marched his troops, the Grenadiers and then the Infantrie, all in near new or new uniforms, their white cross belts freshly clayed. The brass gleamed and their weapons shone in the bright sunlight, Because he had pretensions to being Muslim, Napoléon had invited solemn Muslim prayers of thanks to be offered by black-robed mullahs. It was a political move but it didn't convince the upper echelons of the religious community, who remained very skeptical of this Infidel who had conquered their country so easily. Meanwhile, the festivities continued all over the city with trained monkeys and dancing bears being exercised on the streets leading up to the square. The celebrations and feasting went on for three nights and concluded with a fireworks display that for the most part fizzled because of the poor quality of the powder with which the engineers had to work.

It all went extremely well. The only uncomfortable moment for Bonaparte came when a local pasha asked him why the number of soldiers in the parade was so small. He covered it well by saying that he'd only brought a small number of men with him, that most of the units had been left in Alexandria and in the delta to guard against a possible Turkish invasion.

It was true that a large part of his force had been left behind. At Acre, they were still burying the dead.

After the parade, Corporal Émile and his companions marched to the barracks and for the first time in months were able to avail themselves of the limited delights of Cairo. Since the French had arrived, the ever opportunistic people of the city had learned that cafés which provided a little more in the way of drink than coffee were deeply appreciated by their conquerors. Not only that, the time honored profession of prostitution had been revived and actively encouraged by the authorities. Émile, newly promoted to Sergeant, and his companions intended to take advantage of all of this for as long as their coin lasted.

After they had deposited their arms in the barracks, the Infantrie set about getting as drunk as they could on the wine and spirits the cafés provided. Claude led the way along the narrow smelly streets of the city to their favorite haunt. The Infantrie considered this café and its girls their property to the exclusion of the Grenadiers.

They arrived in an exuberant mood and the men of Clément's company spread out around the ground floor room, occupying most of the tables and chairs. It didn't take long for the lady who owned the café, Madame Farage, to appear, still touching up her hair and pulling her dress into place. Their arrival had caught her by surprise. The parade had barely ended and here they were, thirsty and ready for the girls upstairs.

She could not fail to notice how thin they were; their new uniforms were hanging off most of the men, but there could be no mistaking the weathered hardness on their young faces.

These men had coin and that was all that mattered. Her small, dark, sharp eyes noted that there were NCOs among the group, so the likelihood of violence was minimized. She put on a bright smile baring bad teeth and welcomed them all. It wasn't long before the rooms upstairs were fully occupied and the men seated at the tables were singing bawdy songs and very drunk. They had few memories that they wanted to keep, and drunkenness was one form of escape. The squeals of girls and the raucous laughter of the sex-starved soldiers who had ventured upstairs reverberated through the house.

It couldn't last, of course. There were many more Grenadiers in the city than there were Infantrie, and there were only a limited number of cafés and drinking holes in the city of Cairo. Sergeant Émile became aware of impending trouble while he was talking to Claude and Jean-Baptiste, who were well into their cups, when the room went silent. Uncharacteristically he had his back to the door —he was keeping an eye on the stairway, to see who went upstairs and when they came down again—but now he turned his head and saw the reason for the quiet.

Some bluecoats were standing at the doorway, clutching bottles, with more behind them, and they were wildly drunk. He gave a sigh of annoyance.

"They look as though they want trouble," Jean slurred and began to stand up.

"Don't stand up on our account, Green-bottle," one of the blue-coated Grenadiers shouted and swayed into the room, his mates crowding in around him.

"I think we can deal with this," Claude said, and stood up.

The men boiling into the room were too drunk to realize just how big the man was who beckoned to them with his fingers. "Come on, you lot. This is our place, go and fuck each other somewhere else," he invited them.

"Did that idiot say something?" one of the more cocky Grenadiers asked his comrades in an exaggerated tone. "Doesn't he realize that the real soldiers have arrived?"

He received a cackle of supportive laughter from his equally drunk friends, but now Sergeant Émile stood up. "You men can leave now and nothing will be said. Get out and go back to barracks," he warned them.

One of the Grenadiers waved a finger at him. "Go back to barracks!" he mimicked. "You Green-bottles need to go back and learn how to soldier, so it's time for you to leave. The real men are here to fuck everyone and we'll fuck you too if you get in the way."

"All right, men. It's time to find out who is who," Jean said. "Arrest me later, Sergeant." He strode up to the man who had wagged his finger and slammed his fist into the smirking face. The man went down bleeding from his mouth, and a tooth fell onto the floor.

"You don't insult my sergeant, you pig's arse," Jean said, as he waggled his hand, wincing from the pain. He got no further. With a roar the Grenadiers charged. The café erupted into a frantic brawl as men from upstairs, hearing the noise below, came to investigate and then joined in. Bluecoats from the street, hearing that there was a fight taking place, ran to support their comrades.

Émile kept pace with Claude, who was hammering a path deep into the surging tide of blue, his fists moving like huge pistons, tossing men to the side as he pounded them. Soon there was not a stick of furniture left undamaged, as men used stools as bludgeons, broke tables as they fell, and then grabbed broken legs to use as weapons. Bleeding men of both colored jackets were soon lying unconscious or moaning with bloody heads on the glass-strewn floor

The shouting and yelling groups of green jackets and blue punched and kicked at one another as they fought for possession of the room and its dubious booty. The shrill screams and shrieks of the women and servants only added to the mayhem, but they were ignored as the French soldiers went for one another, teeth bared and fists jabbing at glaring, yelling faces. A stool was thrown, missing its mark and smashing into a very expensive mirror, which shattered into tiny pieces.

Madame Farage stood on the first steps of the stairway, clutching the banister, shrieking and wailing with rage and despair as she watched the French soldiers utterly demolish her furniture and smash every mirror and piece of glass in the room. Poupard raced down the stairs with his trousers only half-buttoned, pulling up his braces. Madame Farage snatched at his sleeve with a claw. "Stop them!" she shrieked at him. He shrugged her off and dived into the fray with a yell.

The battle finally spilled out into the street where Émile, conscious of the danger from the garrison patrol and the potential loss of his new rank, started to haul his men together. When they heard whistles and calls of "Patrol! Patrol!" shouted at the end of the street, he knew it was time to leave.

The girls had by now overcome their initial panic and were lining the balcony, pointing and even laughing at the struggle going on below. Glancing up, Émile could have sworn some were laying wagers on the outcome of individual fights. "Cheeky whores!" he shouted up at them, but all they did was to blow him kisses. "Come back soon!" one called to him. He shook his head, laughing.

"Come away Claude, Poupard! Come on Jean, where are the others?" he panted, pulling on Claude's sleeve. Claude was busy pounding two bluecoats' faces to pulp while holding both semi-conscious men with one hand by the front of their jackets.

"Leave them!" Émile ordered. Claude gave him a wild uncomprehending look. "But I'm having a good time!" he protested.

"It's the patrol, you fool! You won't enjoy being in the jail if they catch us," Émile shouted at him. Out of the corner of his eye he noticed a movement. Then he had to duck as a Grenadier swung a table leg at him. Émile whirled, his fist lashed out and punched once. The man was thrown backwards, his eyes rolling up into his head as he fell.

Claude dropped both of his victims, who collapsed to the cobbles in a heap. Other men were beginning to separate themselves from the fray and look for avenues of escape. Some were too drunk to know where they were, so they stumbled into the path of the patrol, hindering its passage long enough for Émile and his men, along with many other Grenadiers and Infantrie, to flee down the street in the opposite direction and out of harm's way.

"Good fight, Green-bottle!" one of the larger Grenadiers shouted as he departed with a wave and a laugh.

"It was, you bastards!" Jean shouted back. He had a black eye but seemed pleased. "Honor satisfied, I think. Ha ha!" He laughed and waved, and then they ran as fast as they could to get away from any more trouble. Carabiniere Infantrie men tumbled along after them and the mob of laughing, singing and staggering men finally arrived back at the gates to their barracks: bruised, bloody, and very satisfied with the day.

Chapter 6

Supplies

Captain Joseph Clément and a young officer, Ensign Andre Du Pont from Gascony, sought out a restaurant frequented by officers. They were greeted by old comrades, both from their own brigade and from the garrison, and settled down at a small table to drink and discuss events. This was one of the first opportunities they had had to find out what had been going on in their absence.

Major Baudouin walked over to their table and joined them. Clément knew him from the assault on Cairo that had taken the city. Baudouin's green jacket and elaborate silver frogging indicated that he was a cavalryman from Général Lanusse's Brigade.

"We have heard rumors that there were rebellions while we were away," Clément said as he shook hands with the major. Once they were settled again, he sipped a glass of what he called Vin plus ordinaire. It was the best he was likely to find in Cairo so he couldn't really complain, but he still winced at the arid taste it left in his mouth.

"Sometimes I think I would prefer to bite upon a cartridge than to drink this desert piss," he muttered. "It tastes about the same."

The major grinned but ignored the comment. "We've been more busy than you might think. While you were lazing about in the desert and lolling about in front of Acre, which I want to hear about, we've had our hands full. I'll tell you something of our time while you were away," he told them.

"Did Général Desaix manage to capture the Murad Bey and his horsemen?"

"Not yet, but there are so many rumors coming out of the south right now it is amazing," Major Baudouin said reflectively. "The Savants"—he was referring to the engineers—"have apparently made some fascinating discoveries. Our Général is going to be busy as hell once he has had his time off with that lady of his in the palace." He smirked.

"So tell us what happened when we left?" Clément ignored the major's insinuation.

"In his infinite wisdom our illustrious leader took most of the money with him when you left, and Poussielgue, our chief financial advisor, was at his wit's end, so he tried to raise taxes in this area. He wanted to place an early tax on the wheat harvest, which didn't go down well, and if you consider that the French army was mostly absent it is perhaps not surprising that not just one but two uprisings took place. I'll never understand those fellaheen. We actually pay them for the work they do, for God's sake, but still they rise up and murder our people." The major sounded bitter.

"Well, what did happen?" Clément demanded.

The major took a swig of his wine and wiped his huge mustache with the back of his hand.

"I was there for the first one, which was led by a man called Mustafa. He had been appointed Emir el-Hadj in place of Murad Bey, who is still running about in the south trying not to get caught by Desaix. Napoléon ordered him to report to Syria, but he hung back and eventually used the excuse that he wanted to go on a pilgrimage to Mecca!"

Ensign Andre snickered. "Some excuse!"

The major nodded slowly. "You're right, he didn't go to Mecca. As you know, rumors are rife anywhere in this horrible place. One of them was that Napoléon had been killed at Acre!"

His listeners looked startled.

"Oh yes indeed. That was the least of it. We never seemed to hear the truth from anywhere while you were gone. Even today most of the intelligence we receive from the South is suspect. You should hear what the rumors are saying about what the Savants are supposed to have discovered down there. They talk of huge palaces and temples! We'll see. I cannot imagine these people building the kind of places being described." His tone was acid. Clearly the major had a low opinion of the Egyptians.

"What then?" Clément asked. He waved over to the servants for more wine. Whatever its questionable taste, it gave him a buzz which was as much as he could ask for at present.

"It was a complete lie, of course, but it was enough, when spread around, to help him begin an insurgency. Mustafa got busy with the tribes people and won most of them over but fortunately for us, in this instance, the fellaheen stayed on the fence. We do pay them, which is more than the Turks ever did, so they didn't want to lose that option I suppose.

"Mustafa couldn't raise enough men to be a serious problem for us but he did go on the rampage and began to ambush our convoys to and from Alexandria, which finally became too much. I was with Général Lanusse when we eventually caught up with Mustafa and chased him off into the desert. Hardly a shot was fired, either! It should not surprise any of you that he was betrayed by the very sheikhs whom he had tried to bribe. These people simply cannot remain loyal to anyone for very long." He shook his head in disgust.

"I hear we are running short of weapons everywhere," Clément remarked. "Our own are almost worn out. I am worried about the condition of some of the muskets my men carry right now."

"Our Savants are working on trying to manufacture replacements, but the concept of a 'factory' in these parts is unknown so they are not doing very well," Major Baudouin responded.

"My contacts within the main bureau in Cairo tell me that our general wrote to the governor of the island of Reunion asking for muskets, swords and pistols."

"Do they have factories there?"

"Probably not; it's just an island port, but there are French ships that can run supplies from France, although it is a long way. If they want to bring them to us here, though, they have to run the gauntlet of the British, who now have ships in the Red Sea." He looked glum. "We are very much on our own here since the British defeated our fleet at Abukir Lake."

Napoléon sought the arms of his mistress and femme fatale, Pauline Foures, in his residence, the palace of Elfi Bey. Their reunion was joyous and she, conscious that he was tired and preoccupied, did her best to distract him, and for a time succeeded.

For Napoléon it was a welcome respite from the unpleasant memories of the defeat at Acre and the subsequent march. His officers made sure he was undisturbed, so they strolled together in the large palace gardens with their peacocks and fountains. While she prattled on about her days alone in this inhospitable city, he allowed his thoughts to wander.

But he had little time to relax, as the affairs of state made heavy demands upon him. To all intents and purposes he was the ruler of Egypt: hence there was much to do.

His preoccupation was now on how he could extract himself from Egypt without causing an uproar or even a mutiny, and get back to France where he could deal with the insipid men who governed her. There was no news from Europe, and had not been for some time, and this worried him. Perhaps his absence had produced someone else to take his place?

After thinking it through, Napoléon made some preparations to cover his options on how best to leave the country. He sent a secret message to Admiral Ganteaume in Alexandria to have two frigates, La Muiron and La Carriere, to be in a permanent state of preparedness to sail. He was very careful not to let it out that he was considering this option.

He had other administrative issues to deal with, not least of them being the shortage of supplies of almost every kind. The British blockade by Sir Sidney Smith and his ships was beginning to bite, and even ammunition was running low.

It became so critical that the execution procedure of shooting those condemned in the recent uprisings came up for discussion. Dugua, the chief of police in the city, came to see him with a written request.

"With the firing squads becoming more frequent at the Citadel, I suggest, mon Général, that we replace them with a machine for cutting off heads. This would save on our bullets and make much less noise." Without naming it, Dugua was referring to the French guillotine of ill-repute.

The dawn firing squads could hardly win over the hearts and minds of the local population, which was still restive, although for the time being all major threats had been dispersed or eliminated.

Napoléon wrote in the margin of the written request, "Agreed."

Dugua and Général Lanusse reported their activity to him during many subsequent meetings he had with his staff. He was not reassured to hear about the recent uprising instigated by a Libyan called Ahmed, who claimed he was invincible to the musket balls of the French. After he and his mob of tribesmen and fellaheen had massacred the garrison in Damanhur and set fire to the mosque where the survivors had taken refuge, Lanusse had been sent to deal with it.

Général Lanusse was a tough, experienced officer who knew that this insurgency threatened the entire occupation of Egypt. His brigade had arrived with unexpected swiftness and then, upon his orders, proceeded to slaughter the insurgents and, as a reprisal, burned the town to the ground, killing all its inhabitants. Lanusse stated in his report that:

"..we wreaked vengeance on the town and the inhabitants of Damanhur. Around 200 -300 of its inhabitants were killed as they fled; after that I abandoned this wretched town to the horrors of pillage and carnage. Damanhur no longer exists and between 1200 and 1500 of its inhabitants have been burnt or shot."

There was no sign of Ahmed el-Mehdi, who either fled or was killed; he was never seen again. This left lower Egypt pacified until Napoléon finally returned with his army from Syria.

It was hardly the best way to keep the peace, but Napoléon and his generals were rapidly learning that in order to keep the unruly fellaheen and their Arab and Turkish leaders in check they had to be ruthless.

Napoléon nodded his approval as the report was completed. Adherence to the rule of law didn't seem to have much effect in this strange country.

He and his officers were aware that there were odd contradictions at play: although the fellaheen all agreed that the French brought order and employment to the country and actually paid for the labor they required, something hitherto unheard of, they would nevertheless follow their religious and tribal leaders from one disastrous rebellion to another.

There was no forced labor; with hired labor several bridges were completed in good time, which served to impress the local population. It was noted, too, that the French stone-cutting tools were far superior to anything to be found in Egypt.

Général Desaix kept control of upper Egypt in this manner, keeping Murad Bey and his Mameluke cavalry off balance to the point where they had to subsist in the desert on the outskirts of the country, unable to be an effective force against the French.

Napoléon was soon to have other more pressing concerns to deal with.

CHAPTER 7

THE ABUKIR PENINSULAR

The three British ships of the line, with three frigates led by *HMS Tigre* and commanded by Sir Sidney Smith, crept through the calm water of the eastern Mediterranean with barely a whisper of wind to keep them in motion. Dawn was still four hours away and the sliver of moon appeared and disappeared as light clouds moved across its surface at irregular intervals. When it was not covered, the dim light of the moon barely illuminated the dark shadow of the British naval vessels as they sailed cautiously toward the coast of Egypt.

Their destination was the cape of Abukir, just to the north and east of Alexandria, where they were to support the Turkish army commanded by Mustafa Pasha when it landed. Their objective was to take the fort of Abukir from the French and establish a beachhead for the rest of the Turkish army.

The men on the quarter deck were tense and watchful. Sailors high in the cross trees and top sail yards were alert for the dark mass or white line of surf that would signal the mainland of Egypt to the south.

After several hours of slow movement the call came, and almost immediately the men on the quarterdeck could see a long dark line that indicated the coast of Egypt ahead. Sir Sidney Smith gave a nod of satisfaction. It had been seen in the right place, just off their starboard bow. Signal lanterns were lit and hoisted to inform the ships behind the *Tigre* that land was sighted. Now they

56

had to make landfall just before the peninsula called Abukir, where the Turkish flotilla was destined to land and then capture the fort, providing a beachhead for the rest of the army and eventual full invasion of Egypt.

Sir Sidney Smith could not see very much of the fleet in this light but was keenly aware of the large number of ships, sloops, feluccas and other small craft which were all heading for the coast. In the case of his own ship, he was mindful of the fact that the charts were all extremely old and therefore unreliable. One thing was clear: the shallows extended several miles out to sea, and had very likely moved around with storms and tide. There was a real danger that the larger ships might run aground if they did not take great care, so the call of the leadsman from the bows was being listened for with great attention.

The lead was being used to take soundings and the depth called back quietly via relay to the quarter deck. The first streak of dawn had appeared in the eastern sky when the urgent call came from the bow. "Four fathoms only, we are on sand!"

The men on that watch instantly sprang into action and raced up the shrouds to the upper rigging as the officer called out the order for the ship to halt its forward motion and drop anchor. There was a splash near the bow and the rumble and hiss of the cable on its eyes as the anchor was let go. Another anchor had been manhandled to the after part of the ship and this too was lowered into the sea. The top sails, which were all that had carried them forward these last nautical miles, were hurriedly furled. Within a few tense minutes the ship was still; the ships in line behind inched forward to range themselves in a line parallel with the shoreline.

As the first streaks of dawn began to lighten the eastern sky, the long low black line of the coast, approximately two and a half miles away, began to reveal more detail. So far there appeared to have been no alarms raised on shore.

Sir Sidney Smith and Lieutenant Canes stared at the distant shore unhappily.

"It is a pity that we have not been able to get any closer," Smith said.

"Aye, Sir, it is doubtful that the guns of the ship can support an assault on the peninsula from where we are at present. It's almost two miles away! In the morning we might be able to gain a little more ground using the cables and boats, but that would be dangerous in this poor light."

Sir Sidney nodded reluctant agreement. "In that case we should signal the other ships to lower boats in the morning and mount guns on their bows so that we can support the Turks in that manner," he said.

"Aye Aye, Sir," said Lt Canes.

Sir Sidney went below to get a couple of hours' sleep and prepare for the day to come.

As the ship *HMS Tigre* swung at anchor with the rise and fall of the sea, the night watch took their posts under the gimlet eyes of Lt Bowles; sentries were posted on both sides and lookouts stationed in the top masts.

Below decks the crew and officers took their ease. For most it was a welcome chance to get some sleep, as few doubted that they would have a busy day on the morrow. In the midshipmen's berth, however, a couple of lanterns still burned and a game of cards was being played in the stifling space where they lived.

The game was Whist and the stakes were a farthing a point. Of the four midshipmen only two were playing, while the youngest, Mr Standforth, watched with keen interest. The fourth midshipman, Mr Brown, was on the first watch. Snores from the nearby surgeon's assistant on the other side of the canvas wall was the only sound, other than the slap of cards on the flat surface of one of the Midshipmen's trunks.

The two players, Duncan and Mr Tewksby, were focused upon their game and paid Standforth no attention. Duncan was winning, and by some margin. Tewksby was a poor player and appeared to be a hopeless gambler. He had bragged once that his father had lost a thousand in a night at White's of London. Duncan hardly saw a loss of that size to be a recommendation for good play, thus was determined to take what he could off the arrogant boy. When the he laid out his hand of tricks for the fourth time Mr Edward Tewksby finally had enough. He threw his cards onto the table and sat back on his own trunk with a curse. The cards flew all over the place and young Standforth, with a sharp exclamation, scrambled for the precious items. A new set of cards could cost a whole shilling.

"You should settle down, Tewky," Graham told his opponent in a low voice. Card playing was strictly forbidden on board, so they didn't want to draw any unnecessary attention to themselves at this very late hour. Even as he spoke the bell rung for the middle watch and the patter of distant feet was heard on the deck above as the watch carried out some order.

"I have no need to 'settle down', you Scottish oaf," Tewksby snarled in his high-pitched voice.

"Scot I'm a damned Scot. When will you ever learn to say it properly, or do I have to teach you the hard way?" Graham said in a deceptively mild way, his dark blue eyes narrowed.

"There is no need to sound like you came from the gutter, although I am sure you did," Tewksby told him with a sneer. "You have won my allowance and now you seek to teach me how to speak?"

"I'll take a pair of your fancy silk stockings in lieu of teaching you English. That would be a forlorn hope in any case," Graham offered. "This is a game where one has to be able to count. That's my gain, and more's the pity that you cannot."

"Demme! They cost me at least a guinea. I dare say you cheated, demn your eyes," Tewksby muttered, his lisp getting the better of him.

"What's that you said?" Graham gritted. He leaned forward until his face was close to that of Tewksby. The heavier and stronger face confronted the thinner and less resolute features. Graham poked Tewksby in the chest with a grubby forefinger.

"I shall demand satisfaction for that scurrilous remark, you toad. I do not cheat. You simply cannot play, and I will not accept an IOU either. The debt will only be settled after I have shot you to death or pinked you till you bleed like a stuck pig. We would be well rid of you," he told the older boy.

Tewksby drew back and licked his thin lips; he looked uncertain. His eyes wouldn't meet those of Graham, who narrowed his own and scowled fiercely—a look that he had cultivated since a very young boy to look dangerous and threatening. He regularly practiced this when on watch: intimidation of one's enemies was not purely in the skill of a good shot or the use of a sword, his father had once told him. No one could look as fierce as his father could when in full kilt, brandishing a claymore, having drunk a full bottle of spirits.

Tewksby glared back at Graham. One could never quite tell when this freckle-faced Scottish boy with the mop of reddish hair and broad shoulders was joking. Standforth chose this moment to add to the looming disaster. He hated Tewksby with a passion, as the older boy never let an occasion go by when he didn't bully the youngster of fourteen.

"I shall be your second, Graham," he offered.

"Shut up, you little prick!" Tewksby snarled at him.

"I shall welcome your support, Minnow," Graham gave a solemn nod to his volunteer second, "and you will try to behave like a Gentleman, Mister Tewksby, even though it might be an effort," he admonished with a curl of his lip, never taking his eyes off the boy opposite. "Well? I want satisfaction, Mister Tewksby; will you grant it to me? I even have a witness to your scurrilous accusation. Or do I add coward to your other worthless titles? Primp, Fop, Dandy among others come to mind."

"I, I, er, it's forbidden to duel. We could be court marshaled for it," Edward Tewksby, heir to a fortune in northern England and a title declared, looking satisfied with his reasoning.

Graham sat back and scraped the small coins that were still on the chest into the palm of his hand, looking thoughtful. "Only if we are caught at it," he stated. "I don't care how long it takes but satisfaction I will have, Mr Tewksby. Mr Brown can act for you when the time comes. Mr Standforth is already taken, I believe."

"You have to choose your weapons," Standforth reminded them, his voice squeaking with the excitement of the moment. He was enjoying the discomfort of his sworn enemy enormously. He could not count the number of times he had imagined getting rid of Tewksby, from helping him overboard in a high sea to shooting him in the back during a fierce engagement with the Frenchies. Unfortunately neither bad weather nor any reckless boarding attempts by the French had occurred, so he remained frustrated, but now ... he was almost beside himself with glee. Graham, who was difficult to read most of the time, really seemed to mean it in this instance.

Duncan nodded and said, "You are right, Minnow." He seemed to be pondering this for a moment. Then he looked up and smiled. "Swords, I think. Yes, much more satisfying than a noisy pistol. Swords it is, then. What do you say Tewky? Its your choice anyway."

Mr Tewksby looked shocked. "You really mean it, don't you? You mad Sc—" he nearly said the offending word again, but then he noticed the a gleam in Graham's eye.

"Of course I do. How did you expect me to respond to your accusation? You were saying?" he prompted.

"Nothing, no, nothing. When, er, where?" Tewksby mumbled, as though he couldn't believe what he was hearing. "I'll, I'll take swords..."

"On shore, don't you think? We'll find a way, I'm sure." Graham yawned. "Now it's late and I'm tired. Time for the hammock. We'll settle the details in the morning."

Mr Tewksby left to commence his duty. He was late already.

Chapter 8

Invasion of Abukir June 1799

The Turkish armada was composed of Turkish owned warships and fifty smaller vessels carrying upward of 15,000 troops and artillery. The troops had been drawn from Constantinople and other garrisons and assembled on the island of Rhodes prior to embarking for Egypt.

The Turks were supposed to commence the assault on the peninsula in the very early hours of the morning, but there were many inexplicable delays, which Sir Sidney attributed to the Pasha, who it seemed had no inclination to move with any speed to capture a vital foothold on the mainland.

Sir Sidney fumed while messages went back and forth between the British fleet and the ships of the Turkish high command, but eventually, quite late in the morning, the flotilla began to move towards the beaches. It was headed by the Turkish gunboats with the British boats in support. Sir Sidney was quite unable to sit out the assault, so despite the pleading of his senior officers he took his place on one of the *Tigre's* two Longboats and ordered the crew to row hard to ensure that he had a good view of the battle to come.

Midshipman Graham was thrilled to be detailed off for one of the jolly boats. He was made aware of this happy event by Lieutenant Jekyll Canes, who beckoned him over to the quarterdeck and fixed him with a disapproving eye. He looked the young midshipman up and down, from his blue hat to his not-too-clean and scuffed shoes, noting the short sword and pistol slipped into the belt.

"I've got my eye on you, Mr Graham. You are in command of the jolly boat," he said, his tone cold. "Normally Lt Fowler would be in charge, but he is indisposed today. You have a responsibility to your men and the boat. Do not act the fool; bring the boat and the men back in one piece, do you hear me?"

"Aye Aye, Sir!" Graham touched his hat respectfully. His eyes slid to where Tewksby was standing. The boy glowered at him. It took a great deal of self-control for Duncan not to wink at him.

"Dismissed," snapped Lt Canes.

"Thank you, Sir."

"Good luck, Graham!" called out young Standforth from the after part of the quarterdeck. He received a glare from Tewksby, and Lt Bowles frowned in annoyance.

Duncan grinned at Standforth, then hurried over to the starboard side where he was all but dragged into the longboat just as the order came to lower the boats. He got a grin from the bosun's mate as he picked himself up from among the crew and tried to regain his dignity.

"Get a lecture from his nibs, did we, Sorr?" the man asked in an undertone. Graham glowered at the seaman and then couldn't help himself: he grinned. "Nothing unusual about that, Chan." He used nicknames for most of the men he knew well. The men chuckled around him. They liked this young fighting cock of a Scot.

The boats were in the water within moments and unhooked. "Push off and watch what yo'r doin', or you'll be on the paint detail for the rest of the voyage!" Chauncey, the bosun's mate, admonished the men. Then they were rowing hard to keep up with the admiral and his longboat, which was trying to join up with the now hurrying Turks.

Graham moved forward to join the gunner and his mate at the bows. "Are we ready, Guns?"

"Loaded and ready, Sorr," he responded. Graham looked over the four-pounder that was mounted in the bows. Anything larger would have broken the boat in two with its recoil. As it was, placing this kind of gun in a small boat had its own risks. It took forever to re-load, so the placing of its shot was important. He stared forward at the Admiral's boat.

"Come on, come on, you lazy buggers!" he fretted out loud. "It's all going to be over before we even get there! I should have ye all bloody keel-hauled!"

The men grinned but pulled that much harder; they were well used to the boy's ways and enjoyed his blunt language. They pulled abreast of the Admiral's boat and were told to stand off some fifty yards from the shore once the Turks had landed.

From here Graham and his crew had a grandstand view of the landing, and were thus witnesses to an appalling event.

The peninsular known as Abukir stuck out of the coast like a thick thumb, its location was east of Alexandria. For the most part a flat almost featureless sand bar, half a league wide, that extended into the sea by about a league. At its very end there was a small citadel which could hold a tiny garrison while camped on the sand in front of the citadel there was a contingent of soldiers.

Though a cannon boomed from the fortress, it quickly became clear to the British sailors that the garrison was very small. Besides the garrison behind the walls there were about 300 French soldiers who barely had time to form up before the flotilla of crowded boats full of Janissaries and other Turkish soldiers arrived in a swarm and splashed onto the beach as a mob. Screaming and brandishing their weapons they charged up the gentle slope towards the tiny group of French soldiers. The men on the boats heard the rattle of musketry over the screams and yells of the Turks but very soon there was no further shooting.

The Turks overwhelmed the French soldiers within minutes, then set about mutilating the bodies of the dead and hacking the heads off the still living victims who had remained alive long enough to face this hideous fate. There were no prisoners.

Graham and his rowers watched with horror from the water's edge, their support quite unnecessary as the Turks completed the massacre of the French soldiers before turning their attention to the fortress. The garrison had no chance either; the walls were scaled by yelling men clambering up ladders hastily placed against the walls. Brandishing their swords and spears and discharging their muskets in all directions, the butchery began again. It was all over within an hour. The Turkish flag was raised on the battlements of the fort and the Turks howled their victory to the heavens.

"Dear God Almighty!" Graham said out loud.

"Bugger me!" Chan breathed, "Them's savages, them is!" Even the hard-bitten sailors well used to the horrors of ship-to-ship battles were shocked at the behavior of their allies.

"Poor buggers, never stood a chance!" another muttered to his rowing mate.

Sir Sidney Smith and his officers arrived back on the *Tigre* with tight expressions on their faces. He barely remembered to tip his hat as they were piped aboard by the bosuns and arms were presented by the marines. Graham and his men hooked up the jolly boat in total silence and then they too climbed aboard. The young midshipman dismissed the men and walked the length of the deck to report to the officer of the watch.

With a face like thunder Sir Sydney called out just before he went below, "Major Bromley and Colonel Douglas, please attend me in my day cabin. I would be glad if you could come too, Lieutenant," he looked over at Lt Canes, then stamped down the stairs toward his cabin.

"Aye Aye, Sir," said the Lieutenant, but paused to wait for Graham.

Graham stopped in front of him and stood to attention. "Permission to be dismissed, Sir," he said.

Lt Canes had observed the events through his glass. He was as shocked as his senior officers, but he greeted Graham without expression.

"Anything to report?" he demanded.

"No, Sir. They're barbarians, Sir!" the boy said in a clear voice. The men on the quarterdeck heard him speak and looked at one another. Lt Canes tightened his lips. The boy was very angry. That was a good thing, but the outspoken lad had to lean to restrain himself.

"Hold your tongue, Sir!" he snapped.

"Yes, Sir. Sorry, Sir," Midshipman Graham came to attention.

"Mr Graham, a word." Lt Canes led the way to the after part of the quarterdeck.

There he turned and said, "You Sir, should understand that war, for the most part, is barbaric, but I will agree with you in this instance. Just learn to keep your feelings to yourself, Mr Graham."

"Yes, Sir. Sorry, Sir. Thank you, Sir."

"You are dismissed."

The officers wasted no time in presenting themselves at the cabin where they were treated to a small glass of precious sherry from Sir Sidney's much depleted supply.

He stood, so they remained standing and waited for him to calm down and discuss the event they had witnessed.

Lt Canes knocked and walked in. "Sorry I'm late, Sir. I was dealing with that scamp, Mr Graham."

"How is he bearing up?"

"He's bearing up very well, I'd say, Sir. Given the circumstances."

"Yes, I agree. Must have been a shock for him. It was for the rest of us, I can tell you."

Sir Sidney took a deep breath and a gulp of sherry, then said, "We have witnessed an act of extreme barbarity today and I am ashamed to admit that we are a part of it."

"Indeed Sir, we did. I share your sentiments completely." Colonel Douglas spoke for both himself and the Major, who looked equally distressed. Lt Canes looked at the three men and said nothing.

Sir Smith continued. "Unfortunately they are our allies in this endeavor, but I am very unhappy that I was not able to be on the ground to perhaps protect the French prisoners. It was inexcusable butchery!"

"Sir, there was no way on earth that you could have stopped that carnage. None at all!" Major Bromley protested.

"Well, now I must put on a good face and visit with the Pasha to discuss the next step, I suppose," Sir Sidney said, glancing out of the window toward the peninsula.

"If our intelligence is correct and Boney is back in Cairo, we might have a chance to consolidate the defense before he has time to react," Colonel Douglas said tentatively. He wanted to move past the horror of what they had witnessed that morning.

"You are perfectly right of course, Colonel," Sir Sidney said. "It is too late to dwell on remorse, we now have to take advantage of the situation and make sure these ... these people can take the next step toward regaining their empire. Although God knows how brutal they will be once they achieve that. I would not like to be an Egyptian when the Turks rule."

"We were given a taste of their behavior at Acre, Sir. But the French have been uncommonly badly behaved themselves at times, as for example at Jaffa." Colonel Douglas was referring to the massacre of thousands of Turks by the French on their way through the coastal town of Jaffa. Napoléon had decided that he could not contain nor hold that many prisoners, so he had ordered them bayonetted and shot on the beaches.

"You don't need to remind me, Major. What goes around can come around, and we were witness to it in small part today."

Sir Sydney sighed, then said, "We must put all this behind us, and the first thing to do to ensure that the beachhead is retained, after which it is vital to ensure that it is adequately protected by better defenses than it possesses at present. Both cavalry and light artillery, which the French still possess, would be able to barrel in without opposition at this moment in time.

"I want both of you to help with this endeavor, and I shall do my best to provide you with a conduit to the Pasha in order that you have his full support. Please wait until I have seen him and then we can begin. One thing we can safely rely upon is that Boney is not going to sit idly by while we are here."

The officers nodded agreement and left to attend to their duties. Lt Canes remained behind. It was stifling hot in the cabin even with the window open. The heat at this time of year was fierce and there was almost no wind to cool the ship. Sir Sidney wiped his brow with a handkerchief.

"Have we any chance of moving the ships farther in toward the fortress, Edward?" he asked.

"We have already moved just under half a cable closer, Sir. I dare not move any closer; we only have two fathoms beneath our hull at present." He left unsaid the peril of being this close, should a storm spring up from the north, or any direction for that matter. The Mediterranean Sea was unpredictable. They would be in dire straits with no leeway to get the ships off the shore. That could mean a disaster for the British squadron.

Sir Sidney nodded reluctant agreement. "Very well then, we must load the boats and make sure that they can perform as gun boats. This is the only way we can protect the flanks of the Turks should Boney arrive at an inopportune time."

"I have already seen the Turk unload many guns, Sir. There doesn't appear to be a shortage of those," Lt Canes said.

"If our training officers are correct then it is unlikely that they will position them well. We will have to show them how, I fear."

"Indeed, Sir. I shall also see to it that the boats are well-supplied with shot and powder in case of need."

Graham had gone below in a state of shock. He felt like crawling into a dark corner of the ship and crouching there. What he had witnessed horrified him. The pleading of the victims and the savagery of their attackers, clearly heard and seen across the sort distance to the boats, was something he would never forget.

Yet there was little time to feel sorry for himself. His watch was on and he needed to brush his coat and clean himself up before presenting himself to the quarterdeck and the unsympathetic eye of Lt Fowler.

The rest of his watch was spent overseeing the men and preparing the boats for the next day. The guns were checked, the rounds stacked and the powder and grape bags sorted and wads prepared. He examined the gun tools, the ram rods for wear and chipping, the wet wads for their sheepskin wraps, rejecting some for wear; anything to keep his mind off what he had witnessed, although on occasion he would glance out over the glittering waters towards the peninsula which was now seething with activity where the Turks were busy erecting tents and defenses. It was comforting that Bosun's Mate Chauncey came up to him during one quiet moment and muttered, "You did fine today, Sir. None of us could have foreseen such a thing."

Duncan nodded. "Thanks, Chan. I agree," he murmured, then walked the length of the busy deck staring morosely at the distant fort.

That night he sat alone absently chewing on his biscuit and a bowl of soup with shreds of salted beef floating in it. His companions noted his preoccupation and left him alone. Even Standforth, eager to know what Graham had witnessed, was hesitant to ask. He didn't possess a glass, so he had merely seen the activity from a distance as a general muddle. The reaction of the officers and Tewksby, who had a glass, had caught his interest. Tewksby had had exclaimed out loud but had not shared his knowledge with the younger boy.

"What's the matter, Scottish?" Tewksby now asked with a sneer. "Did you toss your breakfast? Couldn't take the sight of blood?"

He didn't get any further. A large hand reached out and seized him by his jacket lapel, and he was hauled almost over the table. Spoons and bowls spilled to fall with a clatter onto the deck, but

Duncan ignored the mess as he glared into the eyes of his would-be tormentor.

"Do not talk to me of what happened over there, ye Sassenash prick! You were not there," he whispered. He pushed Tewksby back so hard that he fell off his stool onto the floor. Such was the menace in Graham's voice that no one spoke. Standforth picked up the utensils and bowls and replaced them on the table with a wide-eyed look on his young face.

CHAPTER 9

OCCUPATION

Sir Sidney waited till the next day before he visited the Pasha, who by this time had landed with his elaborate entourage and established himself in a huge tent in front of the fortress. His accommodation was surrounded by so many others that the effect was of a pageant, with flags and banners snapping in the morning breeze and men in a wild assortment of uniforms and dress moving about all over the ground that had only just been cleared of the signs of the battle the day before.

Sir Sidney was ushered into the tent, which was still cool, and bowed to the Pasha who was seated on a raised dais among large and colorful silk cushions. He was surrounded by his glowering bodyguards, and Sir Sidney recognized several of the senior officers who were present.

He greeted Sir Sidney with a wave of his hand and through an interpreter bade him be seated and to take some coffee. Sir Sidney would rather have stood to deliver his comments but knew it would be impolite to do so. He seated himself on the carpet before the Pasha and asked after his health.

"My health is excellent, Sir Smith! As you can see we had little difficulty with the Frans. My Janissaries are invincible!We overcame the enemy in no time at all."

"Congratulations, Your Eminence, on such a victory. I trust there were not too many casualties suffered in the process?" Sir Sidney asked, his tone dry.

"There were some, but that is to be expected. My men are brave as lions and understand the risks when they go into battle. No one can withstand them, as you can see."

Sir Sidney nodded his head thoughtfully and sipped the steaming cardamom-laced coffee he had been offered. "I must complement your servants for this coffee, Your Eminence, it is superb."

"Yes, yes, Sir Sidney, but what do you think of our landing? Was it not superb?"

"Sir, it was very well executed, but if I may mention...."

Sir Sidney had been disgusted by the behavior of the Turks, but too much hung upon good relations with the Pasha to make this known. He paused, uncertain how to proceed.

Mustafa Pasha, emboldened by the presence of the British battle squadron, swelled with pride and self-confidence.

"I have no doubt at all that we will soon destroy the Infidel Army of the French and reconquer Egypt for my Imperial Master," he stated through the interpreter. "I, above all the other servants of the Grand Seignior, have been chosen for my wisdom and courage to perform this honorable mission."

"May I ask about the possibility of cavalry support from General Murad Bey, Sir?" Sir Sidney asked.

"You are a tactician, Sir Sidney. Murad Bey was notified that we had arrived and I expect him to bring with him a formidable force of three thousand Mameluke cavalry from Upper Egypt. They are the best there is and will make mince meat of the French. But I am sure that we can do very nicely on our own, should he be delayed for any reason."

Sir Sidney held his tongue as to that. He never liked to underestimate the French. He fidgeted with his coffee cup. "May I mention something quite important, Sir?" he asked the Pasha.

"What is it?" The Pasha sounded impatient.

"There are two items, Your Eminence. Firstly, the British ships of the line are out of range of the peninsula and would not be able to support you should there be a battle here. We can and will offer support with our gun boats, which can be positioned off shore on your flanks, but the ships of the line will not be in range.

My second point is that despite the courage and skill your men showed yesterday it might be advisable to reinforce the defenses and perhaps to build a forward defense ... just in case the French decide to attack us?"

The Pasha thought for a while, then nodded his head. "You are right, Sir Sidney. I shall give orders that the defenses are to be reinforced."

"Perhaps I might offer the services of my two officers, Colonel Douglas and Major Bromley, to assist your officers in this endeavor, Sir?" Sir Sidney said diffidently.

"Yes, that would be possible, Sir Sidney. I shall send out orders to my officers to expect them." It was clear to Sir Sidney that the Pasha didn't think it was very necessary to carry out the work but he would do as asked.

They talked about other things, but soon the interview was at an end. Sir Sidney bowed himself out and went off to find the two officers and let them know the situation.

It was nearly noon by the time he found them, sitting in the shade of one of the tents near the shore. Both were sweating in their tight uniforms but jumped up respectfully when he arrived.

"How did it go with the Pasha, Sir?"

Sir Sidney slapped his thigh with exasperation. "Why is it that these Eastern leaders are so arrogant?" he asked the world at large.

Neither man felt the need to reply. They waited.

"I have offered your services to the Pasha, who does not believe that they are needed, but do your best." He looked around him. The entire area was almost deserted, as it was nearly noon and the Turkish army was taking its ease in any shade the men could find. The heat hammered down on the beach and the glare of the sun overhead, reflected off the sea, only added to the general discomfort.

"Rather doubt that you will be able to get them to do much before tomorrow morning," Sir Sidney said with a grimace. "However, there is an urgency to ensure that the defenses are completed before Boney arrives. He will have heard of the invasion by now. No matter how exhausted his army is from the Syrian debacle, he must come here or lose it all if this army disperses into the interior."

Both his officers nodded their heads. "We will do our best to have them build a forward redoubt and place as many guns there as possible with a fall back to a second redoubt just in front of that bunch of tents," Colonel Douglas remarked.

"I agree, Sir," Major Bromley said. "If the French do come, they can spend their energies on the first. If they do get through, then the second redoubt with guns using grape will create a killing field and that should stop them."

But despite the Pasha's offhand assurances, this excellent plan did not materialize. Colonel Douglas and Major Bromley came to Sir Sidney on numerous occasions to complain that this or that commander had not bothered to allocate men for a particular task, ignoring their pleas that it was urgent.

During this time there was tension in the Midshipmen's berth. The two would be antagonists avoided one another whenever possible but it was difficult in their cramped space. Duncan's biggest worry was whether Tewksby would rat out on him and they would then be court-martialed as dueling was strictly forbidden. But Tewksby, other than being cold and distant didn't take it to a higher level. Standforth and the other juniors studiously avoided any mention of the subject making for very quiet meals whenever they were thrown together. However work and duty kept the young men very busy and the events unfolding on shore provided more than a distraction for them. The eminent arrival of the French, expected any day now was cause for great excitement.

An exhausted messenger arrived two days later at the camp of Mustafa. Sir Sidney Smith was summoned by the Pasha and informed of events that had taken place to the south.

Murad Bey had been defeated in a fierce battle with the French to the point where he no longer possessed a useful army of horsemen.

Pasha Mustafa wrote a letter to the brave Mameluke prince that was both patronizing and offensive. His boast was: "A very different fate will meet the Infidel dog of Frank from that of the their battle with you and the Mamelukes, if they ever dare to appear before me and my invincible Janissaries."

The indignant Murad Bey wrote from his refuge, "Pasha, render thanks to the Prophet that they have not appeared, for when they do, you will vanish like dust before them."

In the middle of the month of July Sir Sidney and his officers again took to the boats to go and see the Pasha, who received them with all the hospitality of a Sultan. Duncan was this time witness to the opulence of the Pasha's tent, as he and Tewksby accompanied Lt Fowler and a detail of armed sailors, brought along for the protection of the admiral. Sir Sydney's officers were very concerned for his safety, which he completely disregarded, but he tolerated the presence of his sailors.

The Pasha was, as usual, comfortably settled among huge cushions strewn around expensive carpets and low tables laden with fruit. Instead of coffee he offered the hot Englishmen sherbet drinks, which they gratefully accepted. The servants even brought some glasses of the cooling drink to the three naval officers , which included Duncan and Tewksby who were standing at the entrance to the tent. Sipping suspiciously from the glass, Duncan was pleased to find that the drink was cool and refreshing. He wondered how on earth the Pasha's staff managed to keep it so cool.

The naval officers were able to observe the discussion taking place inside, slowed by the need for the interpreters to catch up as either side made its point. It was a strained conversation, and soon Duncan could see that Sir Sydney was fuming, as were his two Marine Officers.

The Pasha, on the other hand, appeared to be totally unconcerned, employing flowery phrases that the interpreter had difficulty translating into useful English. He appeared equally confused, even offended, by the terse replies from the Englishmen and therefore took time to turn them into long, more elegant phrases better suited to the Pasha's ears.

True to form, the meeting had begun with pleasantries and compliments on both sides. Sir Sydney Smith had a brother in Constantinople who was a Consul and had schooled him in protocol. His time in Acre had also taught him that to hurry these meetings was unproductive, because the Turks would become offended and then would sulk and sometimes retaliate in a spiteful manner.

Sir Sidney was astonished to see how undaunted and even arrogantly the Pasha reacted to the news of Murad Bey's defeat. They each saw the event in a very different light. Sir Sidney realized that Napoléon was on the march and would arrive any day now, unhindered by the Mamelukes. The Pasha simply thought he would destroy the French when they arrived. Eventually the admiral was able to come to the main point.

"We simply must speed up the work on the fortifications, Your Honor," he said, wiping the sweat off his brow. "There is now no longer any time left to delay our work. It is most urgent that we are fully prepared for Napoléon's army."

He received a haughty reply. "My dear Admiral,"—the Pasha always called Sir Sidney "Admiral"—"I am very well aware that the French are on their way. Although Murad Bey failed to carry out his mission to delay the French, I have no doubt that my invincible Janissaries will destroy Napoléon the moment he shows his face before my walls."

"But Sir!" Sydney remonstrated. "These are not walls! They are barely constructed sand banks which, in their present condition, will be ineffective against the French! My officers...."

It was no use. The Pasha waved away the warnings. Tired of the meeting, and perhaps the admonishing tone taken by the British officers, he closed it by directing them yet again to go and talk to his commanders Duncan and Tewksby, holding to an unspoken truce, followed the admiral and his small group of senior officers as they renewed their efforts to persuade the Turkish commanders to focus on the defenses.

The two young men stood on the second redoubt and stared south at the desultory work being done on the first sand bank. Duncan noted a line of low hills even further south of the first redoubt. True, there were gun emplacements already positioned, but even to his inexperienced eye the sand bank upon which they were placed was not well supported and would crumble away if there was a determined artillery attack. Moreover, the cannon seemed to lack the requisite stack of balls, and in some cases there was no evidence of any powder cache nearby.

"They should listen to the Marines," he said to Tewksby, who for once agreed.

Major Bromley came up alongside and leaned on the crude emplacement wall with a grunt of exasperation. He was sweating in the hot June sun. With a jerk of his thumb he muttered, "That Turkish officer actually had the gall to tell the Colonel that he is confident that his men will deal with any assault the French can mount, they don't really need to hide behind sand walls!" he shook his head. "Look over there!" he pointed to the right, towards the place where the second redoubt drew down to the beach.

"They haven't even thought to extend the redoubt into the sea, not even with pilings! The French will be able to simply walk around it if they don't mind getting their feet wet! " He snorted with derision.

"What about the French guns, Sir?" Tewksby asked him. He ran a finger around his collar. He too was sweating inside his serge uniform. Duncan wished he could take off his own jacket.

"They'll use field cannon, not these heavy things we have on this center part. These people have never seen the French field pieces at work. I have. It's not pretty being on the receiving end of them. We will most assuredly need the gun boats in support, no matter what."

Later that afternoon, as they finally made their way back to the boats the conversation continued.

"As you can see, Sir," the Marine colonel said to Sir Sidney, sounding very irritated, "we have managed to get the first redoubt half completed, but there is still much to be done to make these fortifications solid. The men stop work at noon, complaining about the heat, and we cannot get them back for the rest of the day!"

"I can see what you mean, Colonel. The only thing we can do under the circumstances is to persist and hope that they will begin to listen," Sydney said, as they tramped down the sandy beach to the waiting boats.

"I have tried to make them place their guns well, but the commanders keep changing the positions. They do not see what I am trying to tell them about cross fire and overlapping fire," Major Bromley added, looking harassed. The heat was taking its toll of the men who were finally, following Sir Sidney's example and stripping down to their shirt sleeves. The naval officers along with their nautical men followed suit, but by now Turks had once again disappeared into the shade and were nowhere to be found.

"Sneaked back under their rocks, I dare say," Graham whispered to Tewksby, who snickered.

"If the French arrive at noon of any given day they could just walk in and take the place," Sir Sidney muttered angrily, then flicked a glance at the two midshipmen. "As you have succinctly pointed out, they will perhaps find the Turks under the rocks." He gave a wry half smile as they boarded their boats for the ships anchored several miles away.

Duncan and Tewksby rolled their eyes at one another, and Duncan resolved to be more careful about saying anything within earshot of his leader henceforth.

Chapter 10

Forced March to Abukir

On July 15th an Arab horseman galloped up to Napoléon and his retinue, who were at that time still in pursuit of Murad Bey and the remnants of his army. The horseman delivered an urgent message.

Napoléon read the missive and then turned to his officers. "The governor of Alexandria, Général Marmont, has witnessed the arrival of the British fleet. It bombarded the city of Alexandria for a short while, then the Turkish army, accompanied by the British squadron under the command of Sir Sidney Smith, made a landing on the peninsula of Abukir."

He paused to let that sink in. Then he said, "Three hundred of our comrades have been massacred and mutilated. The fortress was besieged by the ships at sea and taken by the Turks, who numbered about fifteen thousand on the landward side."

There were mutters of anger from the officers when they heard this. The shame of their retreat from Acre was still fresh in their minds. There was clearly not going to be any form of mercy applied on either side when they encountered one another.

Napoléon had been taking his ease with his senior officers at the time the message arrived. The men were tired from an exhausting few days of hunting for Murad Bey and his remaining horsemen. Napoléon's own Général Murat and his squadrons of cavalry were scattered in all directions.

"Send a message to Général Murat at once to assemble his cavalry and horse artillery and prepare to block any attempt by Murad Bey to come upon my rear while I march north. I do not want to have enemy cavalry nipping at our heels while we deal with the Turks."

The aide rushed off to find the general and pass along the orders.

Napoléon exclaimed, "Eighty ships have dared to attack Alexandria but were beaten back by the artillery in that place. Having been driven off, they have gone to anchor in Abukir Bay, where they began disembarking their men. My intention is to attack them, to kill all those who do not wish to surrender, and to leave others alive to be led in triumph to Cairo. That will be a great spectacle for the city and lay any doubts to rest that we are conquerors."

It was a gross exaggeration to say that eighty ships had been trying to bombard Alexandria, as Sir Sidney possessed only five ships that could be called naval vessels while the Turks had only a few capital ships of their own. However, it was more dramatic to announce it this way for an audience. Napoléon didn't scruple to exaggerate when it suited him, as most of his senior officers already were aware.

This kind of speech was typical of the man, but behind the bombast there was a shrewd and calculating mind. The news was no great surprise, as he had been expecting something of the kind to occur ever since he arrived back in Egypt.

Sir Sidney Smith was not a man to allow the French any kind of respite, and had without any doubt been able to convince the Sultan of Constantinople to provide an invasion force. Smith had foreseen the opportunity, knowing full well how exhausted the French army had to be after the debacle at Acre and the long and painful retreat across the Sinai desert back to Cairo.

To complicate things further, Napoléon's army was spread out all over the country. He had to act quickly, demonstrating his caliber to his men once again as leader and a military commander.

He immediately sent out gallopers. to recall Murat and his squadrons and to join him on the march to Abukir. But first Murat was to make sure that Murad Bey was not a threat to Napoléon's rear.

He sent messengers to Alexandria, commanding Général Marmot to remain in the city and to defend it but not to attack the Turks. As information was sparse, he also sent horsemen north posthaste to ascertain the strength and disposition of the Turks and to verify whether they had moved inland from Abukir. That he had to prevent at all costs, as once the Turks gained the hinterland they could move around at will and would be very difficult to stop.

When he returned to Cairo to collect his men together, Napoléon thought carefully about the strategy he would put in place. He had the rare ability to conjure up a map of Egypt in his head and could envisage exactly where his resources were placed. Général Kléber and his division were in the eastern delta, protecting his right flank from any possibility of a land invasion from the Sinai.

He gave a mental shrug. Well, the counter land invasion had taken place, so he sent out fast riders to Général Kléber with orders to bring his entire division to Damanhur, forty miles southeast of Abukir, there to meet up with Murat.

Napoléon himself would assemble an army from Cairo and meet them both there.

"Call together every available able-bodied man," he ordered. "Only the sick and the lame are to stay behind and defend the city while I am away."

His aides rushed off to carry out the orders while Napoléon continued to stride about his office, now and again glancing at the real map pinned to the wall to ascertain the accuracy of his memory and to evaluate the options available.

He was taking a huge risk by throwing all his available men at the Turks in this one gambit and he was worried. He had no option but to trust his generals, all hand-picked and battle-wise, to comply with his plans and hold up their corner of the whole enterprise. He also worried about leaving his mistress behind, and before the day was out he was back at the palace of Elfi Bey attempting to reassure her about the unavoidable departure.

"But my Général, my Prince! Do you not have generals aplenty who can take care of these barbarians? Why do you leave me so soon?" she gave him a petulant moue. "Have I not pleased you?"

"My Darling Pauline, I shall miss you every minute of the time I am away." He reached for an embrace, but she turned her back, holding up a hand to stop him, the other wrist across her brow in a dramatic pose. "You do not love me, I ... I am sure of it," she pretended to weep. "You are going to Alexandria where you have unimaginable numbers of women waiting for you! They will jump into bed with you the moment you appear. Perhaps you will even be killed!" she shrilled, looking as though she was about to faint at the very thought.

Napoléon shook his head vehemently and tugged at his jacket in the warm room. Cairo at this time of year was a sweat hole and he was perspiring with annoyance as much as from the heat. "No. No, my Darling, my nymph. I am not going there, I simply have to be at Abukir or we will lose all we have accomplished to the Turks. This one I cannot hand off to the generals," he said with a hint of impatience.

"You must promise that you will return immediately, the moment you have disposed of those ... those barbarians, my Prince!" She turned to him and rushed back into his arms, clinging to him fiercely. There followed a long passionate series of kisses and many whispered endearments before he was able to eventually disengage himself and reluctantly take his leave for the rest of the day. There was so very much to do.

During this time Napoléon sent messages south to Desaix, who was up in the higher reaches of the Nile with his army and the hoard of Savants, ordering him to make his way north as speedily as possible, to ensure that if the Turks broke past Napoléon they could be stopped before they arrived at the gates of Cairo.

In just over five days Napoléon had completed his preparations, assembled a sizeable force, and was marching it to Damanhur. He took with him almost all the French troops there were in the city, leaving Cairo largely in the control of his Greek officer Barthelemy, who ran the notorious police force. The Greek would doubtless become even more ruthless while his commander was away: it was in his nature to prefer fear to persuasion. The guillotine's mechanism was being greased with lard even as the soldiers were leaving the city walls.

The men under Captain Joseph Clément were unhappy to be leaving the flesh pots of Cairo so soon after they had arrived. They packed their knapsacks only with essentials, as this was to be a long forced march. They filled their two water canteens, checked that their pouches were full of ball and cartridges and that their fine-grain priming powder was safe and dry. Then they assembled on parade in preparation for the march with their weapons smartly alongside. Their other baggage would travel more slowly via carts.

"Wonder where we're going now?" muttered Poupard to his next in line, Christophe, who was craning his neck to see down the long green and blue line.

"Damn if I know," Christophe replied in a low voice. "Off for another try for Acre maybe?"

"Merde," grunted Pierre. "I've had enough of those bastard Arabs!"

"Silence!" growled Sergeant Émile who, since he had been promoted, could hear a whisper in the ranks from a hundred paces.

"Prepare to march! Attention!" roared Lieutenant Lefevre, standing next to Captain Clément halfway down the length of the column.

There was a loud rattle of musket straps as the weapons were jerked upwards with a sharp movement and placed on right shoulders, then smacked with the left hand which, after a short pause, was just as smartly snapped to the side. "Right turn!" Lefevre shouted, and the entire column swiveled sharply to the right and hundreds of hob-nailed boots crashed to attention.

"Forward march!"

The column began to move off, resembling some enormous blue and white caterpillar interspersed with the green jackets of the Infantry regiment. The bayonets which were fixed for this occasion flashed in the sunlight. The soldier's left arms moved in exact sequence and every man was in step. To the Arabs, the citizens of Cairo, and the Europeans watching this spectacle of French martial strength, they presented a brave sight: the army of Napoléon tramping off to fight yet another battle. The ration wagons, quartermaster stores, ambulances and water carts trundled along behind.

The long line of horsemen who followed Murad Bey moved rapidly along the western side of the Nile, keeping well to the edge of the cultivated region where men on horses would attract less attention. Murat Bey had no illusions as to what might happen should his column be detected. He had gone to great pains to conceal any sign of his small army from the untrustworthy fellaheen peasants. He hoped to arrive intact at Abukir, where he assumed the Turks under Mustafa Pasha would have landed by now, according to the excited messenger. He assumed too that the Turks would have established a firm hold on Abukir prior to marching on Alexandria.

The goal was for him to join Mustafa Pasha and provide cavalry support when the Turkish army set out from Abukir for Cairo to destroy the French once and for all. Unfortunately, the passage of such a large force of cavalry, even though they kept away from habitation as much as possible, could not escape the vigilance of Bonaparte's alert chasseurs and even the Arabs who spied for the French. The Turks were not popular with all Egyptians.

They were nearing the lake called Natron, some distance to the west of the Great Pyramid of Giza, when his forward scouts shouted back at him that there was a cloud of dust ahead.

CHAPTER II

GéNéRAL MURAT AND THE MAMELUKES

Général Murat of the French cavalry snapped shut his glass and turned to his officers.

"We have found them, gentlemen. Prepare for an attack. They will try to punch through our lines and advance to Abukir. I do not need to tell you that this cannot be permitted."

Although young, Général Murat was a skilled cavalry officer and shrewd judge of the lay of the land, and by now wise in the way in which the Arabs fought battles. He had positioned his brigade so that the Mamelukes had the lake to their right when they advanced. He had placed his horse artillery on his own right flank where they could inflict the most damage and themselves move very rapidly to points of most resistance. His men, well used to moving efficiently, were in position within a few minutes. The field artillery were loaded and the horses behind cover, but close enough to be harnessed within a matter of minutes should the need arise.

Général Murat judged that the Mamelukes would rely upon their most common tactic to carry the day and that would be a headlong charge straight at the center of his own forces. The artillery were there to ensure that they were caught between the guns and the lake while his own cavalry would hold the front and stop the Mamelukes from breaking through to the North.

To Murat's intense satisfaction this did indeed happen. From a rise to the west of the lake waters Murat Bey and his riders saw the French ahead of them and with a roar put spurs to their horses. With wild war cries and much waving of spears and swords the turbaned mass of brightly clothed horsemen galloped recklessly straight at the motionless ranks of the French cavalry. They were so intent upon the enemy to their front that they quite failed to notice the horse artillery concealed behind other mounds on their left flank until it was far too late.

As the screaming mass of Mameluke horsemen came within a hundred yards of the French forces, the guns of the horse artillery opened fire with a horrendous roar. Shells and grapeshot were fired at almost point-blank range into the galloping mob of riders, who at first did not hear the bellow of the artillery over the noise of their own charge, until their ranks began to be torn apart by the grape shot and the shells exploded overhead, hurling shards of iron into their ranks. As they faltered from the shock of the gun fire, Murat gave the signal for his own massed cavalry to charge. The distance was short, barely fifty yards by this time, and effect was devastating.

The tight ranks of French horsemen crashed into the Mamelukes and the close-quarter battle began in earnest. It was a savage fight where men slashed and stabbed at one another in a ferocious melee. For a short while it seemed in doubt that the French could hold the Mamelukes, for they fought fiercely, were excellent horsemen, furthermore they outnumbered the French almost two to one. But the French cavalry discipline held as the guns continued to take their toll, whittling away at Mameluke's flank and tearing gaps in their ranks that they could not fill.

Général Murat, with superb timing, then committed his reserve companies to the fight. These horsemen swept through their own artillery positions to crash into the left flank of the Turks, driving them into the lake. The horse artillery had meanwhile, with great efficiency and speed, hauled their guns out of the way of the fighters and re-appeared like harbingers of death further along the Mameluke flank to destroy the men at the rear.

Every time the Turks tried to get to the guns they were met with a wall of fire and destroyed. Horses and men were thrown about like bloody rag dolls by the blasts of grape, torn to pieces as they galloped with insane courage at the guns of the French.

The Mamelukes fighting desperately by the lake shore had lost the impetus of their charge and were now being pushed back into the water or slaughtered by the long, heavy sabers of the French cuirassiers. The tangle of dead and wounded hampered both sides as they fought desperately for possession of the field of battle. The screams of the wounded and dying men and horses were now louder than the war cries of both sides.

The Mamelukes were reduced from three thousand mounted men to less than a few hundred. Murad Bey realized to his despair that he no longer possessed an army of any use to the invasion. He now had to preserve what was left and signaled to his remaining men to flee. They were chased out into the desert to the West where they could no longer do any harm. He now had the humiliating task of sending a messenger around the French army to Mustafa Pasha and inform him that he would not be able to support him any further.

Still exhilarated by the battle and sorely tempted to chase them all down, Général Murat halted his men's pursuit with the bugles and regrouped. His brigade had not come away unscathed. He himself was covered with blood, although none of it was his own. Most of his men were in similar bloody and dusty condition. Though Murat had taken losses and there were many wounded, he had accomplished what his commander had asked of him and still had a good thousand men for the task ahead. There was no doubt that his assiduous use of the horse artillery had helped win the day. Satisfied with the conclusion of the battle, he sent his wounded back to Cairo under escort and set out for Damanhur to catch up with Napoléon's army.

Napoléon arrived in Damanhur within four days of leaving the area of Cairo. It was an extraordinary forced march, carried out by men who had barely recovered from the Syrian campaign, but once again these hard-bitten veterans demonstrated that they were anything but a worn out army. In Damanhur, while his men rested, Napoléon and his generals completed the assembly of the army of nine thousand men and mounted artillery, augmented by the thousand remaining cavalrymen that Murat brought with him from the western deserts.

Unfortunately Kléber had not yet arrived with his division, so Napoléon was faced with a difficult decision. The intelligence he received was that the leader of the Turks was the renowned Sayid Mustafa Pasha, now past middle age but with a long record of victories against the Russians in the past.

Napoléon and his officers discussed this at length.

"According to our intelligence, the Turk, with the help of the British, landed a force of fifteen thousand men who took possession of the peninsula, including the fortress," Général Lanusse offered.

"Then his men butchered our people defending it, and put their heads on display," Général Lannes growled. His tone was grim.

"How brave they are!" someone sneered from the assembled group of officers.

"We should make sure all the men are aware of this outrage," Napoléon stated to the assembled officers in the tent. "Nothing incenses a soldier more than that kind of barbaric behavior. We need to have an enraged army attacking these Turks. I want our men to drive them into the sea. There will be no quarter until they are decisively beaten."

His generals agreed soberly. Although they might have been party to the horrors of Jaffe, that was quickly forgotten as they contemplated the task ahead of them.

"Our scouts and spies have seen that the Turks have thrown up major lines of defense across that flat half-league-wide neck, and they've installed artillery," Lanusse said, pointing to the map on the table in front of them. "That is most likely the work of those British officers, who are with Sydney Smith, of that I am sure," he finished.

"Their flanks are protected, particularly on the east side by Turkish gun boats, but the British ships are laid off at a two-mile distance. I have to say I am surprised and very happy to discover that the British ships might not be able to contribute much by way of support," Napoléon said to his men. "They cannot fire up to two leagues can they?"

"Unlikely, Mon Général," an aide said, shaking his head. "But their gun boats can come in very close to the shore."

"We should fight our way right into their center and open a way for my cavalry," Murat said.

Pondering this information, Napoléon tried to put himself in the place of the Pasha. The Pasha, who was an experienced general, would know full well the strengths of the man he knew he would face. The French were known for the phenomenal speed: they could maneuver their famous columns on the battle field, bringing light field artillery to exploit weak areas of defense, and force strong points to break when confronted by an army on the open field. Their battle squares were impervious to the Turkish or Mameluke cavalry charges. The enemy literally destroyed themselves on the bayonets and rapid fire of the French squares, as had been demonstrated ever since they had arrived in Egypt.

"So what will the Pasha do?" he mused out loud for the benefit of his officers.

"He should have gone out and taken Dalmatia and even laid siege to Alexandria, but he has not," Général Lanusse said in response.

"Instead he has remained idle, and has built walls in the hope that we will throw men at his defenses and destroy our army in a futile effort to capture them," an aide said. "After which Egypt would lie open to the Pasha."

Napoléon tapped his finger on the map in front of them with a pensive look on his face.

"I don't think it will be that long before our enemy does sally out from this beachhead, and then it will be a very different situation and much harder to control," he said.

"Whereas if our army strikes now, the Pasha could be contained in Abukir. His back will be to the sea, and he has nowhere to go unless the British can help him," Murat said. He was eager to get to grips with the Turks after his success at the Lake. Napoléon nodded approval.

"Our spies tell us that the ships are anchored a long way out to sea. Perhaps the sea is very shallow at that place. I suspect that if the British ships were able to help they would be much closer to the shore than they are today. Remember how effective they were at Acre?" one of the staff officers ventured.

No one commented. They remembered only too well how efficiently Sir Sydney had used his ships to support the fortress of Acre. Napoléon himself worried about those vessels. They had been murderously effective against his army.

"Time is of the essence; we can no longer wait even an extra day for Kléber to appear," he stated, watching their reaction. No one was prepared to contradict him, but they were clearly unhappy. With Kléber's additional forces they could assault the defenses with much more confidence.

It never occurred to Napoléon that he might be defeated by larger numbers behind impregnable defenses. He knew with certainty that he did not have an alternative.

"We have no choice but to march on Abukir before they can really dig in. To wait for them to sally forth would be a disaster, and that I am not prepared to risk," he said. "We march on Abukir."

There was a collective sigh from his officers. The die was cast.

The men had marched hard over a hundred miles in four days, but these were hardened veterans who were able to march and fight as few others could. He issued the order to march that very day for Abukir.

They arrived on June 24th at the base of the peninsula and set up camp in the low hills that formed a protective barrier from Turkish guns. Napoléon rode with his officers to a high point that overlooked the neck of the peninsula and stared at the earthworks thrown up only a league ahead of him. To his relief and that of his men it was clear that the Turks had not exited their beachhead but had remained where they were.

"They must be very confident that they can hold us," he remarked to the men around him. "All to the good," he finished.

He meant that if the French could defeat them here it would be significant.

To the professional eyes of his officers the defenses looked makeshift and poorly finished. The officers examined the redoubts through their glasses while they discussed weak points and noted them for future reference. The general conclusion was that earthworks could be torn down or over run by determined men with field guns for support.

The officers also noted with relief that the defenses on the western side had not even been completed as far as the sea. Général Lanusse, who would be on that flank, issued orders to his officers to note carefully where these weak points were.

Ignoring the murmurs of his officers, Napoléon turned his telescope out to sea where he could observe the British ships anchored well away from the fortress.

"Why are they not closer, as they were at Acre? They appear to be too far away to be effective," he demanded of his staff.

"It is likely they cannot come closer, Sir," said one of his aides. "If you look out there, the sea is light colored, almost brown, and hence possibly too shallow for them to come closer."

Napoléon smiled with satisfaction. This was sure to be a frustration for Sir Sidney Smith, he surmised. If the British ships were able to bring their guns to bear on the peninsula, as they had done at Acre, it would very hard for the French, but it appeared that their previous speculations were confirmed and the British ships were indeed too far off to bombard his army.

"The Turks have gun boats on the water, mainly on the east side of the peninsula, Général. They could present a problem for our flanks should we be successful at overcoming the defenses," another aide pointed out.

"Then the light artillery need to be aware of this and ready to respond when and if there is occasion," Napoléon stated. Indeed, there were as many as twenty of the boats, each with a gun mounted in the bows, floating on the water. The larger number were presently on the eastern side. The Turks doubtless had British seamen manning those but they also had a good many of their own.

"Prepare the divisions for battle. We will attack tomorrow," he told his men.

The army marched into place that evening, then settled down for the night. Général Lanusse's division took the left flank on the west side while Lannes larger division took the right flank, with Murat's cavalry placed in the middle.

That evening Napoléon hosted his generals for a Spartan dinner. They were not boisterous, but there was an atmosphere of optimism. On the morrow they would fight and quite possibly die, but their leader was clearly confident that they could overcome serious odds, even though the rules of war usually required that the attacker of a defensive position have more men. In their favor and despite the odds they knew their foe, and there was also the question of vengeance for the deaths of their comrades at the hands of the barbaric Turk. There was an undercurrent of ferocious determination.

Napoléon wanted to hear from Murat how the battle against Bey had gone and was delighted at the way his general had dealt with the Mamelukes. As they discussed the battle plans he said, "This battle will decide the fate of the world."

Murat was puzzled, but decided that he meant that should they win this battle they could then complete the conquest of Constantinople despite the setback at Acre.

The French veterans of the Company of Carabiniere Infantrie did as many thousand others had: they settled in that night around fires made from scavenged driftwood. The neck of the peninsula of Abukir was dotted with camp fires, but the army had pickets out and was prepared for anything that might come from the North and the Turkish lines during the night.

Around one of these fires Private Poupard, Sergeant Émile and their comrades munched on their biscuits and smoked goat's meat. Some of the men who still possessed a clay pipe lit up and smoked, while others had desultory conversations or stared into the embers of the fire.

These men, the survivors of multiple battles with the Turk and the Arabs, were as tough as any soldiers can be who have endured and fought against often impossible odds. The flames illuminated their sun-darkened, lean, almost emaciated features that had a wolf-like aspect. The light thrown off the embers gleamed off their dark, deep set eyes, giving them all the look of predators at rest, as they contemplated yet another encounter with the Turk.

There was not a man among them who had not killed and killed often. To them this was their raison d'être, their very existence, with death a constant companion. They were experts at using their weapons, both the musket and the bayonet. Nevertheless it was always a tense period just before a battle.

"I wonder how many of those Turks there are behind those barricades?" Poupard pondered out loud. He was the youngest of the group. He had cleaned his musket at least twice now and had checked to make sure that the flint was sharp and produced a good stream of sparks in the pan. He would not pour the precious, fine priming powder into the pan before dawn, to keep it from getting damp. Their musket barrels were as bright as their bayonets, the original dark patina from the factories having been worn away with handling. The wood of their stocks, although chipped, was also polished to a deep brown from much use, while the brass of the butts was dented and scored from contact with sand and rock. Their uniforms were relatively new, having been re-issued for the march into Cairo, but were already sun-faded and dusty from the forced march, while their leather belts and knapsacks were scuffed and in places worn through from numerous campaigns.

"You can bet there are more of them than us. Nothing new about that. Merde," Sergeant Émile said as he tamped down the precious tobacco shreds into his pipe bowl with a scarred forefinger. Then he used his metal spoon to lift a tiny ember from the fire which he placed with great care on top. He drew carefully on the pipe and luxuriated in the bitter taste of the tobacco as he drew it into his lungs. He released a long slow stream of smoke from his nostrils with a satisfied sigh of contentment. Émile had learned that the simple things in life were the most important for a soldier. There was no point in dwelling upon those things he could not change.

"Well, I suppose they won't be any different to the ones we met in Jaffa, Acre and those other hell holes," Gérard said.

They knew they were every bit as good as their opponents on the battlefield, better in fact, but there was always the nagging thought that the sheer randomness of battle could take down any one of them without warning. The prospect of being wounded and abandoned was something that haunted them all. The Turk was merciless towards the wounded, rarely taking prisoners. The men seated around the fire were stoical about it; they were soldiers of France and whatever their reservations about their commander they at least trusted him to lead them well.

"Are they just going to throw us at the defenses and hope for the best?" Poupard asked. He was, like his comrades, a survivor of Acre, so he could afford to sound skeptical.

"Probably. I can't wait to get at them for what they did to our comrades. Savages, they are. No mercy from these people if you're wounded, so why should we give them any?" Claude demanded.

It was one thing to be within a square with the howling Turks all around; it was quite another to move in a column against a redoubt. They all knew this but none spoke of it.

"I could see those damn and blasted Roast Beef ships out at sea, but they are a long way out. I hope that is where they stay when we get to the barricades," Andre grunted. "The Goddams destroyed us at Acre."

"Cannon fodder, that's us. We do as we are told and we die ... or live, but that's in the hands of fate. So shut up and get some rest. We are going to be up at dawn. I want every man to have his musket ready and the pan cleaned for inspection. You'll be showing me your balls, the ones in your pouches, not in your pants, and I want to be sure you have enough powder before we march ... or else," Sergeant Émile told them in his mild voice, but no one doubted the threat.

He tapped out his pipe put it away carefully into his knapsack, then reached for his blanket and rolled up in it. He was asleep within a minute. Soon after the others did the same.

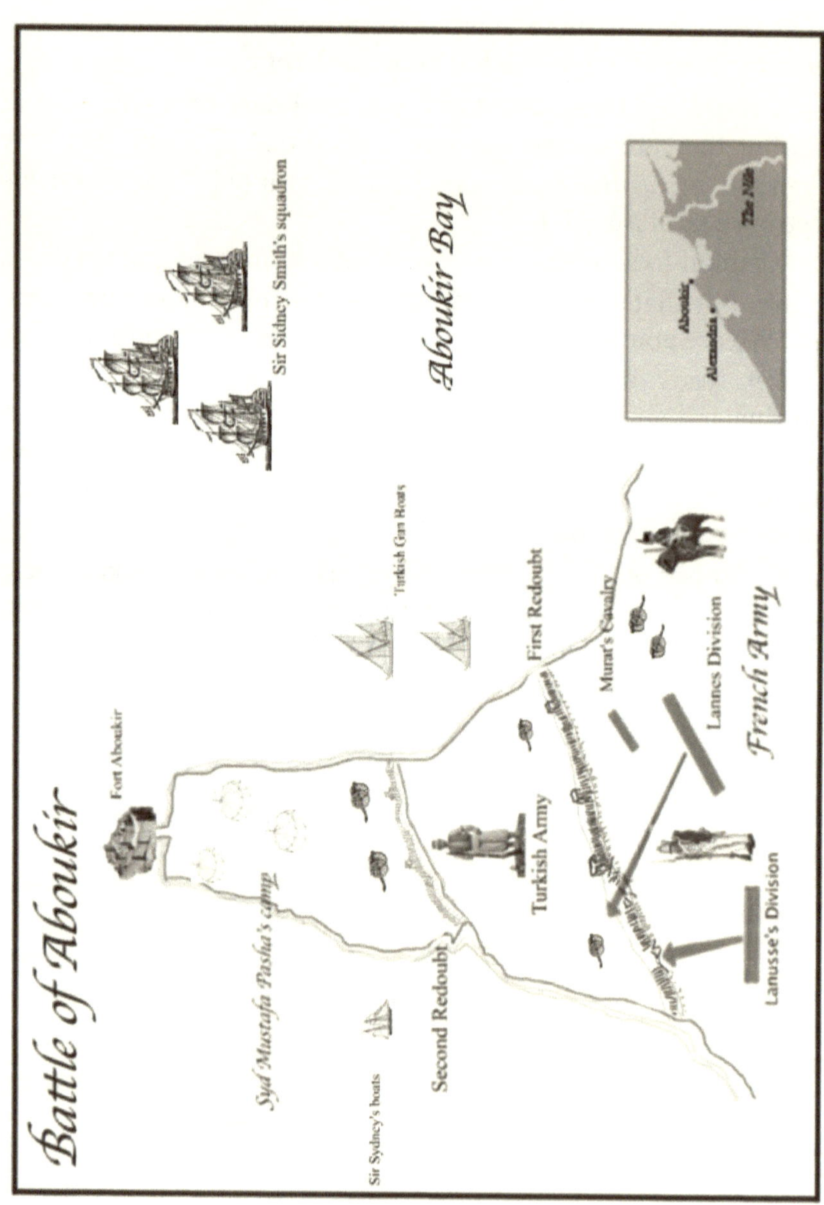

The Battle of Abukir

Chapter 12

The Battle for Abukir

In the very early hours of a cloudless dawn on July 25th the French divisions formed up in columns ready to move into the attack. The columns were four men wide and one hundred men long. The order came to fix bayonets and check pans. There was a flurry of activity and the metallic rattle as the long blades were snapped into place on the ends of the muskets. They were all veterans who didn't need to be told to check their firing pans; they had already done so, and any officer who might have cared to inspect them would have found this to be true. The long lines of blue and green uniforms with white cross belts stood silent and still, waiting for the order to move forward. A chill wind drifted in from the sea, bringing a thin mist.

The men of Général Lannes' division were well prepared and now that the battle was imminent they were impatient to get on with it. As was customary when the French columns advanced, the start of the march was ordered without drums, but as they began to close with the Turkish lines the drums began to beat so that their approach was accompanied by the ominous sound. The mounted artillery drove in on either side of the columns, ready to dismount, align and fire their rounds moments before the columns began the actual assault of the Turkish lines.

Behind the columns and mounted artillery, the larger guns opened fire. The crash and boom of their firing announced to the Turks and the spectators in the ships that the battle had commenced. The crews aimed the big guns at the redoubts in front of the marching column, and after some ranging shots they began to pound the defenses to pieces. The heavy balls howled through the air and smashed into the poorly constructed earthworks, throwing up pillars of sand and sending pilings flying into the air. Sometimes a direct hit occurred and several of the Turkish emplacements were destroyed along with the men occupying them; the French artillery was devastatingly accurate. Soon the rear of the French army was shrouded in smoke and the first redoubt was beginning to fall apart in two places in front of the columns of men marching impassively towards them.

Général Lannes' column made straight for the center of the Turkish defenses. while Général Lanusse made for the uncompleted trenches and redoubts on the western edge of the Turkish lines.

The way in which the French approached the defenses served its purpose well. Seemingly indifferent to the erratic cannon fire from the first redoubt the columns simply closed ranks on those who fell and kept on coming. It was unnerving for the defenders, who had never before encountered a force of this nature.

There was no disciplined defense from the Turkish forces. The few British officers, Major Bromley among them, simply could not persuade the Turks to wait for the French to come closer before they opened fire. The result was a lot of defiant shouting and the discharge of muskets from everywhere which had little effect on the remorseless advance. They were no better organized with their artillery. Balls howled harmlessly overhead or plowed into the sand, throwing up sprays of sand and tufts of grass before bouncing to a stop in front of the implacable advance.

The company commanded by Captain Clément was part of the column that attacked the western redoubt. Sergeant Émile felt his new responsibilities keenly. He, like all his comrades, had done this many times before. The fear that lurked on the periphery of his mind had tentacles that threatened to reach out and take hold of his basic common sense and tell him to flee from this hell. It all had to be suppressed and the objective focused upon; you lived or you died, but your chances were better if you maintained rigid discipline.

He knew that some of his comrades would fall. Some always did, and when it happened it was almost as though they had not existed. When a gap opened up he and the other sergeants would shout, "Close ranks. Keep marching." Their comrades forgotten, the men continued to march towards the smoke and the fire.

Hubert was muttering prayers while Bertrand was swearing out loud as they marched in perfect order towards the sand bank they were to assault. Gilbert vomited, he usually did when they were close to the enemy. He told his comrades that a cleared stomach gave him freedom to act. The firing intensified as they approached the bank and balls hummed overhead or smacked into flesh and bone on either side of them. Armand was struck and tumbled backwards with a cry. His comrades ignored him and marched on. There were men behind the column whose work it was to recover the wounded. The dead would be left where they were but their weapons would be picked up, along with their precious ammunition. French weaponry was in short supply these days.

The columns were almost at the base of the redoubt. As soon the gunners saw their infantry closing the artillery at the rear ceased firing and the mounted artillery galloped forward to new positions, rapidly dismounted and set up their light guns. In very little time at all they began to fire accurately towards the damaged redoubt to keep the Turkish heads down.

On a bellowed command from their officers the men in the infantry gave a great shout and charged. The sheer strain of having to continue in the face of the fire directed at them was loosed against the enemy, who now had a face, and the soldiers were feeling murderous. The leaden fear was gone, replaced by a ferocious need to get at the enemy.

"Kill them! Kill them!" screamed Captain Clément as he led the way, brandishing his sword over his head. They had about twenty yards to run before they arrived at the broken redoubt and the scattered pilings. Captain Clément charged forward, and with loud battle yells the rest of the company charged after him.

The first obstacles they needed to negotiate were the shallow trenches that had been occupied by Janissaries but which had been quickly abandoned as the horse artillery came within striking distance. The trenches were half full of sand that had fallen in. The blue and green coated Infantry and Grenadiers leapt over these and swept up to the base of the redoubt. Sergeant Émile and his small group stayed together, their section following Captain Clément to the base of the first redoubt on the west with Lanusse's brigade.

"I cannot believe that it was only Armand!" the panting Hubert gasped.

They were all surprised that only Armand had been hit while the rest of them so far had not been even slightly wounded.

"Hope to God he makes it," Claude commented, as he glanced up at the top of the berm. They paused to catch their breath for a few moments in this position of relative safety, as the cumbersome guns could not be depressed to fire down upon them. Even now when they were at close quarters the defenders' fire was sporadic and inaccurate. The brightly dressed Janissaries with their huge mustaches, red turbans and fez, their voluminous pants and embroidered waistcoats looked very fierce. They brandished their curved swords and pikes, screaming invectives at the French clustered at the base of the redoubt.

But these veterans had met them before and ignored their shrieking, concentrating on their objectives instead. "Do you see those heads up there?" Clément shouted over the din, pointing. They could see the heads of their former comrades on spikes all along the redoubt and a groan of hate began.

"They are our comrades," Clément roared. "It is time for revenge! No quarter!"

Clément ordered some of the company sections to shoot up at the Turks while he and the others clambered over the half destroyed logs and scrambled up sand banks. The whole structure seemed to be makeshift, which was just fine as long as they could get to the top. Their comrades behind them kept up a wicked rate of fire to keep the Turks' heads down.

Poupard, Alain, and hundreds of other men gained the top of the crude sand wall. Panting, they paused briefly at the top, then fired point blank at the Turks grouped on the other side. Captain Clément joined them in an undignified manner: propelled by a hand on his buttocks pushing him from behind, and a voice shouting, "Get on up there, Mon Capitaine, and leave some Turks for me!" Clément recognized Claude's voice, ever an impatient man.

Shouting encouragement to one another and those behind them, they drove down and into the Turkish ranks with their bayonets extended, and their gristly work began. The French soldiers had seen the rows of heads mounted on spikes all along the redoubt, placed there by the Turks to terrify them as they approached. Unfortunately for the Janissaries it had the opposite effect. The French veterans were incensed.

"No quarter! Forward, forward comrades! Pour La France!" came the shouts from all around. Poupard and Sergeant Émile were among those who took up the cry.

The artillery barrage had shaken the Turks. The appearance of the horse artillery at close quarters and their speed and accuracy had distracted the Turkish gunners so that they had been totally ineffective in mounting a response. Now the appearance of blue and green coats on the top of the redoubt startled the Turks long enough for the French soldiers behind the first rank of infantrymen to clamber up and reinforce them at the top. It became a savage hand-to-hand battle; but Poupard and his comrades, Gérard, Sergeant Émile, Claude and the others in the company led by Captain Clément, who was using his saber to good effect, were battle-hardened soldiers with a cold hatred in their hearts. They were going to avenge their comrades at any cost.

The company of men who had survived the retreat across the desert, now stayed together and exacted their revenge. They presented a bristling, impenetrable array of bloody bayonets that deflected wildly swung sabers and poorly aimed pikes, then stabbed with deadly accuracy at exposed Turkish bodies. They and the line of men behind them reloaded and fired so rapidly that the crash and flame of musket fire seemed almost continuous. Sergeant Émile worked alongside his comrades, grunting, cursing, and sweating, and sometimes snarling at his victims with the rage of battle, as he and they worked their bloody trade.

Sometimes a Turk was lucky with either a pistol or a musket and a French soldier would stagger and begin to fall, but his comrades would snatch at his cross straps and haul him unceremoniously back behind them, then they would close ranks, whereupon, if anything, the bayoneting became even more savage.

While the Turks displayed wild courage as they defended their positions it soon became evident to them that they could make little or no impression on the steady, mechanical thrust and stabbing tactics of the veteran French soldiers, behind whom others poured a relentless hail of lead. The noise of gunfire, the smack of lead on flesh and bone at close range, and the screams and sobs of the wounded was overlaid with a growing pall of choking, acrid gun smoke.

Before very long the dead and dying lay in colorful, bloody heaps over which the Infantrie and Grenadiers tramped, bayonetting those who still lived to ensure they were not going to be a problem from behind. Although it seemed like an eternity to the men fighting, the whole engagement had only taken a few long minutes since the first columns broke through. Now they were followed by the rest of the brigade as Général Lanusse saw his opportunity and ordered them in.

Sergeant Émile was hoarse from shouting and the cloying smoke that made his throat raw. "Stay close," he rasped, "do not stray. Stay close! Reload! Reload!"

His comrades did, along with hundreds of the other troops of infantry, and they stayed close together in the confusion of the battle, always pushing forward and closing ranks whenever one of their men fell. Inevitably the barricades began to fall apart as men behind the front ranks tore at them with picks and shovels to open up a gap to allow the cavalry and horse gunners through.

The infantry would halt every now and then at a bellowed command from the Captain.

"Halt! Front rank kneel. Fire! Reload. Rear rank, fire! Reload. Forward!"

The men would fumble for a cartridge, bite off the end, pour the dark gray powder down a scorching hot barrel, then use the paper of the cartridge as a wad to ram it behind the powder. A lead ball was hammered home after that. The men spat out the residue of the paper from bone dry mouths and parched, cracked lips. Then the hammer was cocked and fine powder shaken into the pan.

A short pause, then the shout: "Tirez!" The deafening crash of muskets at close range and the sharp jolt of the recoil. Roils of smoke, then a hoarse shout from the captain. "Avancez." The men stamped forward one, two, three paces with their bayonets leveled, driving into the massed ranks of the screaming and roaring Turks in front of them. The smell of blood and shit, vomit and sweat mingled with the smoke, clogging the nostrils of the living, making for the putrid stink of hell.

There was no quarter expected nor given by either side, and the Turks resisted fiercely. Very often one of the Janissaries, screaming to Allah, would hurl himself at the bristling array in a mad charge, screaming and slashing with his sword, only to be spitted by one or other of the advancing men who, with a snarl of his own, would stab the man with his long bayonet. The Janissary would fall and be trampled by those French soldiers behind as they marched forward, some slipping to their knees in the puddles of blood and the entrails of the gutted. The Turkish line held their makeshift defenses for some time before the concentrated weight of the French numbers began to tell, and then the defense crumbled and quickly become a rout.

With triumphant shouts Lanusse's brigade clambered over the half demolished redoubts and the trenches while the Turks fled the area. Worse was to come for the Janissaries, however, for the fall of the western side distracted their comrades in the center, and before long Général Lannes' division, taking advantage of the confusion, broke through and the rout of the entire first line of defense began.

Chapter 13

The Rout

Thousands of the Turks were slaughtered as they turned and fled the first redoubt. They fell in bloody piles of bodies as the French poured fire into their retreating backs with no mercy whatsoever. They initially fled towards their comrades in the second line of defense but when most of them were denied admission because the French were so close behind them, they died. The French soldiers shot them down, so the tide of fleeing men swerved and took to the sea. The screams of the wounded and dying filled the air all around the combatants, but the French were implacable and drove on.

It soon became a stampede; Janissaries abandoned their weapons and equipment, then died before they could get to the water. Those that could make it were screaming and clawing at one another as they tried to reach the gunboats which were standing out from the beaches.

Earlier that day, Sir Sidney Smith had ordered the ships to send boats to stand off from the sea shore and on Lake Maadieh with cannon and carronades, with orders to harry the French on their flanks.

Seeing the defenses on the west side begin to crumble, Sir Sidney called over to the other boat commanders to bring the British boats round to the west of the peninsula and to get closer to try to arrest the French progress. The men on his boat pulled hard to bring the boat within fifty yards of the shore. As bullets began to zip past them, Sir Sidney ordered the gunners to fire at clusters of the French army, who were forming up in the space between the two defense lines.

The junior officers on the other boats lined up with his, and their guns opened up, adding to the deafening din and dense smoke of battle. Squinting through the smoke, Sir Sidney tried to assess the situation on the shore. To a certain extent the gun boats were successful and the French began to take casualties. But they moved rapidly out of the way, and then the men on the boats beheld an awful sight. The Turks on the first redoubt had been routed long before the gun boats were able to do much good, and they were now between the British and the French. The British had to cease firing or risk killing their own allies.

Thousands of the Turkish men rushed to the beach on the west side, preferring to take their chances with the sea over the ferocious and vengeful bayonet-wielding French soldiers. They ran screaming and howling into the water where a very few were able to reach the boats. Sir Sidney and his men were suddenly preoccupied with saving Turkish lives as men pleaded from the water for help. They hauled as many as they could onto the boats, but there were many others who could not even swim out as far as the boats, so they drowned in relatively shallow water, as those in front were pushed further out or trampled under foot. Either way they perished, and the sea was clogged with a solid mass of drowned or drowning men whose bodies began to sink to the bottom. Only a few were able to survive long enough to be hauled aboard the gun boats, almost swamping them in the process.

It became impossible for the British gun boats to provide any useful firepower as they ran the risk of simply adding to the destruction of the Turks who obstructed their access to the French.

Worse was to come, for the French light artillery galloped up to the dunes and with cold efficiency unlimbered their guns at practiced speed and began to fire grapeshot into the water all around the boats. Then the captured guns still in the first redoubt were hauled around and their well directed fire was added to that of the cavalry. It soon became obvious that the position of the boats had become untenable. The water all around them was alive with water spouts from gun fire and the panicked splashing of drowning men.

Sir Sidney, seeing that it was a hopeless cause, shouted to the boat crews to pull away and waved the others off. They had no choice, with the water being churned up all around them by shot and shells and the desperate, shrieking Turks reaching for them and threatening to overturn the boats. The crews thankfully and energetically applied themselves to the oars, and although impeded by the wet and wailing Janissaries on board, they managed to pull their boats out of immediate danger.

Appalled, Sir Sidney and his men watched the mass of Janissaries drowning before their very eyes as they pulled away. Although he was outwardly calm he was seething with anger, for the Turkish gun boats had refused to come around the peninsula to join his own boats on the west side where they were most needed. He was sure they could have prevented the rout and perhaps saved the day. The combined firepower of all the boats in one place would have easily out-matched that of the French horse artillery. But those boats were now far out of reach on the other side of the peninsula where they were useless.

He ordered his boatswain to row towards the area behind the second line of defenses and waded ashore with some sailors as a body guard to try and make for the Pasha's tent. He was met by Major Bromley and some marines who had managed to evade the French and get back to the relative shelter of the second redoubt. They were panting and angry at what they had witnessed.

The group of British soldiers and sailors could not make much progress because all around them was chaos. Frightened, wailing slaves and servants mingled with leaderless Janissaries to block the way. The opulence of the camp area was in stark contrast to the madness, filth and gore of the defense lines. Then the gun fire intensified at the second line of defense. The Turks on the walls and barricades screamed defiance and fired off irregular volleys from their muskets, while their remaining cannon banged away at the approaching enemy. Sir Sidney noted with professional disgust how slow they were to reload. His own sailors or the Marines would do much more damage.

Sir Sidney and his small escort hurried towards the redoubt just in time to see the French repulsed, whereupon any remaining discipline the Turks might have had was lost. Thinking the French were beaten, they scrambled down from the redoubt, screaming and howling their battle cries, abandoning their positions to rush back into the area between the defense lines to hack and dismember the dead and wounded French soldiers who had been left behind.

Sir Sidney and his men watched appalled as the Turks mutilated the dead, but then one of the men called over to him.

"Sir! Look over there!" He pointed to towards the first redoubt. "It's the cavalry, they're getting ready to charge!"

Sir Sidney stared over to where the man was pointing, and sure enough he could see clearly that the French cavalry were rapidly forming up just inside the gaps of the first redoubt and indeed were about to launch themselves at the Turkish soldiers who were preoccupied with their gristly tasks.

"We cannot defend this place on our own, Sir Sidney. I am sure that those Frenchies will find the gaps, or make their own and get through. There is no one to stop them, Sir!" Major Bromley shouted over the deafening noise of battle all around them.

"You are right. Where is the Pasha? He should damned well be here!" Sir Sidney snapped with a grimace of disgust. He was shocked that the Pasha had not been at the front of his forces, as then he might have been able to restrain the madness of his men. A catastrophe was unfolding but Sir Sidney and his men could do nothing about it. The time had come to leave and try to take the Pasha with them.

He looked behind him towards the largest tent in the encampment and pointed. "We must see if we can get to him and persuade him to defend the line ... or leave with us," he called, beginning to run towards the tent.

Général Lannes' division, once over the first defenses, turned towards the western beaches to link up with Lannuse and establish a firm grip on the flank of the Turkish lines.

There was a pause while they regrouped, then at a shouted command the French hurled themselves at the second line of defense. These proved to be better built and manned by more determined Janissaries, supported by several British officers and Marines. This time the French soldiers, exhausted by their previous efforts, could not make it past the Turks on the banks.

Captain Clément, along with Sergeant Émile and his troop, were to the forefront of that attack, but they were tired and moved slowly. Casualties began to mount. Gérard caught a bullet in the chest and fell without a word, while Poupard and another fell back wounded. Their comrades seized the three wounded men by their epaulettes and cross straps and dragged them to a space behind them. They knew what would happen should they be left out in front.

The others fired up at the men on the top of the redoubt to keep the Turkish heads down, while the front line attempted to scramble up the slopes. There were many more Turks there than had been on the first redoubt, and their concentrated firepower was too much. The French began to waver.

Émile and his comrades heard the bugle call to retreat, and Captain Clément reluctantly waved his men back with his bloody sword. All the companies executed the retreat in good order, falling back across the blood-soaked, corpse-strewn sand to the first redoubt, where they formed up and faced the enemy while reloading. Émile and another seized Poupard by the shoulder epaulets and dragged him along with them; others along the line pulled as many wounded as they could to safety behind their line.

"We do not leave you behind!" Émile croaked through a mouth that tasted like ashes. He had no illusions as to what the Turks would do to his comrade should they find him. He was right. This retreat was a signal for the Turks to sally forth and begin to behead those French soldiers who were either dead or left wounded on the field. They totally disregarded the French assembled in front of them while they carried out their gristly activities. Their exultant shrieks and the bloody butchery of the wounded and the dead resembled the actions of demons who had temporarily escaped from hell, observed with disgust and rage by the French officers and men gathered at the trenches they had formerly overrun.

The Turks showed no discipline whatsoever, rushing about in a random manner, ignoring the French as though they had already been defeated. But Murat was also at the opening to the first line of defense with his cavalry. He saw an opportunity and seized it.

"Suivez moi! Pour La France!" He shouted, brandishing his saber. Calling upon his men to follow him he put spurs to his mount and led them at a ferocious charge into the space between the two lines, catching the Turks completely by surprise.

They had been so preoccupied with their looting and mutilating the dead that they barely heard the thunder of horses' hooves until it was too late. The cavalry used their heavy sabers with awful efficiency, hacking and stabbing, then running the fleeing Turks down with their horses, crushing them under the iron-shod hooves of their mounts. Within minutes the field was cleared of living Turks. All were either dead, wounded, or fleeing for their lives.

Slashing their way through the massed Turks, Murat and his horsemen arrived at the second line of redoubts and trenches, already being abandoned, and swept over or through the gaps blown by their artillery with minimal resistance from those still manning them. Within a few minutes the second line of defense was wide open, allowing the French infantry to pour through or over and capture the guns, while the cavalry proceeded on to the now exposed Pasha's encampment.

The cheering French Infantrie and the Grenadiers were out for blood and almost no one they encountered on their way to the fort was spared. Clément and his men led the charge, screaming and yelling like madmen, but they ran in a solid group that bristled with blood-stained bayonets. Turks fled before them, knowing that there would be no quarter given by this implacable foe. Despite the need to scatter the enemy and the temptation to break ranks to hunt them down individually, Émile and his companions remained disciplined and grouped together, as did the other companies around them.

Listening to their NCOs and officers, who roared hoarse commands over the din of artillery, the howling balls and the deafening crash of musketry all around, they now advanced at the trot to pause, fire and reload, then move forward and fire again. When close pressed they used their bayonets with devastating effect. Sergeant Émile parried a clumsy lunge from a desperate enemy, then thrusting in and twisting, then stamping on the body that would not release the bayonet. Dragging it free, he called his men to close ranks with their comrades. They obeyed, all with blades dripping with gore and blood-bespattered uniforms. They were caught up in the blood lust of battle and vengeance.

Sir Sidney and his men had no choice but to abandon the redoubt and race towards the Pasha's tent, which was placed just in front of the fortress walls. Glancing up, Sir Sydney and his men could see the Janissaries lining the walls of the fort, shouting and screaming defiance at the enemy. There were also men on the two small towers on either end of the short wall, and overlooking the entire fort was a single stone tower at the very back that abutted into the sea.

Major Bromley shook his head, and as though he had read Sir Sidney's mind, he too glanced upwards. "This will be no real defense against the guns of the French if they get this far, Sir."

Just as he said this they were stopped in their tracks by a huge roar from behind them.

"The charge has begun. It is too late!" the Commodore gasped. In a matter of a few seconds they were overtaken by Janissaries racing towards the elusive safety of the fortress. The remainder of the army manning the defenses had abandoned their posts and were running for their lives. The mass of men grew so quickly that it soon became impossible for Sir Sidney and his men to get anywhere near the tents.

"Sir, Sir! We must make for the boats," Major Bromley called to Smith, his voice cracked with urgency. "They will trample us underfoot if we do not! I don't think the Frenchies are in the mood to take prisoners, not even us!"

It was probably true. While British officers were quite valuable for the exchange of prisoners, the pursuing men had their bloodlust up, and it would not be the first time that potential hostages were slain in the heat and confusion of battle. The charge by the French cavalry had caught the Turks completely by surprise. The wailing and screaming came closer until finally swarms of Janissaries poured back over the redoubt to join those already running for their lives.

Sir Sidney and his men barely made it to the boats before the terrified mob caught up with them. They splashed into the shallow waters and were hauled unceremoniously on board by the anxious British sailors who wanted get away from the clawing hands of the Turkish men who were threatening to overturn their boats and drag them down into the sea with them.

Despite this, as they pulled away Sidney ordered them to haul on board a few more who had come close enough to save, joining those already huddled in the well of the boat. The British rowed away, casting anguished looks at the thousands who wailed and screamed for help that was not forthcoming. Before the horrified spectators' eyes they began to go under and drown in their hundreds. To make matters worse the French mounted artillery once again found the beaches and hurled grape shot at point blank range into the backs of the stricken mob.

Chapter 14

Gunboats

On one of the gunboats manned by the British seamen, Graham and Lt Fellows were huddled with the gunner as he set the heavy 4-pounder in the bows.

"Grape for this one," Lt Fellows said, as he peered over the shoulder of the gunner and his mate at the French who were themselves about to fire their own field piece in the direction of the boat.

"Grape loaded, Sir!" said the gunner almost huffily as though to say, "What else would we use under these circumstances?"

Lt Fellows ignored the tone and instead snapped, "Stop hopping about, Mr Graham, you are rocking the boat!"

Duncan had been hopping from one foot to another in excitement that an actual engagement was about to take place.

"Are they going to shoot at us or at the Turkies, I wonder," said Lt Fellows.

As though in answer there was a puff of smoke that almost obscured the French gun, followed by an awful sound as the round howled through the air just above boat.

Everyone ducked reflexively, then they stared back at the puff of smoke and the light artillery who were reloading. Just then another of the field pieces fired and again there was a howl as the ball came right towards them, and this time the ball took Lt Fellows' head off at the shoulders. The officer's head disappeared in a red spray of blood, bone, and brains, while the body was tossed backwards in among the rowers.

There were exclamations of "Kerist!" and "Bugger this!" from the sailors as they tried to push away the inert body that still pumped blood everywhere. The tough sailors, well used to carnage in sea battles, shook their heads and helped to lay the twitching body on the bottom of the boat. "Poor bugger, anyone got somethin' to cover 'im with?" asked one.

"Silence back there!" shouted the bosun's mate. He automatically looked to the next officer in line.

Duncan had felt the wind of the ball as it killed his commanding officer; he stared in uncomprehending shock at the remnants of Lt Fellows body lying among the rowers.

"Sir! Sir! What do we do now?" Chauncey prodded him. "Orders, Sir?"

Duncan gulped for air and forced himself not to vomit. "Ready... ready to fire?" he demanded with a tremor in his voice.

"Aye Aye, Sorr," responded the gunner, sliding sideways out of the path the gun would take on its recoil.

Duncan felt a rising anger. "Then fire the Goddamned thing!" he shouted, and pointed towards the enemy who had re-emerged from the smoke and were frantically reloading.

"Fire, Goddammit!" he repeated.

The gunner nodded, gave him a gap-toothed grin and jerked the lanyard. The 4-pounder boomed. The whole boat shuddered. Smoke from the gun briefly obscured the target and the cannon hammered backwards onto its stops. "Reload!" shouted Graham unnecessarily. The gunner and his mate had already leapt to the work.

Then they saw the effect of the grape. Their gun had been well laid. The packed shot from the gun had all but obliterated the French gunners. "Well done, Gunner!" Duncan exclaimed, contemplated with satisfaction the destruction they had wrought while the men cheered.

"That's for Lieutenant Fellows, ye bastards," he called out. The men behind him grinned. Duncan ignored for the moment the screaming and floundering Janissaries all around them who were now clamoring to get into the boat, but then Chauncey called out urgently, "Sir! Do we take them aboard?" He looked apprehensively at the splashing and screaming Turks approaching the boat.

"Later!" Graham called back. He glanced over to the right where more Turks were struggling in the water and several French artillery pieces were raking them with grapeshot.

"Get us out of here, Chan, and over there where we will give the Frenchies a taste of our lead, then we can pick up some of this sorry lot," he waved his sword in the general direction of the Janissaries.

The oarsmen bent to the task with a will. They knew that if they tarried they would likely be swamped. The boat shot back out to deeper water and then was skillfully spun around to dart a few hundred yards in along the shoreline. Meanwhile the gunner turned to Duncan. "She's ready, Sorr."

Grahame nodded and peered through the smoke that was drifting over the sea towards the coastline. It appeared to be full of blue colored uniforms, while the sea was dense with the red of the Janissaries' fezzes, many of which were drifting about in the water after their owners had sunk to the bottom. The noise of screaming and wailing Turks, the rocketing sound of passing shot and the distant boom of the guns all added to the chaos around the boat. It was hard to even think but Duncan could barely contain his own excitement. He pointed. "In there, hurry. We'll give it to them and then get hold of some of those Turkies!" he yelled

The boat shot in among the Janissaries, who were splashing about more and more desperately as their comrades behind forced them into ever deeper water. Duncan dropped his hand, Chauncey bawled an order, oarsmen braked the longboat in a flurry of foaming water and Duncan shouted in the gunner's ear. "Fire!"

Again the earsplitting bang, an acrid billow of smoke, and the boat jerked as the gun recoiled. "Back! Back up!" yelled Duncan, waving his sword in a circle over his head, and the oarsmen bent to the task.

There was some return fire but the shot rocketed overhead, causing the oarsmen to cringe as they rowed hard to get away. Duncan stood in the bows, high with exhilaration, refusing to flinch, feeling somehow invincible. His blood was singing. The bosun's mate, Chauncey, nodded to his men and chuckled as he pointed to the young midshipman. He shook his head.

"Likes it 'e does, that one."

There were chuckles from the rowers who were close enough to hear.

They picked up twenty of the soaked and bedraggled Turks, dragging some aboard who had almost given up and were resigned to their fate. These lay gasping and moaning in the well of the boat, babbling in their own language. Allah received a lot of mention.

The now silent oarsmen pulled hard for the distant ships. They could see the horror of death in the sea all around the peninsular as the vengeful French infantry and field gunners caught up with the fleeing Turks, who fled to the water where they drowned because they could not swim.

Duncan, after watching for a while, felt the high of battle drain away and turned away, sickened. He didn't want to watch as the ranks of wailing Janissaries slowed and subsided beneath the small waves, leaving their red fezzes and turbans to float away on the current.

They dropped off their sodden and demoralized charges at one of the Turkish transport ships, then made their way back to the *HMS Tigre* where, upon being informed of the death of Lt Fellows, the crew above dropped a canvas sheet to the men in the boat below. They wrapped his body in the canvas and tied it well before having it hauled aboard the ship.

Duncan clambered aboard and saluted the quarterdeck to find Second Lt Bowles waiting for him.

"What happened?" he demanded brusquely of the powder-blackened young man standing before him.

Duncan told him of the event and what he had done following the death.

Bowles looked grudgingly pleased. "Go below and clean yourself up, Mr Graham. I will want a written report by Six Bells this evening." Then, knowing how hard that would be in the gloomy cave that housed the midshipmen, he said, "Get the Purser to provide you with paper and ink, and write it in his cubby."

"Yes, Sir." Duncan saluted and staggered off.

Bowles turned his attention to the corpse and the hovering crew of the boat. He wanted to know from them what had occurred.

"Just as the young gentleman told you, Sir. A ball took off the lieutenant's 'ead and then the Middie just took over as though nothin' had happened. Gave them Frenchies something to think about 'e did, Sir." Chauncey shook his head and grinned. "Seems to like a fight, does that one, Sir."

Bowles noted the approval in his voice. He turned away to pass along the sad news of Fowler's death to his superior.

Such was the rout of the encampment that the Pasha was almost alone when Murat arrived at his splendid tent. Curious to see who might still be there, Murat dismounted and handed his horse off to one of his men and strode into the tent. There he found the Pasha standing quite alone and confronted him. "Surrender! You are my prisoner," he called to the overweight Turkish leader facing him. "Your army is defeated."

At the very moment that Murat called upon the Pasha to surrender, the Pasha pointed a small pistol at him and fired it. The ball ploughed a furrow on Murat's jaw, inflicting a slight wound. Ignoring the pain Murat wasted no time; he lunged forward and struck back with his already bloody saber at the Pasha's hand, removing two fingers and the pistol. Murat called upon his men. "Seize him and take him to Général Bonaparte." Then, fingering his wound, he remarked, "The women of Paris have no need to worry, my lips are intact!"

His men, who admired and loved their commander, roared with laughter, and then some of them escorted the Pasha—none too gently—away to present him to Napoléon, while the rest of them set about chasing the remainder of the Turks, either into the sea or back into the fortress at the end of the peninsula. There was plenty of looting along the way to keep them busy.

In front of the fortress, the battle was all but over. The Turks were routed and fled in all directions, again abandoning their weapons and equipment. Supposing that they would be subjected to the same treatment that they had meted out they were in no hurry to surrender to the coldly ferocious French, but instead tried to flee to wherever they could.

Unfortunately there were no good exits, only the sea or the fortress, where a few thousand managed to gain entrance before the rest were stopped as the gates were slammed shut in their faces. They beat on the doors, frantically pleading with and cursing the occupants as they contemplated their imminent fate, staring over their shoulders in terror at the implacable blue and green uniforms coming ever closer. The grim, powder-blackened faces and bloody bayonets spelled their doom.

Captain Clément had not heard any bugles calling for a halt and was not inclined to listen for any either. Nor were his men. Caught up in a frenzy of killing they butchered anyone in their path. The humiliation of the long and terrible march back to Egypt, harried and picked off by the marauding Arabs, and then the senseless killing of their comrades here in Abukir were sufficient reason for these men to give no quarter.

Finally the bugle did sound, but not before the men of the first column had almost reached the walls of the fortress. They had swept through the encampment barely noticing it, but now Captain Clément and his men realized what booty they might be giving up for the sake of their blood lust. The call came just in time for them to change direction, abandon the cringing enemy and seek loot instead. Incredibly, their discipline had held despite all the chaos. Their captain and sergeant merely ordered them into another direction and off they went.

In their place the light artillery swiftly took up positions in front of the citadel and proceeded to blast the Turks grouped at the base of its walls at close range. The terrified and demoralized Turks repeated what had occurred before at the first and second redoubts and fled en masse into the sea. Once again the shoreline was packed with men hurling themselves into the water only to die as they were trampled by those pushing up behind them or they sank out of their depth and drowned. The vast majority could not swim, so they perished in their thousands. The British boats plied back and forth as fast as they were able, picking up men still able to stay afloat, but this number dwindled and soon there were none left alive to save. The red plumed hats, turbans and fez of the Janissaries who had drowned left the bodies and floated to the surface to bob on the waves in a dense crimson mass, many hundreds of yards wide. It was a horrifying sight for the men on the ships who witnessed the whole event.

The British watched appalled as those left on land were shot or bayonetted by the French, who were in no mood to take prisoners, so several thousand more died. Very few were allowed to surrender. Captain Clément simply shook his head when his men looked at him with the question as they stood over yet another Janissary pleading for his life on his knees. The vision of the heads on the redoubts were too recent for any chance of forgiveness.

The battle was in all respects over by 11:00 a.m., leaving the French army in charge of the field in front of the fort of Abukir. The French cannon finally ceased firing, leaving an eerie calm to settle over the sand dunes and the area of the former redoubts. Slowly the pall of battle cleared; tendrils of gun smoke drifted off with the light wind, leaving a battlefield strewn with the dead. Corpses and abandoned equipment were piled high, and the vast majority of them were Turkish. Of an army of 15,000 men who had landed a few days before there were perhaps only 6,000 left alive: either in the fortress, saved by the British, or captured.

CHAPTER 15

AFTERMATH

The British boats rowed back to the ships anchored two miles away with shocked and silent crews. Sir Sidney climbed the side of his ship *Tigre* feeling too tired to pay much attention to the shrill sound of the bosun's pipes that welcomed him aboard.

"Major Bromley, please accompany me to my cabin," he said to the major, who followed him over the side and onto the deck.

Sir Sidney turned to the young officer on duty.

"Please ask Lieutenant Canes and Captain Williams to come to my cabin as soon as is convenient, Lieutenant," he said, and then without looking to his left or right he made straight for his day cabin.

Sir Sidney was standing by the large bay windows of the day cabin and Major Bromley was seated on one of the chairs in front of the desk when there was a knock on the door.

"Come," he called.

Lieutenant Canes opened the door and advanced into the cabin, followed by Captain John Williams.

When Smith turned and faced the two men he looked haggard. "Gentlemen. Take a seat," he said. "Can I offer you something to drink? I for one am in need of something to wash away the taste of today."

He sat down heavily at the desk and drew the decanter and glasses towards him without waiting for their replies. In the silence that followed Sidney busied himself with pouring the sherry into the small glasses. They all took one and he raised his to them.

"Here is to one of the greatest disasters I have ever had the misfortune to witness, and I pray I never do again. I would say 'Confusion to the French,' but they do not appear to be confused. Indeed they have upheld their reputation for being one of the best armies in the world today, to the chagrin of the Turk and myself."

Major Bromley nodded agreement, his face drawn and glum.

"What happened over there, Sir?" Williams asked his commander.

"Why John, the Turks landed their many men, butchered the defenders of the fort and encampment, as we all witnessed, and then would not listen to Colonel Douglas nor Major Bromley here, who both know the French well and tried to get the Turks to prepare for them. Boney arrived and with his usual discernment found the weak spots that we tried to warn the Turks about. He wasted no time in attacking those very points, and not long after the first redoubt was overrun. His men are utterly without fear and incredibly disciplined.

"Sadly we in the gun boats realized this too late, as we were on the eastern side when the French attacked. I ordered our boats to pull for the West and ordered the Turkish gun boats to follow, which they did not." He sighed and pressed his lips tight in a bitter grimace.

"We arrived with only a few boats just in time to witness a shameful rout. We did all we could, but the French had taken the first line and the Turks were either milling about, being killed by the French, or trying to swim back to our boats.

"It didn't take the French long to exploit that situation and attack the second redoubt. The major and I were there on the fortifications to witness not only the utter lack of discipline by the Turkish forces when the French withdrew from that attack to regroup. Even then the Turk might have won the day by holding their ground, but no, they had to rush out and start behaving like savages again, butchering the wounded and mutilating the dead.

"That was when the French attacked with their cavalry. Général Murat, I think it is, who commands them. The French were enraged and the Turks are mostly dead, except for those cowering in the fort."

"I have never seen anything like it before," Major Bromley said. "Their turbans and Fez floated to the surface as they drowned. The water is like a sea of poppies all around; I have never seen the like!" he exclaimed again, shaking his head as though trying to banish the sight. "It was terrible to witness the panic and disarray," he added, taking a sip of his Madeira; then he shook his head again as though he still could not comprehend what horrors he had seen.

"We could see most of the battle from the ships with our glasses! It seemed as though the French were invincible!" Lieutenant Canes said. There was real respect in his voice as he spoke.

"We have to assume the Pasha has been taken prisoner, although we tried to reach him. He was not even on the redoubt directing the battle!" Sidney said tonelessly. "I cannot understand how a man of the Pasha's reputation could be so disinterested, inept, and so utterly irresponsible. There was no leadership whatsoever on the Turkish side, while the French knew exactly what they were about at all times."

"Their horse artillery did much damage. They are very experienced and came right on the heels of the Turks and destroyed them by the hundreds as they fled," Major Bromley stated with barely suppressed admiration.

"That, too, we witnessed from the ship. Those horse artillery were a decider. God, I wish we could have supported with our own ship's guns! It would have made all the difference," Lieutenant Canes said, nodding his head.

"Can the Turks hold out in the fort, Sir? Is there still a chance?" Williams asked.

"There would be a very good chance of driving the French off the peninsula even now if we could only bring the ships in closer and support the fort with our own guns, but we are stranded out here unable to do anything."

Sir Sidney slammed his hand down on the desk, making the glass rattle. It was a rare demonstration of anger on his part. His frustration was palpable, and contagious.

"We cannot just give up, gentlemen, but I fear that this engagement went the way of Boney and we must do our best to salvage what we can of it."

The others wondered what on earth he meant. How was it possible to salvage anything from this debacle?

He looked at Lieutenant Canes. "Lieutenant, I want all the boats to take water to the fort. Employ all the midshipmen and senior warrant officers to command them.

"There are now several thousand men in a place that can only accommodate about five hundred at best. They will be very short of both water and provisions. We must do all we can to help them hold out. Please arrange for this to take place immediately. And we must send boats to find if anyone is still alive in the water, although I rather doubt it. Major Bromley, please assist Lieutenant Canes. At the very least we must try to evacuate as many as possible tonight."

"Aye Aye, Sir." Lieutenant Canes stood up, as did Major Bromley, who gulped down the remainder of his sherry. They saluted Smith and left. Captain Williams stayed behind.

In the silence that followed Captain Williams observed that his commander. looked exhausted. There were dark rings under his haunted looking eyes. He had not yet changed his clothes, which were soaked, blackened with burnt powder and torn in places, exposing the garments underneath.

"You should change out of those clothes as soon as you can, Sir," Williams suggested.

Sidney wiped a hand across his forehead, also smudged with powder and grime.

"It was an utter disaster, John. Those Turks have to be led by the most arrogant and stupid of people. Major Bromley and Colonel Douglas pleaded with the Pasha to listen to what they had to say. In the end I had to plead personally with the senior officers and even the Pasha himself before the battle, and only then did they do anything at all; and as we have seen, it was far too little."

"You did all you could. The ships would have made a huge difference if they could have come in to help, but a ship grounded is of no use, and indeed immediately becomes a target itself," Lt Canes said. He had returned just in time to hear the last words.

Sydney sighed. "If only we could have, or if only their gun boats had come to assist us! We might have turned the tide. Yes indeed, a lot of 'if only's'. We are witness to a catastrophe!"

"The Pasha was unspeakably arrogant and has now paid for it dearly. I imagine that he might be better off as a prisoner rather than having to go back to the Sultan and explain things."

"That's just the problem, Lieutenant. We will get the blame, as they do not know how to examine their own consciences and draw the true conclusions. Furthermore, I am very sure that Nelson and his merry crew of sycophants will chortle about this when they get to hear about it," he sighed.

Captain Williams feared his senior officer was only too right. Then they heard the sound of guns again. It was something of a surprise, as there had been a ghostly calm for some hours. The boom of the French guns pounding the little fort was an unwelcome reminder that the battle was clearly over for the British.

Sir Sidney listened to the guns for a moment before remarking, "The Turks can eventually replace their losses; the French cannot."

As he was to write in his report to Admiral Nelson, "Even under these untoward circumstances, we have the satisfaction of observing the enemy's losses to be such that a few more victories like this will annihilate the French army."

CHAPTER 16

VICTORY

During the time when the guns were quiet The Pasha , his right hand heavily bandaged was brought before Napoléon. They stood on the same rise that Napoléon had occupied for most of the day as he watched the progress of his army. Now the Pasha was forced to see the humiliating consequences of his neglect.

Bonaparte was courteous in victory. "I would be glad to send a letter to your master in Istanbul and tell him of your courage, Your Highness." This was said not without some satisfaction, as Napoléon intended to parade the Pasha in Cairo when he made his victory march.

The Pasha lived up to his arrogance with the reply, "Thou mayest save thyself the trouble. My master knows me better than thou canst."

After that statement Napoléon had no more thoughts of magnanimity.

"Take him away and guard him well. I shall have him paraded in Cairo. Continue with the bombardment!" he ordered.

Indeed it had been a fine victory, and Napoléon was pleased to give credit for the seized moment to Murat, who was promoted to the rank of divisional general. Napoléon also gave most of the glory to Murat's brigade; he told them they had achieved the impossible.

Général Kléber arrived with his brigade that afternoon to join Napoléon. The tall Alsatian embraced Napoléon and told him, "Général your greatness is beyond all bounds, you are out of this world!"

"Murat was the man who turned the tide, and even captured the Pasha on his very own!" Napoléon crowed. "Our casualties were minimal. Two hundred or so dead and about seven hundred wounded in some fashion or other. The enemy? Thousands and thousands! But we are not yet done with this spit of land, my Général. The invasion is not fully repulsed yet, as the fort of Abukir is still in the hands of the Turks," Napoléon stated. "However, I am told that many Turks took refuge and the fort is full to bursting with men who have neither the food nor the water resources to withstand a long siege." Napoléon laughed. "I can just imagine Sir Sidney Smith over there in that ship of his, biting his nails with frustration."

Kléber nodded agreement. "We now have the captured guns and our own artillery. It will not be long."

"Bring our artillery and mortars up and demolish their walls. This will not be another Acre."

"No indeed, mon Général," said Général Lannes. "Look out to sea. They could not bring their ships in closer as they could at Acre."

"I can imagine how impotent that Sir Sidney Smith must be at this moment!" Napoléon said with satisfaction. "He must watch as we destroy the Turkish survivors and drive them into the sea to join their cowardly comrades who are already there. Revenge is sweet at this moment."

Within a few hours both the light horse artillery, the captured cannon and some more larger field guns brought by Kléber were in place behind the very redoubt made by the Turks as their second line of defense, and the bombardment began. Napoléon ordered the barrage to continue all through the night.

Chapter 17

Water for the Besieged

After he had cleaned up and taken a short but restless nap, Sir Sidney appeared back on deck and began to observe the British ship's boats, which had switched from gun boat duty to supply vessels which now plied the water between the ships and the distant citadel. The roar of the French guns continued unabated leaving a pall of yellowish smoke that hung over the former battlefield.

"There must be thousands of men in that tiny fort, Lieutenant," he said, peering at the now darkened peninsula through his glass. The bright streaks of flame from the French cannon and the pall of white smoke that obscured the battle field were clearly visible to the men on the ships.

Midshipman Graham was in command of a longboat with the bosun's mate Chauncey in charge; not far away, Tewksby and Standforth were in charge of jolly boats. All the boats were loaded with water casks destined for the fort. It was distracting to hear the wailing of the survivors and those who had watched the ghastly tragedy taking place from the Turkish boats and ships standing out to sea alongside the British ships.

On board the Turkish transporters and their war ships the survivors and sailors called out to their God.

"Oh Allah! Allah!" they wailed. "The Faithful have this day perished in thy sight, and thine Hand was not lifted to save them! Tonight thy servants sleep beneath the waves, while the proud Infidels are resting in their tents, and trailing thy standards in the dust! Woe! Thrice woe, is Islam this day!"

"What are they wailing about this time, Sir?" Lt Canes asked Captain Williams.

When he was told he muttered under his breath. "Perhaps they should have listened to Sir Sidney then they wouldn't be in this situation would they?"

As the boats approached the shoreline, using the fort as a cover between themselves and the French guns, something none of the young officers could have anticipated occurred.

The Turks who had taken refuge in the fort appeared to think that rescue had arrived and boiled out of the back gates of the fort and ran down among the rocks, trying to reach the arrivals. Duncan and his men had to yell at the Janissaries to stand back, for they appeared to be determined to swim to the boat.

"Get the barrels over the side, men!" Duncan yelled over the screaming of the Turks.

"Keep them off the sides of the boat or they'll swamp us!" Chauncey bellowed, as he thumped down the flat of a cutlass on the hands of a man struggling to haul himself onboard.

"Water!" Duncan yelled at the Turks, pointing at the barrels that splashed into the water alongside them. "Drink water!" he mimed drinking the clean water from the half floating barrels. But then, to the surprise and horror of the men on the boat, the wild-eyed Janissaries dragged the barrels onto the rocks and the short strip of sand and, using axes, began to smash the barrels open, spilling the precious water out onto the beach.

"Goddam the stupid buggers don't listen!" Duncan exclaimed, looking back at his own men who were gaping at the chaos that unfolded in the shoreline before them.

Frantic Janissaries on their knees tried to capture some of the drinking water in their hands, only to be shoved aside by others, desperate to have a drink themselves. Within moments two large barrels of fresh water were shattered and their contents lost. The Turks then turned their attention to the boats. But Duncan had been in this situation before.

"Get us out of here, Chan!" he yelled, and using the butt of a musket he rammed at the panicked Janissaries attempting to clamber aboard. Other members of the crew rapped the Turks on their heads or their hands with their oars as they pulled away. Given the chance, the mad Janissaries would all try to board, swamping the boat and sinking them all.

As they drew abreast of the jolly boat with Standforth in charge, Duncan pointed back to the Turks who were now fighting over staves of the barrels.

"Its madness over there, Minnow!" Duncan shouted. "You'll have to get in and out fast. Do not tarry and don't let them swamp you!"

Standforth nodded, his face was pale under his oversized blue hat, and he fingered his short sword nervously. They all watched incredulously as some of the Janissaries, having seized some staves, began to run into the sea and try to use the wood to support them as they floundered out towards the resting boats.

"We'll stay here and support you," Duncan assured his younger companion. "Get in there and dump the barrels overboard. It's up to those idiots to do with them what they will."

Standforth nodded and called back an order to his crew, who heaved on the oars. The boat shot forward and almost beached itself. While several of the crew held off the yelling Turks with their oars, others manhandled the two barrels overboard. One of them landed on a couple of struggling Janissaries, who went under. One didn't resurface. Others of the screaming and howling Turks seized the barrels and hauled them ashore. Once again the boat crews watched in amazement as the barrels were hacked to pieces by the insane Janissaries. The drinking water pouring out over their outstretched hands and gasping faces, to be lost yet again in the sand and on the rocks.

Wondering what Tewksby might be facing, Duncan cast a look to his left where other boats were drawing close to the shore. Without exception they experienced the same insanity and were forced to dump their barrels in the sea and hurriedly withdraw out to deeper water, from where they watched the madness taking place on the beach. Each boat tried to help several of the more desperate Turks aboard who had made it far enough out to sea but were now in danger of drowning.

But now the French had seen what was going on and raced some of their light guns forward to open fire on the boats standing out to sea. It was time to go and leave the luckless Janissaries to their fate.

"Stupid bastards!" Duncan exclaimed, as Standforth's jolly boat pulled alongside.

Standforth looked like he was going to be sick. "It's madness over there!" he jerked his sword point at the beach. "How can we help them when they behave like that?" he asked, sounding shaken.

At that moment another boat came close. "Ahoy there, Graham, Standforth!" a voice called.

They both turned and saw that it was Tewksby, in charge of another of the ship's boats.

"I wondered where you were," Duncan called back.

"We were over there on that side of the point." Tewksby waved his sword to their left. He sounded shaken too. "They are completely mad! They destroyed their own drinking water! Never seen the like before!" He shook his head in amazement. "What do we do now? We cannot help them if they are stupid enough to do that."

A small water spout rose into the air between the boats, followed by another spout twenty yards away. None had heard the guns firing, but this got their attention.

"Demme! Row for the *Tigre*, the French have our range! Nothing more we can do here," Tewksby yelled. As he was the senior officer in the location, and they all heartily agreed with his assessment, his command was obeyed with alacrity.

"Get us the fock out of here, Chan," Duncan called back to the bosun, who grinned and looked relieved. "Aye Aye, Sorr," he called back. "Row lads!" he shouted, and put the helm over hard. The rowers bent to their task with a will, and the three boats hauled off towards the distant ships, every man relieved to be gone from that hellish beach.

Duncan noticed Major Bromley on the other longboat, well behind them as they drew closer to the main ships. He assumed that the Major would pass along the tragic news directly to the Commodore. Duncan didn't envy the man.

After dismissing their crews the midshipmen clambered aboard, leaving the boats tied off. There would be more work for them later.

It was a very subdued group of midshipmen who touched their hats to the quarterdeck and reported to Lt Bowles.

Although the thunder of the French guns continued into the evening there was complete silence on the British ships other than necessary commands.

Later, when dusk was falling, Major Bromley came aboard to report. After saluting Sir Sidney, who turned away from moodily contemplating the peninsula to greet him, he opened his mouth to begin his report, but Sidney took him by the arm and guided him below to his day cabin.

"You look done in, Major. Have a drink and tell me how it is going over there."

"The disaster continues unabated, Sir," Major Bromley said with cough. His face was streaked with grime and sweat and his uniform was in tatters. "There is absolutely no discipline whatsoever. It is very distressing to witness, but there is very little we can do. We bring casks of water to them, whereupon they fight and tear at each other to get at them. I took some men ashore to try and put a stop to it, but they either ignored us or they tore at us with their bare hands." He gestured at the state of his uniform.

"We had to get back into the boats or be torn limb from limb, Sir! They smashed the casks without even attempting to open them with care and conserve the precious water. It was spilled out and wasted almost before it has come ashore! The maniacs then fought over the empty casks trying swim out to our boats on the staves! We could not take every one, and we had to leave because if we had stayed we would have been swamped and drowned along with them. Not long after that the French realized what we were up to and began to fire upon us."

Sir Sidney had already heard some of this information from Lt Bowles, who had interrogated the midshipmen. The shaken young men had been dismissed with instructions to go below for a rest. Even so, he listened quietly to what the major had to say. Everything was of importance, if he was to salvage anything from this debacle.

The agitated major continued after taking a gulp of the sherry. "It didn't take the French long to figure out what we were doing, so they lined up some of their longer ranged guns just for the purpose of shooting at our boats. They also ran some of the lighter ones using grape onto the beaches. It meant that we had to run the gauntlet of their guns to arrive at the chaos on the shores!" He shook his head again.

Sidney observed Bromley in silence as he took a long sip of his sherry, then replaced the glass on the desk with a shaking hand. "I have never seen the like, Sir... and never want to again."

"How many of them are there in the fort right now?" Sidney asked.

"I would estimate there are five thousand men crammed into that place, which if my memory serves me rightly is now commanded by Mustafa Pasha's son. I rather doubt that he has any control over the situation, Sir."

"Why don't they evacuate most of them, I wonder," Sir Sidney mused. "They will probably have to surrender. Boney isn't going to leave them in control of the fort. Would a detachment of marines make any difference?" he asked.

"It might, but the discipline is so bad that I would fear for their safety if it deteriorates much further."

Sidney pondered this for a few long moments while he stared out at the darkening sea through the open casement window. The routine sounds of a ship full of men drifted in, combined with the thump of the guns on the peninsula. The contrast struck him as ironic: the normal sounds of life on shipboard; and only two and a half miles away men were dying in their hundreds, terrified and panic-stricken, with little chance of rescue. He scowled; he had to do something, even if it proved futile. He could not simply watch the disaster come to its inevitable conclusion without doing something. He turned back to the major.

"Ask Colonel Douglas to attend me, Major. I don't want you to go next time, but make very sure that whoever does go is well aware of the situation and knows how to signal our boats to come and collect them if it goes badly."

Major Bromley stood up and saluted. "Yes, Sir. I will ask the Colonel to come immediately."

"Thank you, Major. Get some rest."

Sidney waited until the major had left and then called out to the Marine outside his door to find Captain Williams and have him report to the cabin.

Williams arrived on the heels of the colonel. "Gentlemen, please be seated, I am in need of your help." They sat up and paid attention.

"Colonel, I want you to send two boats of marines to the shoreline. Pick the men carefully and have an officer lead them. I know it is but a salve, and mainly for my own pained pride, but I want to be seen by our allies as trying to help even at this forlorn moment."

"Yes, Sir. I can arrange it, we can send them over during the darkness."

"We need to have a couple of boats standing by to take them off if things get perilous for their safety, but I need to know from our own people what is happening in that fort, Colonel. A detachment of marines might help stiffen their resolve; you never know."

When the colonel had left Sidney turned to Williams. "Now is a chance for you to test your skill with languages, John. I need a spy out there to tell me what is going on."

"That would be interesting, Sir. What exactly am I going to be looking for?"

"To be quite honest, I am not sure as yet, but I know one thing: even after that disastrous march back from Acre there is still a deadly sting to the French army. We need more intelligence about their morale and the general condition of the occupying forces. We will have to wait out this bloodbath, but then I want to put you ashore and see what is what over there. I feel blind at present."

Days passed and the conditions in the fort deteriorated, as the French bombarded the walls and interior with mortars and artillery day and night. The bodies were piled alongside the mounds of rubble. Men began to die from thirst or dysentery from drinking fouled water or even sea water. The British continued to try to bring fresh water but, as Major Bromley had pointed out, little of it made it to the men inside. The men were crowed into the dark stone passages and against the thick walls, crouching in corners, praying or crying at their fate. Almost none could be persuaded to man the parapet and defend the fortress. Before very long the British Marines had to be evacuated, for they became the target of the madness all around them.

The Colonel reported to Sir Sidney what had transpired.

"The bombardment is highly effective, Sir. The French captured a treasure trove of riches from the Pasha, including all the guns the Turks had, along with all their powder and shot.

Many of the guns were ours, loaned to the Turks. They seem intent upon reducing the fort to rubble, and they have the wherewithal to do so, using our own equipment to accomplish the task.

"I went ashore myself with the marines and can attest to the fact that the conditions in the fort are truly terrible. They are living on top of one another, and on top of the dead, as they have nowhere to put them other than to toss them over the walls into the sea. They have no food and very little water, which they have squandered every time we have tried to provide it."

He sighed and wiped a filthy hand over his grimy face. "We established some form of order for bringing supplies in, but not enough to help the situation very much. Although we managed to evacuate almost a thousand of the Turks, it became too dangerous for us to remain. I fear cannibalism is already rampant in some of the darker corners, and men are going mad from drinking sea water."

"It is clear that we cannot continue to supply them from the ships. That means we have to find some spring or source to fill our own casks on shore," Sidney reflected.

"I see what you mean, Sir. There is, according to our own crude maps, the possibility of a spring to the east of the French positions which the French might not be guarding, but I don't know if that is really the case. Perhaps we should investigate before we send too many boats?"

"Good idea, send Captain Williams in; I'll talk to him."

John Williams appeared with Lt Bowles in tow, both looking curious. Sir Sidney beckoned them over to look out of the starboard after window that gave them a view of the distant land and the peninsula. He pointed to the shoreline to the west.

"I need you to do a couple of things for me, John. We are running short of fresh water, or will be very soon if we have to keep resupplying the Turks in the fort and even their own ships, which came woefully undersupplied. I want to know if there is a water source of some kind to the east of the French positions. There are tributaries from the Nile all over the map in this region.

I'm sending some boats to look for water that we can obtain without letting the French know. You can go ashore at the same time and take stock of the situation on land. Perhaps even look into Alexandria?"

"I have contacts within the city so yes I can see what I can do, Sir." Captain Williams nodded assent.

"A couple of boats, Sir?" Lt Bowles asked. "We have two which have just arrived back from the fort. Midshipman Graham was put in charge of one of them and I have Midshipman Tewksby with the other."

'How are the young men holding up?" Sidney asked.

"Pretty well, I think, Sir. The first day was a shocker but now they know better how to handle the situation. We've had no casualties today, despite the French trying to shoot at them."

"Good, then give them their orders. They are to look for water to the east of the peninsula, well away from the French lines. There is lake of some sort over there but it could just be tidal. I want a safe fresh water outlet that we can tap into, and while they are at it they are to observe whether there are any French patrols along that strip of land. I would send the small ships, but not even the ketch can get close enough to see if there is anything useful, and a ship prowling so close to shore would draw the French like fleas to a dog. The boats will be less conspicuous."

"I agree, Sir. We'll go this evening just before sunset so that there is less chance of being spotted," Captain Williams replied.

"I'll notify the men, Sir," Lt Bowles said, and they departed.

Chapter 18

The Duel

That evening, a good two hours before sunset, two jolly boats left the *Tigre* and joined the other boats plying back and forth between the British ships and the fort. Although the traffic was much reduced there were still casks of water and food being ferried, and the boats often as not returned to the ships with wounded or sick from the hell of the fort.

The two boats commanded by the midshipmen continued in an easterly direction, leaving the fleet and the peninsula behind as they took a bearing on the nub of land that lay to the northeast. The sea was calm out here, so they made good progress for a couple of miles before Williams gave the order to approach the land. He was dressed in Fellaheen clothing: a collarless, long sleeved and skirted robe of light brown cotton and sandals on his feet. It was his intent to land and make contact with some of the locals and then try for Alexandria. later he intended to disappear into the hinterland and do some reconnaissance. Alexandria was his objective on this mission however.

"By my reckoning and the old maps, there is a small lake just inshore in line with our approach. If we can find an inlet we can mark it for future visits, and hopefully the French won't notice," he told Duncan.

"How will you manage on shore, Sir?" Duncan asked him, eyeing the dirty robe and the ragged turban.

"Don't worry about me. You have to make sure we don't get caught landing, so keep all noise to a minimum."

"Yes, Sir," Duncan murmured.

He had discussed an idea with Tewksby before their departure. When Williams was well on his way the two of them were going to walk into the sand dunes and settle their point of honor.

Tewksby had been horrified by the suggestion, his skinny features contorted with a mixture of fear and incredulity, but Duncan had persisted. "All we have to do is walk ahead of the boats, on the pretext that we will be looking for a good place to take on water, and when we are far enough away we can engage."

"You're mad!"

"Don't forget to bring your sword."

"We'll never get away with this!"

"First blood and then it's done."

He had left the cramped quarters for the deck after that. The smell of Tewksby's fear was oppressive.

The low-lying land loomed as the boats approached with care. The sandy bottom was only a few feet below, which meant that a man had to be in the bows keeping an eye open for submerged banks. Duncan and Williams focused on the shoreline, looking for any signs of activity which would abort the operation before they even landed.

At one point they did indeed observe dust rising behind the sand dunes of the shore. They stopped rowing until Williams stood up and waved them on. "I imagine it was a squadron of cavalry on their way to the French encampment," he said, and pointed to their right. Duncan glanced that way towards the continuing siege.

The sound of the guns was like the low mutter of a storm. Somehow the flash of their muzzles was brighter in the glow of the setting sun, now below the horizon of the peninsula. The remaining rays of the sun threw the small fort into sharp relief.

While Duncan could not make out any figures, the repetitive thud of the French guns and the flashes reminded him that there was a terrible reckoning still taking place on Abukir.

They were now coming to the beach and all eyes were intently scrutinizing the shoreline for any danger. Off to his right Duncan noticed a tidal inlet, and he pointed. The coxswain immediately steered them in that direction. If they could get into the inlet they would be less conspicuous to any French patrols.

"Be careful here," Williams admonished Duncan. "I do believe the Frenchies would have patrols out but they might be further inland and not as far out as this. I'll take my chances with that. You focus on the fresh water. Just make sure you are here within two days at the same time."

"Right, Sir," Duncan whispered back.

They pulled into the inlet to find that water was moving out towards the sea, so the men had to row hard to make progress, but eventually they were moving into calmer waters. The estuary was wide but shallow at the throat, but even in the dimming light Duncan could see that further inland the water deepened.

When they had rowed another fifty yards into the inlet and were well out of sight of the beaches on either side, Williams indicated that they should land. Armed men disembarked quietly into the thigh-deep water and drew the boat up onto the beach. Williams jumped out onto the white sand and with barely a wave headed due south towards the scrub and small trees that grew in clumps all around the area. About a mile away Duncan could just make out a grove of palm trees which seemed to be the direction Williams was headed. It wasn't long before he was out of sight and Duncan turned his attention back to his present surroundings.

"It's clean water flowing out to sea, Sir," one of the men whispered. He had taken a cup to the water and sipped it warily. "Smells fine and tastes fine, Sir," said another.

Duncan nodded, this then was a tiny tributary of the Nile, he guessed. His heart was beginning to pump harder and faster, for he had the duel on his mind. He waved the other boat in and

Tewksby jumped ashore. Duncan could tell he too was tense and nervous.

"You men fill those casks with water from here. Myself and Mr Tewksbury are going to reconnoiter," he told the coxswain of his boat. "Keep the noise down, men," he admonished them, when he heard a careless splash from the other boat.

"Sure you don't want an escort, Sir?" Bosun's Mate Chauncey asked, indicating the armed men all around.

Tewksby was about to answer but Duncan forestalled him.

"No. No, that's all right, Chan. We are only going as far as those palm trees to see if there is any habitation," Duncan lied. "Come along, Tewks," he said to the other midshipman, and drew his sword. "Just in case," he explained to Chauncey, who was eyeing the blade with a speculative look. Duncan led the way up over the sand bank, then followed the shoreline using the palm trees as his compass.

They were fully out of sight in a dip of the dunes, half surrounded by the scrubby trees and bushes, when Duncan heard Tewksby rushing up behind him. It disturbed his already tense senses to a state of alarm. He spun around and with an exclamation dove out of the way. Only just in time, as Tewksby had rushed up on him and was about to spit him with a savage lunge at his midriff that, a moment before, would have been pierced his back.

"You bastard!" Duncan snarled. His surprise was quickly overcome by his instinct to survive and his mounting outrage. "Couldn't even wait, eh?" He backed away to find better purchase for his feet in the soft sand.

"You are a pain in my buttocks, you Scottish pudding!" Tewksbury said, barely keeping his voice down, and their swords snapped together with a sharp clink of steel.

They went at it clumsily for a couple of seconds as Duncan found his pace and Tewksby thrashed at him with his weapon. Neither was an expert by any standards, but this was a grudge match and Tewksby, having overcome his initial fears, was committed and savagely determined to finish off his arch enemy.

"Scot, you useless pork rind," Duncan ground out as he ducked a wild swipe from his opponent. He lunged and Tewksby only just managed to parry, then stumbled backwards and turned to run up the slope. Duncan followed, stabbing at Tewksby's buttocks with crude lunges. "Turn and fight or I'll stab you in the arse!" he hissed, and stabbed again at the white trousers just ahead of him, missing by a fraction.

"Erk!" grunted Tewksby and turned, slashing wildly with his sword and advancing on Duncan. "I'll, I'll kill you!" he threatened, as he slashed away.

"Call that sword skill? You couldn't fight your way out of a wet papyrus sack!" Duncan taunted his opponent, who went for Duncan's face with a slash of his sword , the wind of which made Duncan wince. He lunged hard to force Tewksby to keep his distance.

"Take that, toad!" Duncan whispered fiercely. "And that! And that!" he lunged again, but Tewksby fought back desperately, trying to prevent being overwhelmed. His sword slammed Duncan's away on one occasion and he nearly managed with a swipe to cut Duncan in the leg.

"Low blow, bastard!" Duncan raised his voice and renewed his attack. Finally he managed by sheer chance to cut Tewksby on the upper left arm.

"Ah hah! Got you! First blood!" he exclaimed exultantly and stepped back. As far as he was concerned the fight was over.

"Ow, Ouch, Ow!" Tewksby cried out, more in surprise than in pain, and held up his arm staring at the blood beginning to stain the sleeve of his jacket. He clutched at it theatrically. You... you could have killed me!" he cried.

"Honor satisfied." Duncan announced grandly and was about to slide his sword into his scabbard when he realized that Tewksby had other ideas.

Forgetting completely where he was and the danger, he shouted, "I'll kill you for that, you swine!" and charged at Duncan, who retreated under the flurry of wild blows from Tewksby's sword. Duncan's blood was up now and he was angry. "No honor with you, is there, Tewk?" he called at his rival, whose eyes were narrowed with hate.

"Not necessary for a peasant like you!" Tewksby slashed at him again. Their blades rang out in the descending dusk as the two boys danced about, tossing out insults and performing a wild jig on the sand while trying to dismember one another.

They were thus engaged when the French arrived.

Sergeant Émile and his section had been on an evening patrol. They were no longer needed at the fort. where the siege continued unabated. Captain Clément and his company had been pulled back and had rested for a day before being given clean-up duties and patrol work. Preferring patrol work to the grisly business of burials, Émile had volunteered his section for a coastal patrol. His men agreed with this idea, as did his commander, who told him to go as far as the fresh water lake near the beach and then report back.

The patrol up to this point had been uneventful, which was just how they liked it. No lurking Turks bent on massacre, torture and looting, no packs of feral dogs that barked incessantly nor crocodiles. The men, accustomed to forced marches, enjoyed the loitering and relaxed walk that took them along the dirt track just behind the dunes out of sight of the beach itself. They had poked their heads over the top of the sand dunes to look out to sea on one occasion and seen a couple of what they too to be fishing boats ahead of them, then had then moved on. But now Private Poupard held up his hand for silence. The men stopped and became instantly alert. "I hear something," he said. "Over there!" he pointed.

"What is it?" Sergeant Émile demanded.

"You won't believe this, Sergeant, but it sounded like... swords?"

Sergeant Émile trusted his men's instincts, and their sense of hearing even iff somewhat impaired by the din of the battle by now. "Come on! Hurry! We need to find out what it is. Half cock the muskets." The men instantly became a cohesive unit, their eyes and ears alert for anything in the gloom, their muskets at the ready and set at the half cock.

They hurried off the road towards the sound of the clashing steel, which seemed to be growing in intensity. They breasted a rise and saw before them, about eighty yards away and on a bare space half surrounded by shrubs and trees, two figures going at it with swords.

At that moment the fighter facing the soldiers noticed them too and, shouting in alarm, turned and ran away. The one with his back to the French broke off from what appeared to be a duel of sorts and turned, gaping at the oncoming French.

"Its the Froggies! Run!" Tewksby yelped.

Duncan at first didn't believe his opponent, thinking it was some treacherous ploy to distract him, but then Tewksby turned and scampered away in the direction of the boats.

"Come back here, you coward!" Duncan called, but then he decided to see what Tewksby had really seen. He whirled to gape at the oncoming soldiers and his blood ran cold. "Oh God! Oh Bugger! Oh fuck! Run!" he called out unnecessarily, and turned back to run for the boats. Tewksby had already vanished into the trees. "Bugger me!" exclaimed Duncan, amazed at his former opponent's alacrity, then he too began to run as hard as his legs could carry him, his arms flailing with the effort.

There was a shout from the oncoming soldiers, "Aretez vous!" followed by a loud bang, and a ball whistled overhead.

Duncan fled for the bushes and reached them just as he heard another shout and a volley of musket fire. Fortunately he tripped and tumbled face forward to the sand as several balls twitched the branches of the shrubs and small trees just where his head and shoulders had been, showering him with broken twigs.

Fearful but also annoyed, he hauled his pistol out of his belt, cocked it and pointed it in the general direction of the French and pulled the trigger. The flint snapped down on the pan, there was a small flash, and the weapon bucked in his hand as it discharged with a loud bang followed by a puff of smoke. His reward was a shout of surprise but he didn't wait to find out what damage he might have done. He rolled clumsily over to his left and took off in another direction in an attempt to throw the soldiers off his trail.

As he blundered away, trying to make as little noise as possible in the gloom, he heard the French reach the border of the trees and stop. They appeared to be discussing their options, and rather than abandoning the pursuit they seemed to be intent on something they'd found. Duncan stopped and listened. Then he realized that he had lost his hat. It wasn't so much the hat itself as the cost of a new one that would be exacted by the purser if he should ever be lucky enough to return to his ship that made him curse under his breath with chagrin. He thought he heard the words "Chapeau de marine," being spoken by the French soldiers. They had clearly found it. Soon they would be after him again.

Then the sound of shouts could be heard coming from another direction. That of the boats. Although he could not hear what was being said he could quite clearly make out the high-pitched voice of Tewksby, and then more shouts.

Duncan heard the French rapidly move off in the direction of the boats, making no attempt to hide their own noise as they rushed towards the entrance of the estuary. He sat down to contemplate his situation. He was cut off from the boats, Tewksby had seen to that, the bastard; now he was in enemy territory with nowhere to hide!

Chapter 19

A Skirmish

The first sign of trouble the men at the boats became aware of was the sound of a musket being discharged only a few hundred yards south of their position, followed by the popping sound of a pistol going off. Men looked at one another in alarm. Where were the two young officers? They had gone in that direction about twenty minutes ago.

The sailors were instantly on the alert and, at a signal from Bosun's Mate Chauncey, both boats were pushed hurriedly and furtively back out into deeper water. Then men on the boats who had weapons fingered their muskets and stared south into the gathering darkness, apprehensively waiting for their junior officers to reappear. They were all startled to behold Midshipman Tewksby stumbling alone over the west bank, shouting.

"The French are coming! Push off at once!" he yelled as he splashed into the water and tried to get aboard one of the boats. One of the seamen helped him clamber over the thwart by seizing his belt and hauling him over the side, to drop him in an undignified heap at the bottom of the boat.

"Jesus, why don't you tell everyone where we are?" muttered one of the agitated men in a hoarse whisper. "Damned boy officers!"

"Enough of that!" snapped Chauncey. "I'll take names the next one speaks out of turn."

"Pull out, pull out and get us out of here!" Tewksby gasped as he sat up in the boat.

"What about Mr Graham, Sir?" The bosun's mate demanded.

"They... they got him," Tewksby mumbled.

"But Sir! Are you sure?" Chauncey persisted.

"Get going at once! That's an order! They are right behind me!" Tewksby shouted at him, sounding panicked.

His jaw tight with anger at having to abandon the young Scots Midshipman to his fate, Chauncey called an order and the rowers bent to their work. Other men stood in the center of the boat with their muskets pointed back at the diminishing shoreline.

Midshipman Tewksby had been right: figures quickly materialized from out of the bush and lined up on the white beach. The sailors could hear shouted orders and then the flash and bang of muskets. Balls whistled overhead or threshed into the water nearby, encouraging the rowers to pull for their lives.

"Give them a taste of our own," the Bosun's Mate told the musketeers. He didn't even ask permission of the young Midshipman seated nearby. There was something fishy about this whole thing. It was no secret that he and the Scot were not on good terms.

The men on the boats fired with a will but it was now too dark to tell if they had hit anything. The darkness and the distance were not any help. There was another volley from the French in reply with no damage, and by then the boats were out to sea for the long pull back to the ships of the fleet.

After the firing had stopped and the boats had vanished into the night, Corporal Émile assembled his men. "Any injuries?" he demanded.

"No, Corporal. But that fellow back there missed me by a hair," Claude complained.

"What were the Roast Beef doing here?" they asked themselves, the name being the unflattering term the French used for British soldiers.

"My money is on fresh water. That's why the boats were here. That hat you are holding, Sergeant, is a naval hat, and I'm sure I saw casks in the middle of each of the boats," Claude said.

"That doesn't explain the sword play," Émile growled. "I'll recognize the last one to run away anywhere. I've a good memory for faces. He is a carrot head and has a face as pale as snow."

"Perhaps he was so scared he went white when he saw us," Philipe snickered. "We might have just surprised them at practicing," he added.

"What I saw didn't look very much like a practice bout," François replied with a laugh.

"I agree, from what I saw those two were hard at it," Émile agreed. "Anyway, it's back to the road and camp. We are miles from camp and need to get back there before some fellaheen decide we are fair game and chase us instead," he told his men. "Reload en route."

They regained the road and marched off in silence towards the sound of the guns. Émile was going to report that the British were desperate for water and were sniffing around for it. The Roast Beef would find the French waiting for them the next time they tried.

Duncan sat on the sand and tried to comprehend his situation. "Just my kind of luck!" he lamented as he thought about the utter stupidity of the improvised duel. But then he smiled to himself. It had given him enormous satisfaction to pink Tewksby. That alone, he decided, had made it worth while. "Wish I'd got him in the bum!"

he consoled himself, though he realized that he was in a serious pickle now. He had heard the French soldiers and their noisy engagement with the boats and then they strode they strode off to the road still talking among themselves and marched away.

One thing he was sure of, and that was that by morning they would be back and the area would be swarming with French soldiers, as it must have been clear to them that the British were looking for fresh water. He could not remain here for any length of time. Inwardly he cursed Tewksby for his cowardly behavior, but by the sound of it the sailors had made off without too much trouble, even though there had been some shooting. He hoped there had been no casualties. Where was he to go now? In his British naval uniform it could not be very long before he was picked up by a roving patrol.

With a sigh he stood up and brushed off the sand from his pants, then emptied more from his shoes. He tried to get his bearings. Staring up at the blaze of stars in the sky he found the north star and decided that the palm trees had been due south. That was the general direction Captain Williams had taken, he remembered. He set off, using the stars as his guidance, and after some false starts arrived on the track recently used by the French patrol. In the gloom he could see its pale white stripe going in both directions.

Slowly the night settled in, bringing with it a chorus of frog calls that became louder and louder, the deep boom of the bullfrogs answered by the high pitched squeaks of the tree frogs. Duncan gave up all attempts to be quiet; he could barely hear himself moving with all the noise.

He sweated uncomfortably as he pushed his way past thorny bushes and stumbled over tussocks of sharp-bladed grass. His stocking were rent and torn, and his shoes once again full of sand. He hopped about on one leg as he emptied out one shoe after the other while trying to stay alert. He ruefully contemplated his ruined socks but consoled himself with the thought that he was owed a pair by Tewksby. He shivered. While he had been on the move it had been warm enough, but now the desert cold was seeping across the dark land and he didn't have his coat, just his light uniform jacket.

The road appeared to be completely deserted, which was some comfort, and furthermore he could just make out the dark silhouette of the copse of palm trees about half a mile further south. He was just congratulating himself on his navigational skills when he became aware that he was not alone and that someone was watching him. He drew his sword and turned slowly. A figure emerged from the path he had just left to join the road. It was pointing a small pistol at him.

"Is that you, Midshipman Graham?" The tone of Captain Williams's voice was wary and incredulous.

Duncan gulped with relief. His heart was beating furiously. He put up his sword and relaxed.

"Yes, Sir, it's me." Next would come the difficult explanations, he guessed wearily.

"What the hell are you doing here?" Williams demanded. "Where's your hat?"

"Well, Sir. It's... erm... a long story. I lost the hat, Sir. I think the Frenchies got it."

"Hmm, in that case you are fortunate that your hat is all you lost, if the shooting I heard is any indication. Well then, we have to get out of here and be a long way away before dawn. You can tell me all about it while we are doing so. Were you and that other Midshipman sparring? I heard the sound of blades. The boats are gone, I suppose?"

Duncan decided not to answer the question about the sparring. "The French arrived and chased them off. I was... er... stranded and couldn't get to the boats in time, so I made off until the French left, Sir."

"I was in those trees over there," Williams pointed to the palms, "when I heard the noise of what sounded like blades, and I was not far away when I heard the shooting. Not long after that I saw the French heading back towards the peninsula. Then I heard someone blundering about in the bushes and decided to investigate."

"I think they will be back, Sir," Duncan said.

Captain Williams sounded annoyed. "You may bet on it. We won't be making a rendezvous with our own people here any more."

In the darkness he went silent as though considering something. Finally he said, "You are going to stand out like a sore thumb with that uniform, hat or no hat. We'll have to find some other clothing. Come along."

He led the way towards the palm trees with Duncan stumbling along behind him. It amazed Duncan how easily Williams moved in the darkness. Despite the bright mantle of stars above he still could not manage to walk as quietly as his the captain and kept blundering into low bushes, which tried to trip him up or raked his face with their spiteful thorns.

They arrived at the grove within a short time and approached it with caution.

"I have only just left the hut over there, but it always pays to be careful," Williams whispered as they crouched in the shadow of a tree and studied the tiny flat-roofed mud hut ahead of them. It stood on the shore of the lake that fed into the estuary and was surrounded by shrubs and other palms that, Duncan realized, made it almost invisible from the road even in daytime. There was a very small boat lying on the shore. His hopes rose a little. Perhaps they could take that boat! But Captain Williams dispelled that idea soon enough.

As though he had read Duncan's mind he said, "The house is safe; the occupants fled when the French came barging through. It's deserted now and yes, I checked the boat; it has a hole in it the size of a man's head. It's no use to us. Come along now, there are still bits and pieces of clothing in the hut. We will leave just before dawn for Alexandria."

They arrived at the hut without incident whereupon Williams pushed open the cracked and split wooden door and entered the dark interior.

"Come in Graham. Don't want you to be seen outside by anyone." he said.

Duncan sidled into the darkness and the rude door was closed behind him. Williams struck a flint and lit a small oil lamp," Lucky I found this before dark came or we would be unable to see anything. As it is I don't want to keep it on for long. Some fellaheen might still be in the area and the last thing we need is anyone investigating at this moment," he remarked. "Best thing to do is to settle down ad get some rest, he added and then pointed to a crude truckle bed in the corner. 'You can sleep there and we'll work on a disguise at first light."

Graham nodded reluctantly. "Aye Aye Sir and went over to sit down on the bed.

The lamp was blown out. "Good night," came the terse comment from Captain Williams. Duncan tentatively laid down on the bed among the rags.

"Dear God what have I gotten myself into?" he thought to himself before sleep overtook him.

Graham heard the whine of mosquitos even before he felt them bite, but even the deafening noise of the frogs croaking and singing in the marshes could not stop him from eventually falling asleep.

Tewksby and his two boats arrived alongside the *Tigre* late that night. After being challenged by the Royal Marines on guard duty he clambered aboard with the help of a crewman. He then touched his hat to the quarter deck and faced up to Lt Bowles. The lieutenant was shocked at his appearance and by the news, so he took him down to see Sir Sidney immediately.

Sir Sidney had been sleeping but woke up to the discreet knock and called out, "Enter." Lt Bowles poked his head inside the door. "You asked me to notify you the moment the boats returned, Sir. It's Midshipman Tewksby, he's back but there is something you should know."

Sir Sidney Smith sighed. It had been a tiring day and now a long night. "So I did. Bring him in." Sidney rubbed the sleep out of his eyes, got out of bed and put on a silk dressing gown, then called to his steward for some light. He stood waiting as Bowles ushered the young midshipman into the cabin, just as his steward brought two oil lamps and placed them on his desk.

In the glow of the lamps the boy looked disheveled, paler than usual and very nervous. Sidney noticed that his left arm was in a sling. There was still dried blood on the sleeve of his jacket which was draped over his thin shoulders. His shirt and trousers were torn in places and his shoes badly scuffed. Sidney took all this in within a moment and immediately said, "Sit down, boy. You look as though you have been wounded. I hope it's not serious?"

Tewksby gave a brave nod and staggered to the cabin chair. "It's nothing, Sir. Just... just a graze." He winced theatrically as he sat down.

Sidney shot a glance at his lieutenant, but that worthy kept an impassive face. It was almost as though the boy was putting on a little bit of a show.

Nonetheless he quickly poured a tot of brandy from his the precious supply on the side table, offered it to the midshipman and said, "What happened out there? I want to hear all of it, Mr Tewksby."

"We were surprised by the French when we went inland to scout, Sir," Tewksby said, as he sipped the brandy with a shaking hand.

"Where is Mr Graham? Should he not be here too?" Sidney demanded.

"Er... during the confusion he was lost. He... he... er... didn't make it to the boats, Sir."

Sir Sidney exchanged a concerned glance with Lt Bowles.

"You'd better start from the beginning and tell us all about it, Mr Tewksby."

Chapter 20

Chameleon

Duncan and Captain Williams passed a very uncomfortable night in the hut. The original owners having departed, it seemed to Duncan that most of the insect world had decided to take up residence in their stead. After initially sleeping deeply he half woke and scratched and tossed restlessly in his new clothes, wishing fervently that he had not been so stupid as to land himself in this predicament. He eventually fell asleep again, only to be shaken awake immediately after by his bearded companion.

"Come along Graham, it's time to get going," Williams said in a whisper. He left Duncan to crawl groggily to his feet, yawning with fatigue, and went outside. Duncan could hear water splashing and then footsteps. Williams came back into the house just as the sun was peeking over the flat line of the east. He regarded Duncan critically in the pale light.

"You are not too tall, that's one good thing, but you are light of hair and we cannot have that. You'll need to keep the hood of your bisht over your head at all times, and I'll still have to do something about your face and hands." He rummaged about outside for a few moments, and Duncan moved to the entrance to see what he was doing.

Williams was crushing some old charcoal into powder. "Come over here," he commanded. Duncan reluctantly complied. Williams proceeded to smear the charcoal all over his face and forehead, then his neck, and told him to rub the dust into the back of his hands. After that Williams mixed some of the charcoal with some water and rubbed it into Duncan's hair, after which he stood back with a critical look at his handiwork.

"Well, you look more like a fellaheen now, but you are going to have to stoop your shoulders and shuffle. These sandals will help with that." He tossed a couple of old grass sandals onto the ground in front of Duncan. "You're not on the ship now, so do not comport yourself like an officer. And for God's sake don't say a word, nor look at anyone. Keep your eyes on the ground as much as you can. Few people hereabouts have blue eyes," he finished.

Duncan nodded without saying anything. He itched mightily in the filthy robe, and now his face was hot from the charcoal and mud. He rubbed at the bristles of a day old beard with a filthy paw.

"All right, take that bundle of our clothing and carry it draped over your shoulder, and take one of those sticks and we shall be off. For God's sake don't sweat so much, Graham. You'll cause the make-up to streak and we can't have that, can we?"

"No, Sir," Duncan replied glumly.

My name, for your information is now Ahmed. You will be Sindi and we are from the Beni Oufi tribe. Let me do all the talking, should that be necessary."

They came out onto the road just in time to see the dust from a cavalry unit disappearing in the direction of the guns of Abukir, which were still at work but in a more desultory manner, pounding the old fort and its unfortunate inmates to rubble.

Williams and Duncan set off to follow in the tracks of the cavalry, their destination the city just to the south of Abukir.

They saw the cloud of dust before they realized what it was. A small detachment of cavalry were galloping towards them. They hastily departed the road and concealed themselves in some scrub and bushes. The detachment of horsemen thundered past the horse's hooves throwing up a lot of dust but then they disappeared down the road leaving a light pall of dust in the air.

"I'll wager they were going to investigate the incident of last night," Captain Williams stated. "Come along, Graham, we need to get into the city as soon as possible."

After this there was almost no traffic, which Williams put down to the presence of the French army. On one more occasion they had to get out of the way as a large patrol of Blue Coats marched briskly towards them. They were unable to hide anywhere, as the area was flat with irrigation canals crisscrossing the countryside, so they got off the road and down a bank where they huddled, pretending to be poor peasants, while the French marched past. The sergeant and corporal in charge gave them a glance. The sergeant seemed to pause for a few seconds before shaking his head and turning away. Once they were well past and almost out of sight, the two British men regained the road and hurried along.

"Phew!" exclaimed Williams in an undertone. "For a moment there I thought that sergeant wanted to look us over."

As they approached the area occupied by the French army, the road became much more busy with infantry units marching to and fro and cavalry squadrons trotting past. Several field artillery pieces drawn by sweating horses charged by, leaving clouds of choking dust behind. No one paid any attention to the two men, but Williams, in an undertone, told Duncan to pay attention to the numbers and activity.

The French camp was a sea of tents of all sizes with some still being erected. Cooking fires were smoking and men were lining up to be fed while others were inspected by their fastidious NCOs. To their right they could now hear much more clearly the boom of the guns firing at the fort. The firing went on without interruption, leaving a pall of gray smoke hanging over the peninsula.

"We will have to report what we have seen to the admiral once we're out of this mess, and I want to be as accurate as possible," Williams murmured. "This is what is left of the French army in Egypt." He then encouraged Duncan to pick up the pace.

They were almost past the army encampment when they heard the sound of many horses and a shout from behind, and Williams seized Duncan's arm to pull him out of the way of a group of Arab horsemen who were galloping along the road in the direction of the city. The riders paid no attention to the two peasants other than to shout at them.

"Get off the road! Get out of the way of His Honor, the Sheikh Zahsad ibn Ahwad!" The lead riders shouted and waved their whips threateningly.

The road at this point had narrowed and was running along a bank, so they had no choice but to stumble down the low embankment and get their feet muddy while the horsemen boiled past in a cloud of dust. It was poor consolation to see that a straggle of other peasants on the way to the city had to get off the road and stand in the mud too.

"Arrogant bastard," muttered Williams.

"D'you know them, S... Ahmed?' Duncan asked.

"The Sheikh? Yes, everyone does. He is a dangerous man and has signed up with the French. Wouldn't do to fall into his hands. Not many of the Arab chieftains have sided with the French, but some have. That is, until something changes their minds and they switch sides."

They followed the fellaheen who had regained the road, keeping some distance between them, as Captain Williams didn't want to be trapped into a conversation that might expose them. Graham hefted his bundle, wishing desperately for his shoes. They had only to walk a few miles, but the sandals the captain had provided were almost useless, and now with mud all over his feet he could feel blisters beginning to form. He forced himself not to limp and bravely kept up with the striding Williams, who seemed to be observing everything around him with a keen eye.

It was nearly noon by the time they arrived at the gates of the city. Alexandria was a walled city, but there were many dwellings clustered outside the walls, as the city had not been threatened for a very long time. The hovels, some small palm groves and walled-off estates indicated that the area had enjoyed peaceful times. Indeed the gates were not even closed when the growing pedestrian traffic approached and they were allowed through by bored Egyptian guards supported by French Blue coats.

Duncan breathed a sigh of relief as they passed this first test. No one had even glanced at him, and neither did the peasants around them seem to have any interest. As the travelers converged they were surrounded by a dense flock of smelly, wooly sheep and goats that bleated constantly, pushing and shoving their way through the gates along with the peasants. The noise and smell were overpowering, and Duncan could feel the sweat trickling down his face, which set him worrying for his disguise. It would scarcely do for runnels of perspiration to reveal his pale skin and freckles. He pulled his hood further over his head and kept pace with Williams, who was walking just ahead of him.

After passing through the gates, which Williams, in a low voice, said were the Canobic Gates, they joined the throng of people, lumbering camels, and heavily-loaded donkeys walking down what Williams called the Road of Thirty Strada. Straight as an arrow, it ran off into the west of the city, where Duncan could see in the distance ruins sticking up into the sky. The city appeared old and unkempt to his critical eye. While they were walking, Williams paused from time to time as though checking his surroundings. After following the crowd for about three hundred paces, he drew Duncan by his sleeve off to the left side of the main street.

"We are not far from our destination," he murmured in Duncan's ear. "See over there," he pointed with his chin to the south, where some tall ruins jutted up over the other buildings looking like rotten teeth.

"That's the old Gymnasium. We are in the Greek quarter of the city," he said cryptically. Duncan could not have cared less about the ruins but had never been more relieved that they might at last be arriving at their destination.

His feet were killing him and he was sweating copiously under the rough covering of his bisht. He was sure that at any moment they would be exposed. However, the townspeople and the visiting fellaheen had other preoccupations and were well used to ignoring others as they went about their daily tasks. Another filthy fellaheen carrying an awkward bundle did not interest them in the least.

Williams led the way along some very narrow streets; in some places the houses seemed to almost be touching at their top stories, in others crumbling arches with gaps in the stones that looked like missing teeth curved overhead, and then the street would take a sharp turn. Neither was the street well maintained: filth of every description littered the dry streets, giving them a musty odor of neglect and old rot. Duncan had to put his sleeve over his nose in places, the smell was so bad. Wooden doorways that were deeply ingrained by the sun and had never seen a coat of paint and barred windows hid the occupants, although he could hear shouting going on in some houses as they hurried past.

In the distance he heard for the first time since being near or in Egypt the hypnotic sound of the muezzin as the prayers for noon were called all around the city. He became aware of a calm settling over the city, and their back street became if anything more quiet, the only sound now the slap of their sandals and the buzz of thousands of flies around something putrid farther down the street.

Williams paused at a heavy-looking wooden door that was studded with iron nails. It had once been adorned with blue paint which had peeled to mere shreds. He raised a large bronze knocker and banged twice. The sound reverberated along the street. Duncan peered about furtively, hoping no one was paying them any attention. Apart from an old man sleeping in the alcove of another house, and a dog lying in the shade of an archway which cocked an ear at the sound, there was no one. A huge rat, indifferent to both their presence and that of the dog, ambled slowly along the drain in the middle of the street.

It was a relief to hear footsteps on the other side of the door. A voice spoke and Williams responded. Although he should have expected it, Duncan was surprised to hear his officer speaking rapid Arabic. After a brief conversation there was the scraping of iron on iron, the door was pulled open a crack, and a dark, hawk-nosed man peered out at them. He stared at them and then nodded, indicating with one hand that they should enter quickly. After they had eased through the doorway he immediately shut the door and ran some long iron bars into slots in the wall, securing it shut.

He led the way along a dark, vaulted passage to emerge into the velvety silence of a stone-paved courtyard that was empty of people but at the center of which was a small fountain that burbled quietly to itself. Surrounding the small fountain was a well-maintained garden. Several orange trees and a pomegranate shrub with hanging fruit provided shade. The whole was in direct contrast to the shabby and unkempt street outside.

They were ushered into a large airy room on the second floor that overlooked the trees and the fountain, where their guide left them with a brief comment in Arabic. Williams nodded and waved Duncan over to the grill that passed for a verandah window.

"You are going to find things a little different here, Graham. We are safe for the time being, but we must be very careful all the same.

"What is this place, Sir?" Duncan replied, looking around him at the richly decorated silk cushions and low tables of what could only be a wealthy man's house. He thought he saw a water pipe device on one of the tables, while on others there were papers and even books.

"Why, Mr Graham, we are in a brothel," Captain Williams replied with a wry grin.

ALEXANDRIA
(by M. Matter, 1840-44)
MEDITERRANEAN
NICOPOLI (NEAPOLIS JULI
Canobic Gate ?
Road to Eleusis
Thirty Stadia
Stadium
Amphitheatre
Canobic Gate ?
Pharillon or Ruins of a Mosque
Ruins of a dike
Exterior of Principal Palace
Royal Parks and Gardens
Canal
GREEK, JEWISH and MACEDONIAN QUARTER
Royal Harbour
Antirrhodos
Sebasteum
Library
Poseidium
Timonium
Emporium
Arsinoeum
Roman Tower
Caesareum
Mausoleum
Theatre
Museum
Gymnasium
Didaseleum
Road of
BRUCHIUM
Claudium
Homerion
Obelisk
Sema Mausoleum
Ruins of a Temple
Public Garden
Paneum
Dicastery
Walls of the Ancient City
Bridge Area
GREAT HARBOUR
Pharos Light
Walls of the ancient city of Pharos
Castle
Bridge
Moon Gate
Canal
Hiereum
Arab Town
Amphitheatre
Street
Canal
Canopic ARAB QUARTER
EGYPTIAN QUARTER
RHAKOTIS
Serapeum
Column of Diocletian
Sun Gate
PORT of PIRATES
PHAROS
Fort
Castle
Bridge
Julius or Augustus Canal
PORT of EUNOSTOS
Kibotos Harbour
Gate to Necropolis
Walls of the Arab City
Canal
Canal
Stadium
Catacombs
NECROPOLIS

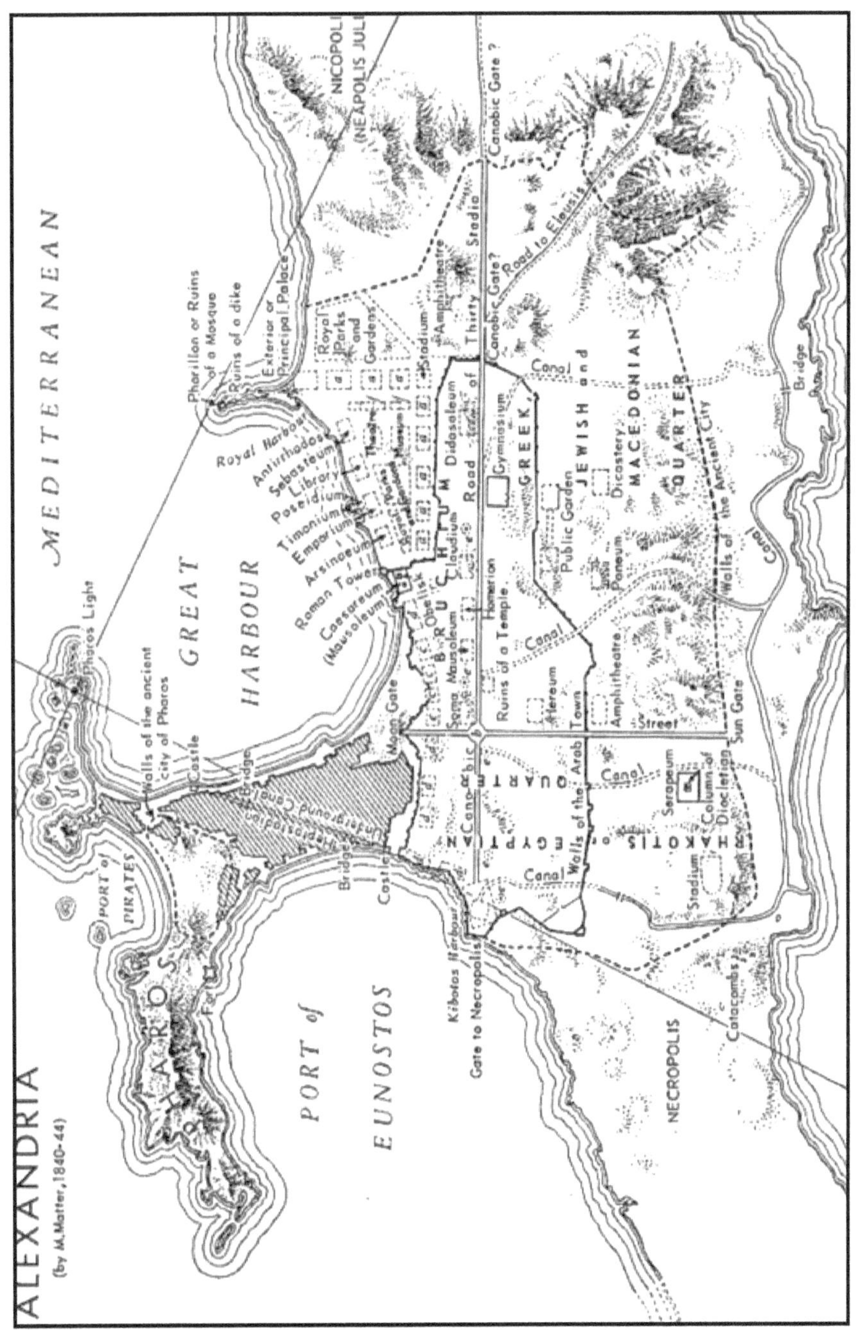

Alexandria

Chapter 21

The House of Paradise

Duncan was still getting over his surprise when a tall, slim man with a greying beard and fine turban walked silently into the room. He was dressed like most of his countrymen in a long loose, collarless robe of fine cotton material and wide sleeves that came down to his wrists. His fingers were bejeweled with gold and precious stones, denoting a man of leisure and wealth.

"Salam Aliekom," he said in a low tone and smiled. His sharp, dark eyes were deep-set in a long, pale face but they were friendly enough.

Williams beamed. "Aliekom Salam, Danush. How good to see you again!"

Danush's smile broadened and he stepped forward to clasp Williams by the hand. "You are always welcome here in my house," he said in French.

"I could wish it were under better circumstances, my friend," Williams responded, and he turned to introduce Duncan, who bowed politely and said, "It is an honor to meet a friend of Mr Williams, Sir."

Danush looked pleased. "Aha, your companion speaks French too. That is useful. But his disguise is... er, rather basic, is it not?" he murmured, staring at Duncan critically. "Who are you that is dressed like a fellaheen but is clearly not one?"

Williams gave him a rueful grin. "It sufficed to get us past the French army and into the city, but I don't think it could have taken us much farther than your house without detection."

"I must ask you, Williams, what does bring you here in these uncertain times? I had not expected to see you for a while yet," Danush said, with a glance at the door to the room. "We are perfectly safe here, but I always like to be careful. The French really do have ears everywhere at present."

"We, or rather my young companion here and his men, were surprised by a patrol of infantry when they were out looking for water. I heard the exchange of fire. I had not gone far, so I came back and found him, whose name by the way is Midshipman Graham, cut off from his boats," he paused. "I think the rest of his men got away, but there was no going back; the French would be waiting and would likely bag us if we returned there to be picked up."

Danush contemplated Graham for a long moment. "Well, the first thing we should do is to provide you with food and a bath. You look as though you could do with both."

Williams smiled his wry smile. "Of that I am sure. He speaks no Arabic, so he must not move around until we can figure out how to leave the city. I had hoped to perhaps bribe a fisherman to take us out to the fleet, which is due to come back sometime to blockade the harbor."

Danush looked surprised. "I thought the fleet would remain at Abukir. Is that not where the fighting is?" he asked. "I know the French defeated the Turks but we can still hear the guns, even from Alexandria. We assumed the British were targeting the French as they did at Acre."

"Alas no. The British ships could not come close enough to support the Turks who were soundly defeated." Captain Williams shook his head ruefully. "The French are bombarding the fort into rubble. So many fleeing men drowned that the water was red as poppies. It was both tragic and horrible to witness, and the smell, even as we left was beginning to be intolerable," Williams said.

"Sir Sidney had planned to come here and resume the blockade once the battle was won. Despite the setback it will be just as important, so I think he will be here fairly soon," Williams assured him.

"You will have a very hard time finding a fishing boat at present. The police are keeping a sharp eye open for runners, almost as keen to stop people leaving as the British are to stop them coming in. So we must await an opportunity, but in the meantime we must figure out how to hide this young man. First things first, however: a bath, then food." Danush clapped his hands.

Two young men almost ran into the room and stood respectfully as Danush rattled off some orders in Arabic.

"Go with them," he told Duncan. "This one knows some French. His name is Kaylah," he pointed to the older of the two. "They will help you bathe, and then we will eat."

While Williams and Danush continued to talk the two servants beckoned Duncan to follow them. He had a chance to see himself in one of the many mirrors lining the walls of the corridor as they padded along the beautifully tiled floor. What he saw shocked him. Staring back at him was a wild-looking creature whose formerly reddish hair, now that the hood was down, was sticking up in places from a blackened, sweat streaked face with staring blue eyes. He almost jerked back at his own image. To his fevered imagination the figure staring back at him looked as though it had just stepped out of some dark African jungle. He hurried on with his new guides.

When they came to the baths, a steaming pool surrounded by low alcoves and slim arched pillars, he hesitated. He was expected to undress in front of these two boys? The older, seeing his reluctance, smiled reassuringly. "It is all right, we are here to make you clean, Effendi," he said and made motions for washing.

It took some effort to overcome his initial modesty, but finally the lure of hot clean water and the infernal itching of his clothes drove him to discard them and hurriedly climb down into the water. It was hot, but a great comfort. He noticed the second boy take a cane and lift his discarded robe and other clothes onto the end of the stick with a look of disgust on his face, then take them away.

He began slowly to relax and wallowed happily in the hot water, feeling his cares ease away. That is, until he saw the oldest boy taking off his bisht and stand naked on the side. Suddenly Duncan realized that the boy was bereft of one important item of his anatomy.

He could not help but stare initially, then averted his eyes, embarrassed, and began to flounder towards the other side of the pool.

The boy called to him, "I clean you, Effendi."

"Oh God!" Duncan groaned, then to add mortification to alarm he heard giggling from behind a curtain on the other side of the room.

The boy said something and it ceased, but the curtain twitched and Duncan was sure there were females lurking behind it. He went red with embarrassment but realized that he was doomed. He passively accepted the sponging he received from Kaylah, who was efficient and scrubbed him hard all over, although Duncan insisted that he deal with his own nether parts, snatching the sponge out of Kaylah's hands to do so and turning his back. Unfortunately he now faced the curtain, which twitched, and the giggling began again.

Casting all discretion to the winds he glowered and grimaced fiercely at the curtain, remembering times in his home in Scotland when modesty was sometimes sacrificed for necessity and his sisters and the maids could see him bathe in a tub down in the warmth of the kitchens. He bared his teeth and rubbed his belly in a more exaggerated manner pretending to look ferocious. This elicited even more giggling and soft peals of laughter, but Kaylah put a stop to it and this time gave a sharp order. The curtain twitched one last time and there was silence.

Kaylah led Duncan, now dressed in a clean soft bisht of light brown cotton, and left him seated on one of the elegant cushions near to the window. Williams had disappeared somewhere with Danush, but Duncan was not left alone for very long. He couldn't help it: his mouth began to salivate at the aroma of the dishes that were now brought to him by the second boy who had vanished with his old clothes.

The boy brought him a bowl of stew with succulent-looking pieces of meat within which Duncan took it to be lamb, with small bubbles of fat drifting around on its surface. Some tasty flat bread accompanied the soup, and he was provided with a wooden spoon. Unable to contain his ravenous appetite, Duncan pounced on the meal and ate with relish, burning his lips in the process. After the awful naval food he had become used to, the taste of this stew was unlike anything he had had since childhood. He devoured the food within minutes under the startled gaze of the two boys.

"Crikey!" he mumbled to himself as he finished off the last of the soup with a piece of bread. "This is the life!"

He barely finished the meal before his eyelids began to droop, ready to go to sleep. He'd had almost no sleep the night before, and it had been a day of extraordinary experiences. As though sensing this, the two boy servants helped him to his feet, then led him off to a comfortable bed which he could not remember falling into. They left him there and locked the door before going off and informing Danush of his whereabouts.

CHAPTER 22

DISGUISE

Duncan woke early in the morning of the next day to the sound of a peacock screaming outside, and for a moment could not think where he might be. By the sounds emanating from the house the day was well advanced, so he clambered to his feet and went to open the door, but it was locked. He began to panic. Where was Captain Williams? He banged on the door and finally heard footsteps. A key turned and Kaylah opened the door with a finger to his lips. "Shh," he whispered. "No one is to know you are here." He carried a tray of fruit and bread with some goat cheese and a small cup of tea.

Duncan devoured the food, but was restless and uncertain in the company of the servant. At that moment there was a light knock on the door, and Williams and Danush entered the room. Kaylah closed the door firmly behind them and stood with his back to it while the two men looked Duncan over.

"I hope you slept well, Mister Graham?" Danush asked solicitously.

Williams was still dressed as before but looked refreshed. "We decided that we would leave you in the care of the servants overnight while we discussed matters," Williams remarked, as he observed the wreckage of the meal Kaylah had brought to Duncan.

"You appear to have eaten and slept well. You also appear to be somewhat cleaner," he remarked drily as he looked Duncan over, who had by now jumped to his feet.

"We are facing a small dilemma, Williams," Danush said.

"How is that?" the captain asked.

"I had not realized your companion would be so... er... light colored. He will stand out anywhere as he is. Even the slaves from the north do not look as pale as he."

"Of course he can't go outside, if that is what you mean, Danush?" Williams responded, glancing at the now clean and scrubbed midshipman. It was true his red hair and very fair features were a giveaway.

"His French is passable enough. Where did you learn it?" he enquired of Duncan.

"At home in Scotland, Sir," Duncan answered, remembering the long tedious hours of labor accompanied by the sting of the ruler when he failed to pronounce words or decline verbs accurately.

"Even so, it is not good enough to pass him off as a Frenchman, and he most definitely is not an Arab, neither in shape nor form." Danush looked at Duncan appraisingly and sucked his teeth.

"Although we might pass him off as an albino, he would still attract a lot of attention. You see, the French police inspect this building on a regular basis," he said. "The doctors come to see the women on occasion, but the police more frequently to seek all manner of things among them, including deserters or men who have failed to appear on parade. This being a house of pleasure, they automatically assume those kind to be here." He scratched his beard thoughtfully. "They are sometimes very thorough. I suspect they are also looking for our agents. Monsieur Le Guennet, the Chief of Police, is nobody's fool." He let that hang in the air for a moment then continued.

"We also have a conundrum on our hands. I have many servants downstairs who do not know at this time of your presence, but that could change very quickly. And as you well know, there are women. More than just a few, and we are often very busy in the evening entertaining the French officers and non-commissioned men. However, there is one place they do not search, out of delicacy, you know?"

They had been speaking French to include the boy in the discussion, but now Danush switched to Arabic and spoke rapidly. Williams blinked and shook his head.

"Impossible! I couldn't hear of it!" He even gave a small uncomfortable laugh and looked at Duncan, who didn't like at all what the look implied.

"It is our only option," Danush said, sounding insistent. He was again speaking French, and there was a curious gleam of amusement in his eye.

"It's... it's ridiculous, he'll never pass it off!" remonstrated Williams, but a smirk was beginning to twitch his mustache. Things sounded ominous to Duncan.

"Sir, what are you talking about?" he demanded. This discussion obviously concerned him. "What can't I pass off?"
"Danush has this crazed idea that we can hide you here in this... this house of pleasure as a woman," Williams said, looking as embarrassed as any man could.

"Oh Lord!" Duncan groaned and grimaced. "You cannot be serious, Sir?" he appealed to his senior officer. Duncan had raised his voice in his mounting agitation which made Captain Williams wave his hand. "Hush not so loud, Graham. Remember where we are!"

Danush spread his hands wide and shrugged. "It's the only way!" he said. "In any other guise you will be quickly discovered and then we will all go to the guillotine." He shot a pleading look at Duncan. "Please, Mister Graham. We were not expecting to have you as our... as our guest. Mr Williams can disappear into the crowd here; he is dark of hair and speaks the Arabic fluently, whereas you!" he shrugged again.

"You cannot even go out into the street before a French man would become curious and perhaps speak to you, and people will stare at you all the time! If you stay as you are within my house, where there are people in and out all the time, including spies, you will soon be noticed and word will get out. If you are seen by one of these wandering spies it will be all over. You need to be hidden in the women's quarters."

"Oh good grief!" Duncan exclaimed. "How on earth will I manage that?" The prospect of being in the forced company of many women terrified him. Cannon and shot he could endure, but this?

He sent a horrified look at Williams, but that worthy had made up his mind. "I agree, reluctantly, mind you." He didn't sound reluctant enough to Duncan. "But Danush is absolutely right, Graham," Williams continued. "You have to become a woman and disappear for a couple of days at least."

For a very brief moment Duncan contemplated mutiny but the captain seemed to read his mind.

"Don't even think about it, Midshipman," he said sharply. "Anyway who knows, you might even enjoy it!" he gave Duncan a wicked smile. Duncan hated him.

Danush clapped his hands again and the two eunuch boys appeared like magic. He issued a long list of commands and made them repeat them to him before finally waving his hand in dismissal.

The boys turned to Duncan and beckoned him to go with them. He could swear that they were smirking as they turned to lead him off yet again into the labyrinth of the building.

As they left he heard Williams chuckle and say, "The boy is more used to the din of battle than what we are now going to put him through. I hope he survives."

He seethed when he heard a return chuckle from Danush. This was going to be awful, he decided, but he put on a brave face and followed the servants.

They took him along many corridors; some opened onto the verandah overlooking the gardens below while others were gloomy and had many rooms on either side. Overall he could smell the not unpleasant aroma of sandalwood and jasmine flowers. This was without doubt the domain of women.

Finally they came to a strong-looking door with a servant standing outside who questioned the two boys, who in turn indicated Duncan in rapid-fire Arabic before he reluctantly opened the door and allowed them entrance.

The room beyond was female territory, the scent in the air alone warned him of that; the hangings, curtains and cushions with young women seated all about told him that he had most certainly arrived in the lion's den. His courage nearly failed him but a firm hand in the small of his back propelled him into the room.

Kaylah called out a name and one of the girls—they were all very young women—appeared from behind a curtain where she had been seated with some embroidery and walked towards them. Her body moved sinuously, her whole being suggesting sexuality which Duncan could not fail to notice. He felt his ears beginning to burn.

Coming to a stop before him she looked right up at him and he looked away guiltily. Something was stirring and he couldn't control it.

Kaylah spoke to the girl, in French this time. "The master wants you to take this man and turn him into a woman," he murmured.

"I beg your pardon!" she exclaimed, putting a hand to her mouth in amused shock.

"You heard me!" Kaylah said, his voice rising. "He has to disappear and be here until he can be moved along. No one is to know, other than you girls." He glowered. "Pain of death, but you will be well rewarded, my sisters. He speaks some French."

The girl rolled her large grey eyes. "You are serious, Kaylah? This isn't one of your nasty little tricks to get us into trouble?"

Kaylah gave an emphatic shake of his head. "No I am not, and yes, you are to do it at once. We do not wish him to be seen as a man in this house from this time on. His... er... her name is going to be Jasmine. We will be busy tonight, as you know, and he must not be seen as he is. The girl from Cairo is here and the house will be full of the French, as most of them know of her and want to see her, so they will be all over the place along with their cursed spies."

"Allah forgive me!" she murmured with an incredulous look on her pretty face. With a shrug of resignation she took Duncan's hand in her slim one and tugged him deeper into the room.

"Come along, ... Jasmine. You do speak French, do you not?"

Duncan gave her a mute nod, too embarrassed to even look around him as he was dragged unprotesting her alcove. He didn't really see the other five girls, who now got to their feet and began to follow them, chattering excitedly all the while. The perfume in the air and proximity of the fresh-smelling girls threatened to overwhelm him and he was sure he was going to faint any minute.

He glanced back pleadingly to where the two eunuchs had been, but they had vanished like a pair of genies. He was quite alone and assuredly in a lion's den. He wondered how he was going to live through this.

"My name is... Leilah. I am from Bulgaria, where I am called another name," she told him, as she sat him down on the low bed. "You are going to get out of those clothes and do as I say from now on." Her tone brooked no argument.

After a quick conference with the other girls, who were eagerly clustered at the entrance, she drew the curtains of the alcove closed in the face of the disappointed females. The chatter, however, continued unabated on the other side.

"Now 'urry, Jasmine," she told him with a cheeky grin. "What is your real name?" she enquired.

"Duncan," he croaked.

Leilah had obviously decided that she was going to make the most of this odd arrangement, no matter what. He stood up and divested himself of the bisht, standing only in his underclothes.

"All of it, Monsieur Dunkin. Don' worry, I 'ave seen men before," she said with a sardonic twist of her full red lips.

"You 'ave 'ad a bath?" she asked skeptically with a raised eyebrow. He nodded.

She sized him up and then called something out to the other girls waiting outside. Before long some women's wear was pushed into the alcove, accompanied by an inquisitive face.

The girl's eyes widened as she caught a glimpse of Duncan standing naked. She gave a startled squeak and was rudely pushed back out of sight by Leilah, who then lifted the silk blouse to check the fit, ignoring the excited chatter outside. Once he was dressed she inspected his face thoughtfully. Then she opened the curtains and the other girls crowded in to stare, cooing and chattering like a flock of pigeons. She hushed them and a long conversation ensued, all of it concerning him, as they studied him critically from every angle.

"You are very light," Leilah concluded. "But not albino. I am glad. We think we can convert you. The right word, yes?"

He nodded, too mortified to speak. "'S'pose so," he managed.

They set to work on his face. First they shaved him very carefully, and then came powder that made him sneeze, followed by an intense hour of work.

Leilah and her colleagues stood back to examine their work with critical eyes. They discussed this and that for a little while longer, making small corrections before they appeared to be satisfied.

Duncan was made to stand in front of a long mirror where he could see himself. What he saw made him catch his breath. That wasn't the cocky, freckle-faced young midshipman anymore: it was a woman, slightly busty whose shoulders were somewhat too broad but a woman nonetheless. An auburn blonde colored wig fell in curls to his shoulders—Leilah assured him it was in the latest Cairo style—a long orange and gold skirt fell in pleats to the floor, and his upper body had of a sudden developed a convincing pair of breasts. His eyebrows were almost gone and his lips were a bright red. There was even some darkening color around his eyes which stared back at the mirror with the haunted expression of a prisoner about to go to his execution. He stared for a long time at the image, muttering repeatedly, "Oh my God!"

"You like what you see?" Leilah asked him tentatively, as though hoping to hear some praise for all the hard work she and her companions had expended on him.

"Er... er... I don't know what to say!" he moaned, wishing he was dead and buried.

"Ye...es, about that voice of yours, and the way you walk. You are not a man now, you understand?" she admonished him. "We all will call you Jasmine now, and you must learn to walk and to talk as we ladies do."

CHAPTER 23

CLOSE ENCOUNTERS

Three days after the debacle on the peninsula, the French army, the British in their ships, and the men still holed up in the fortress witnessed the grand ghastly finale of the battle of Abukir.

The bloated corpses of the drowned soldiers began to rise to the surface between the fort and the vessels, then to drift among the ships still riding at anchor as though appealing to be taken on board again.

The Turkish war-ships and their immense fleet of transports, tenantless now, and without further motive to remain upon the coast of Egypt after the destruction of the fine army they had nourished and supported, spread their sails and fled precipitately from this scene of horror, overwhelmed with grief and despair.

One French officer was to observe later in a letter home:

The dead army of Pasha Mustafa remained behind to bob and drift in the current to slowly and remorselessly come ashore at the very beaches they had left three days before in a renewed invasion of this ill-fated peninsula. An invasion that was unstoppable by the French who had no defense against this horror. As their comrades-in-arms sailed away, the corpses remained swinging back and forth upon the tides, and then began a slow, solemn movement back to the beach whence they had so strangely fled, as though to avenge their wild panic by landing again to renew once more the fierce battle they had just lost.

"They had no fear now of French bayonets, battering cannon, nor musket fire. They were unheralded by drums or the blare of brazen-throated trumpet!—those ghastly battalions, with voiceless lips and weaponless hands, impelled by the tides and the winds, they moved blindly forward with the white breakers upon Abukir's beaches— in long, broken lines and formless masses, advancing and receding, rising and falling, with the restless tides, whose confused jostling cause aimless blows and faint rattle of steel by the scabbards of undrawn sabers still worn in gay-colored sashes, which cease, suddenly, as the wearers drift apart. They made dull, meaningless shocks and strange noises amid the hollow roar of the sea, more terrible than any living tumult of battle—assaults which did not stop with the coming of the hours of darkness, more persistent and determined than those of the bravest columns—careless of repulses, those invincible regiments, reinforced by more corpses with every wave, press onward,—ever press onward!—till they rest in tangled heaps at the foot of those low, sandy heights, yet, only to rot and fester there, beneath the burning rays of an Egyptian mid-summer sun, the prey of the beaks and claws of countless vultures which tear at bloodless lips and sightless eyes!

Conscious of the danger from such an exposure to thousands of corpses, the French troops made every effort, with the enforced help of the Arabs and other natives who had flocked to the scene in hundreds for the sake of plunder, to bury as many of the dead as could be reached during the brief time it was possible to approach or touch them. Corpses were thrown into long trenches hastily hollowed out of the hot, dry sands. But vast numbers of bodies could not be interred, and the horrible stink from decaying flesh and bones would surely poison the waters and shores of Abukir Bay throughout the remainder of that year. No one would want to venture out onto the peninsular for many months. Only vultures and scavenging animals from the desert came to feast. The French army even had to retreat some miles inland to avoid the dreadful stench of death that hovered over the land.

All the while, despite the horror on the shore all around them, the French artillery bombardment of the fort continued unabated, with men in the French army wondering at the awful conditions which must exist in the fort. After eight days there were only about 3000 still alive and they were starving, while many were mad with thirst because they had drunk sea water. At last they could stand it no longer and surrendered, desperate for a swifter death at the hands of their captors than the agony of starvation, even as they dreaded meeting the tortures they had themselves meted out to captured French soldiers.

Captain François of the French army described the scene as the men came out of the fort:

"They came out to offer themselves up to the vengeance of their victors. The son of the Pasha and his lieutenants came out at the head of the Turkish soldiers who looked like ghosts... They threw down their arms that they no longer had the strength to carry, and all of them bowed down, asking for death. But our commanders and soldiers, forgetting their previous hatred of the enemy, felt for them all the compassion and care evoked by their deplorable state. We gave them food and drink. Despite the precautions taken to prevent the illness that comes from eating too much too quickly after having suffered from hunger, three quarters of those 3000 men died of indigestion."

A final irony!

Unaware of this awful conclusion to the battle on the peninsula, in the House of Paradise Leilah spent the best part of the day working on Duncan's walk, his voice and his expression. She gave a small frown as he grimaced at the image he was seeing in the mirror.

"Jasmine!" her tone was sharp. "We girls do not distort our faces into expressions like that. You are not a... a gorilla! You must learn... all times you must keep your face smooth. We 'ave spent much time on your not so pretty face and it is a work of art. If you pull a bad face... the powder, it is going to fall off, and then you will 'ave trouble."

He nodded, afraid to speak; his face felt frozen in place.

"Now speak with high voice and open your eyes... yes, like that!" she applauded him. "Now it looks like you are pleased with someone."

Duncan saw the scanty eyebrows move up, his blue eyes widen and the corners of his mouth curl upwards in an uncertain smile. He still looked like a frightened animal facing a pack of hounds, but with Leilah's coaching, accompanied by many an encouraging comment in Arabic from her companions, they began to make some progress.

Soon Leilah pronounced herself and her friends satisfied that at a distance he might pass.

"There is a test you can make to prove our work," she informed him.

Captain Williams was lounging on the verandah alone, waiting for Danush, when he became aware of a new presence in the room behind him. It was accompanied by the scent of roses, so he assumed it to be a woman and turned.

It was a servant girl who had just entered, carrying a brass tray with small coffee cups and a long-spouted brass jug. She walked a little hesitantly into the room, her long orange dress flowing behind her, and bent over to place the tray on the low table in front of him. He observed that she was auburn-haired under her flimsy veil and a little heavy compared to the slim Arab women he was used to seeing in the house, but was about to dismiss this when realization dawned.

He took a step forward with his hand raised to forestall her departure. "Excuse me," he said in Arabic without thinking. "Are you...? Is that...?" At that moment the girl looked up and he found himself looking straight into the blue eyes of the young midshipman, who had pushed the veil aside. There was a kind of desperation lurking at the back of his eyes that did not go unnoticed by Williams.

"Dear God!" he said and stepped back a pace with his mouth open. "It really is you, Graham?"

"Yes, Sir, 'fraid it is," the apparition standing in front of him said in a glum voice.

Williams was not normally at a loss for words. He hurriedly collected his wits and then said, "Whoever did this work is a genius! You look well... er... just like a... a woman! It's marvelous!"

"It was to be a test. Mademoiselle Leilah sent me in to see what you thought. How long have I to be like this, Sir?"

He noted the pleading in the boy's voice.

Williams had regained his composure somewhat. "My compliments to the ladies who carried out this work," he laughed, but then he sobered a little. "As long as it takes, Graham, I'm afraid. There are rumors that the British fleet has sailed from Abukir. I suspect they will pop up outside the harbor in force, and then we will see. Meanwhile, I think you should enjoy the comforts of the house, not too literally of course, it might upset Danush, but for the time being you at least can relax. I have to go out and check the harbor for an opportunity—should there ever be one."

Captain Williams indeed had work to do. He needed to make contact with some of the other citizens of the city of Alexandria to find out how many soldiers Napoléon had in the country and confirm where most of them were at any given time. Also the defenses of the city would be of interest to the commodore, should an assault be considered.

Danush joined him later in the afternoon over tea. They discussed the tragic situation at Abukir and the pending arrival of the British fleet.

"I would very much like to find out how many soldiers Napoléon has in Egypt and confirm where most of them are at any given time," he told Danush. "If we can get away that knowledge would be useful to Sir Sydney. I suspect that he would like to gain a foothold in Alexandria with British troops rather than use the Turks," he added dryly.

Danush nodded agreement. "Despite his reputation the Pasha Mustafa was not a match for Napoléon. The Turks have not had very reliable leaders of late," he commented. "Général Kléber and that cavalry officer, Général Murat, who I hear captured the Pasha, are superb soldiers. For the moment they are at Abukir, but that will change," he observed. "Then Napoléon will go back to Cairo, leaving Général Marmont to hold Alexandria on his own, I would assume, but we here will be locked in if the British show up, and that could pose problems for you."

"No more than if we were roaming the countryside trying to get back to the fleet, I suspect," Williams said. "I will take a look around the harbor today and see if there is anything there which might help."

"I presume the boy will stay here?" Danush asked.

Williams laughed. "Oh yes. I was very nearly fooled when I saw him. Those girls of yours have done a marvelous job on him."

Danush smiled. "Leilah is a good girl. She can keep an eye on him until it's time to leave."

"You are going to keep him with the girls?" Williams asked, with an incredulous tone that was almost envious.

Danush laughed. "Yes, where else would you have me put him? The house will be swarming with Frenchmen this evening and some will inevitably wander about where they are not supposed to go." he paused and looked at the captain.

"I could always place him under guard in the cellar. but that might be considered very poor hospitality, my friend."

Williams chuckled. "You do what you think best for our safety, Danush."

Chapter 24

Reconnoiter

Williams made his way into the streets of the city in the early evening after prayers had been called. The city was quieter now, the markets empty and the farmer's stalls closed. the meat vendors were beginning to stoke their charcoal fires, preparing chicken or goat meat kababs as well as roasted vegetables for the evening crowds who, despite the presence of the French, would be coming out into the streets to enjoy the cool evening breeze coming off the water.

Observing everything he could, especially the presence and numbers of the French garrison, the spy made his way cautiously towards the new harbor.

Williams knew the history of Alexandria well: Pharaohs supplanted by the arrival of the Greeks followed by Rome and then the Byzantines. Now it was the Turks. He didn't see the presence of the French as being anything but temporary. The various cultures had left their mark on the city's architecture, especially in the old city that had clustered about the old harbor. The Greeks and Romans had been builders, but the Turks had neglected the city, leaving much in disrepair and ruined. The French, however, were taking on some of the re-construction and the fellaheen were being paid to do the work. The old harbor was now being replaced by the far more spacious 'New Harbor', a deeper and wider basin that could accommodate larger war ships.

He arrived at the docks after passing through the ancient archway that gave access to the piers beyond. He moved inconspicuously among the laborers and gawkers along the wide quays, observing the activity and taking mental notes of everything he saw. Where the famous lighthouse of historical fame, the Pharos of Alexandria, had once stood, was now a tall, solid-looking castle called the Citadel of Qaitbay which dominated the entrance to the new harbor. It stood four towers square at the end of a causeway in the general area of the former lighthouse. It also bristled with guns that could rake the harbor as well as the entrance. At its base were even more gun emplacements. Altogether it presented a formidable obstacle to any enemy ship attempting to gain entrance to the harbor.

Nearer to hand Williams observed the long curved border of the new harbor with several French battleships idling at anchor in its spacious pool. There were also merchant ships tied up at the quayside and a small huddle of ships anchored in the middle of the harbor. There was much activity in and around the port itself.

As he stood watching the four French war ships in the harbor basin, wishing he had a glass to look more closely, he heard a command in English. "Get up! You 'ave work to do. Lazy bastards."

He turned slowly about, in time to see a French soldier pointing his musket at some men who had been crouching at rest in the shade of a building nearby.

He watched as the prisoners scrambled to their feet with the clink of chains and shuffled off towards a merchantman which was just docking about a hundred yards along the pier. Full of curiosity, Williams decided to follow the gang and their two accompanying guards. The prisoners were chained by their ankles in a line set roughly six feet apart; each man held the chain in front of him as he shuffled along the stone pier. They looked tired and ill-fed, their clothes were ragged, but by the way they moved he could tell that they were former sailors—and by his guess, British sailors at that.

Now his curiosity was thoroughly piqued. He had not known there were British prisoners of war here in Alexandria. He joined the people who were passing the slow-moving prisoners, and while a guard was looking another way he sidled up to one of the men.

"Are you British?" he asked in a low voice.

The man began to turn towards him in surprise. "Don't acknowledge me," Williams snapped. "Just answer the question," he commanded.

"Ship's Master Jones. Off the Monitor, taken four months ago."

"How many of you?"

"Just us. Who are you?"

"Never mind that. Do you—"

The guard turned back saw Williams walking too close to the prisoners. "What are you doing? Keep away from them, you Arab pig!" he shouted and brandished his musket at the captain, who ducked his head and shambled away.

Williams drifted off. At least the sentry had not seen through his disguise. But just as he left he murmured,, "You here every night?" He got a nod from the prisoner.

Satisfied, he disappeared into the crowd and made his way forward to find an observation point where he could watch them at work.

His mind was moving furiously, but first he needed to find a means of transport. He spent the next four hours watching and observing until it was too dark to see, then made his way back towards the brothel.

CHAPTER 25

THE DANCER

As evening closed in on the city of Alexandria, a different world awoke: that of the night and its dubious population of entertainers, thieves, cut-throats and other nefarious characters who lived for the darkness. The house of pleasure, "The Garden of Paradise," belonging to Danush and a consortium of pragmatic Greek merchants, opened its doors just as the sun set, and it was not long before there were discreet knocks on the main entrance, which was located on a more respectable street than the one Williams had used to gain access.

The person or persons who wanted entry would tap on the solid, iron-studded door with wrought iron decorations nailed into its paneling, and a small grate would open. An impassive face with a huge hooked nose would inspect the would-be guests, and if they were acceptable the door would be opened and the visitors allowed entry. If the man at the grill decided he didn't like the visitors he would deny them access and, if necessary, have two enormous black Nubians chase them off with loud threats. No one wanted to tangle with these two heavyweights.

Those who were allowed in, and this included any officer or a senior NCO, were shown to the spacious seating area where they could purchase a bottle of wine—or something more powerful. Food was offered on an elaborately decorated thick paper menu, although it was very dependent upon what might be available in the market. Alexandria was essentially a blockaded city where food was no longer in plentiful supply, especially delicacies such as beef and pâté, which were desired by the hungry French soldiers, some of whom were prepared to pay well for their luxuries. Nevertheless, this was a house of entertainment and wine was not yet hard to find, although the good wines were very expensive.

Most of men came for other reasons, and not least was the prospect of watching their favorite belly dancer, who had arrived from Cairo the night before, to perform here at this prestigious house of pleasure. Later other forms of entertainment would be provided, and some of the crowd were eager to experience those as well.

Captain Joseph Clément and Lieutenant Alain Lefevre arrived an hour after sunset.

"I hope we are not late for the show!" Lefevre said, as the door was opened for them.

"The show is about to begin, gentlemen. Please enter and you will be shown a seat," the unctuous servant standing on the steps to the main entrance stated in good French, having overheard them, and he led the way into the well-lighted foyer. They walked on past the heavyset, intimidating guards standing on either side of an arched doorway and into a large, low-roofed room full of people. The vast majority were Frenchmen in uniform. All were conversing in loud voices, well lubricated by wine and spirits by this time. The warm air was thick with pipe smoke. At the far end of the room was a low stage with a curtain drawn across, unoccupied. There was an air of expectancy that crackled in the room.

The two men found a small table near to the back of the room —the tables at the front were all taken by more senior officers— and ordered a bottle of wine. Then they sat back to watch. The wine arrived just as some reedy music began behind the curtain, which was now drawn slowly back to reveal a small group of musicians seated on the back left-hand corner of there stage. Without preamble they began to play. The musicians continued playing their pipes and stringed instruments while the audience fidgeted and drank more wine. The thin reedy music had no appeal to Captain Clément, who favored his own nation's music above all others.

He leaned over to his Sergeant. "How do they play such horrible music?" he asked.

Lefevre wiped his enormous mustaches and laughed. "My Captain, no one is going to pay attention to the music once the show gets started. I saw her in in Cairo, she is quite something. Be patient, it'll get better."

Clément sipped the wine with caution. It wasn't as bad as he had expected. It at least matched the wine they had found in Cairo, which could be described as reasonable cooking wine. He relaxed and watched the stage like every other man in the house.

She slipped onto the stage like a wraith. There was no introduction; the music gave only the slightest clue with a few rapid finger taps on a tiny drum and there she was in front of the expectant audience. The response was immediate: they cheered and clapped applauding her for simply being there. Some men even stood up and cheered, clapping furiously. Others shouted at them to sit down as they could not see. The dancer stood with her long legs slightly apart and her arms held outwards.

Back in the wings, observing the electric effect that his Fatima had upon the audience, Danush gave a small smile of satisfaction. Business would be brisk later on.

Meanwhile, Fatima had begun. The colors she wore were of shimmering turquoise with silver threads and glittering pearl buttons sewn into the fabric which reflected the light of the lamps, a ring of sparkling light about her waist. She was clad only in an alluring separate top which displayed her naked midriff almost to her mons, and the bright paste diamond in her belly button glittered in the lamplight. Her well developed breasts were held captive in sequined silk and nothing more. She wore an ankle-length, flowing skirt that was divided all the way up to her hips to the briefest of sequined pants that in turn displayed her long thighs as far up as her well-fleshed bottom. Around her waist was a thin belt with silver decorations that held colored beads, while fine gold bracelets clinked on her wrists and ankles.

From her elbows to her wrists she wore fine decorated lace and filigree silver threads. Her right hand was tied with a gold thread to the bottom of one trailing length of her split gossamer dress that flowed about her as she moved her hand.

On her head she wore a transparent veil held in place on her rich flowing, ebony hair by a small round hairpiece, richly sewn. The veil did little to hide the dusky, oval features of a very beautiful woman with large, sensual lips and huge eyes. She was a very wild and sexually captivating creature who smiled with white teeth in appreciation of the applause.

Already in motion, her tiny feet, which were encased in turquoise slippers of the finest doeskin, were never still. There was a hush from the men who were enraptured by this vision that had appeared before them so suddenly, and the swaying and undulation of her hips hypnotized the entire audience. She effortlessly caused her dress to swirl about her thighs, accentuating her long and shapely legs; the crowd loved it and tapped the tables with their fingers to keep time.

"Dieu, Dieu!" sighed Lefevre. "I swear I have died and gone to heaven!"

The music, which had never stopped, began to very slowly increase in tempo, drawing out the moment. As she danced, the drum became more insistent and the girl in front of them matched the musicians beat for beat. Her entire figure was in motion as, with the music, slowly at first, she undulated her belly and hips, and then her upper body seemingly independently of her waist, upon which most men's eyes were riveted.

One moment her hips were undulating towards the sweating men while her torso was thrown back at an almost impossible angle and her breasts were vibrating, then she spun away to present her back and her buttocks teased the gasping audience. Around she twirled, and then it was her torso which held them riveted with their mouths drooling.

"How does she do it?" Lefevre breathed, unheard in the noise. "How can anyone move their backbone like that?"

"I can't take my eyes off her legs!" exclaimed someone at the next table. "No one can have legs that long!"

"No one has a bottom like that!" shouted another.

"I'm going to have an attack of the heart if this goes on much longer!" yet another wag shouted.

One moment her breasts were jiggling at the wildly excited crowd before her, and the next her lower body was in motion in what could not be anything other than a blatant sexual invitation, the bright paste diamond in her belly button winking lewdly at the sex-starved crowd of soldiers below her.

The music wailed ever louder, with the beat of the finger drum becoming more frantic as the tension built and the girl on the stage appeared to vibrate into a frenzy of motion, her dress flying around her in shimmering waves. At just the moment when every eye was locked on this whirling vision of light and motion, the music stopped, the lamps were extinguished and the curtain was quickly drawn closed to hide the stage. The girl was gone, leaving the audience gasping, sweating and rampant. There was a long stunned silence, but then the crowd erupted into applause, clapping, whistling and shouting for the dancer to come back.

That was not to be. The lamps around the room were relit or their flames turned up to display the dazed audience of officers and NCOs, most with the collars and buttons of their tunics undone and their hats lying on the tables alongside the empty bottles of wine.

The men were excited and had a sense of being left hanging, but the waiters were moving around with cool efficiency offering more wine and spirits to thirsty men.

"Come on. It's time to leave before someone starts a fight," Captain Clément stated and got up.

He was none too soon, as a group of men near to the stage began to shout at one another and before long fists were flying. The group of men surged back and forth, some trying to restrain others who simply wanted to hit someone, something, anything to relieve the tension that had built up in them.

The two men pushed their way towards the exit while more and more men rushed towards the fighting mass of shouting and yelling men. Men fell crashing against wooden tables, which collapsed under them. Just as they were leaving Clément glanced back and saw the two black giants wading in among the fighting men, tossing them aside as though they were wooden toys as they headed for the center of the fight.

"It always amazes me the power of a woman! There will be some broken heads tonight!" He laughed as he followed his companions out into the darkness.

"I don't want to be anywhere near here when the night patrol arrives," Lefevre stated. "We are on furlough for two evenings and I want to enjoy them both. For sure I am coming back tomorrow!"

His amused companion agreed, and they put as much distance between themselves and the house of pleasure as they could.

Meanwhile, in the brothel some of the soldiers had escaped from the clutches of the servants and the two giants, and were now roaming. A few even managed to make it up to the third floor.

Chapter 26

Chivalry

Duncan had spent the best part of the evening by himself in the women's quarters having been told to stay there by Leilah and under no circumstances to leave. He was bored and the cloying scents of the room had given him a headache, so he wandered about the place restlessly, idly inspecting the room. There was nothing to do and he wondered where Williams might be.

Then he heard the muted sound of music far below and the roars of the appreciative crowd. His curiosity got the better of him.

"God dammit I'm going out of my mind sitting here!" he muttered. But he remembered to check himself at the mirror on the door before he slipped out, satisfied by the image of a well-proportioned, auburn-haired woman with bright red lips.

"See yew, ye pretty bitch!" he preened placing his right hand behind his head and the other on his hip which he wiggled with a cackle at the absurdity of the image. He was by now somewhat familiar with the corridors and eventually found himself standing on the verandah overlooking the now dark gardens below.

Then the music stopped, leaving an abrupt silence, followed by a roar that shook the house, after which he could hear shouts and then crashes and more shouts. He was just about to hurry away, fearing that the noise might bring unwelcome persons to where he was standing, when there were hurried footsteps outside and an apparition appeared at the entrance to the room. A lightly-veiled woman of extraordinary beauty pushed through the curtains with an exclamation of annoyance, looking behind her as she entered.

She turned and faced Duncan and exclaimed again in surprise but also relief at seeing another person in the room. She hurried further into the room, all the while studying him with a slightly puzzled expression on her face, and said something that sounded like a question. She spoke again in Arabic and lifted her veil. Duncan realized with a shock that not only was he staring at a scantily-clad woman in a stunning costume but that she was talking to him and appeared to assume he was a woman too. He began to stutter a reply in French when another person appeared at the entrance.

This time it was a French soldier. "Ah-hah! There you are, my darling beauty!" he called out, then he noticed it was not one but two women standing near to one another by the verandah.

"By God! Have I found the harem at last? The belly dancing angel, my God! Oh, my angel! I've been wandering these corridors forever and now at last I have found you!" he staggered towards them, twirling his huge waxed mustache and reached for the flap on his pants.

"Two-in-one! Who will be first for Captain Kermaret?" he cackled as he came towards them.

The girl shrank from his approach with a cry of alarm. barely realizing it, she had almost fallen into Duncan's arms.

Without thinking, Duncan reached forward, pulled the girl closer and then pushed her behind him after which he took a step forward.

"Hah! So Blondie wants it first, eh? Fantastic. But you," he pointed to the girl, "don't go away. There's a lot of stamina left in this old warrior." The officer fumbled some more with his trousers, almost tripping over his sword as he stumbled the last few yards.

Duncan seized his chance. He took one more step forward and launched a punch from the waist. It landed exactly where he had hoped, on the side of the man's lower jaw. It was a wicked blow that carried with it all the humiliation and pent-up anger the boy had had to endure for the last two days. There was an audible crack as his fist connected and it threw the soldier backwards to crash in an untidy heap on the floor.

"Bugger, that hurt!" Duncan cried out loud and flapped his hand, which hurt like hell. The midshipman stepped forward to check on his victim, but the man was out cold. He became aware of another disturbance, but this time it came from the girl, staring at him with her hands over her lower face with a look of shock on her face. She appeared to be on the verge of hysterics.

"Oh bugger, no!" Duncan groaned. He reached for her, but she shrank back from him, her eyes wide with surprise and not a little fear as she stared at him. He had time to note that although she had lovely features her nose was just a little too big.

Several of the girls appeared at the entrance to the room and ran to join the girl, all chattering at once and commiserating with her, as she pointed at the Frenchman lying on the floor and then at Duncan, speaking in choking Arabic all the while, after which she began to weep. Leilah appeared at the entrance and rushed up to Duncan, almost tripping over the fallen soldier at his feet.

"Oh, merde!" she exclaimed as she looked down on the man.

"What are you doing 'ere, Jasmine?" she demanded of Duncan, her gray eyes wide. They flicked to the dancer with a question for the other girls, who shook their heads and went back to consoling the weeping dancer and turning her away from Duncan. She held up an imperious hand for silence and the excited babble ceased. Then she asked, "What is 'e doing 'ere?" she demanded of Duncan in a hushed tone, pointing at the Frenchman.

"I... er, he was... er, going to attack the girl over there. I... um, had to protect her," Duncan mumbled, stumbling for the words.

She was clearly furious with him. "You go back to the room, right now, Dunkin or I am in trouble! I see you later," she ordered, and pointed to the door.

Duncan slunk off, leaving a hysterical belly dancer and her consoling companions behind, and the unconscious soldier still lying on the floor.

His travails were not over this evening, however. He had just arrived at the stairway leading up to the top floor where the girls lived when two French soldiers appeared at the other end of the corridor and, spotting Graham in his disguise, gave a shout and began to give chase.

With a startled look at the two men running towards him, shouting with glee at having found a woman in the labyrinth of rooms and floors, Graham took off. It occurred to him to go upwards but he realized instinctively that this would lead the two drunken soldiers to the wrong place, so he took a chance and headed down the stairs.

This proved to be a mistake, as he had no idea where he was going, and the two soldiers, now decidedly excited by the chase of a blonde woman, were rapidly gaining on him. He sped down the steps and took a blind right into a narrow corridor along which he raced. One of the soldiers was faster than the other and caught up with Graham, grabbing for his shoulder. Duncan wrenched himself away, but in the process the soldier tore his blouse.

The two of them crashed through a thick dark leather curtain to collapse onto the stage that had been the center of entertainment only a few minutes before.

The officers and men who had been scuffling and milling on the main floor caught sight of the two figures on the stage and, thinking that there was anther act coming, cheered wildly and began to separate themselves in the expectation of a show. It didn't seem to occur to any of them that it might be somewhat incongruous to see a French soldier on stage.

For his part, after an appalled and wild-eyed look at the crowd below, clutching his now badly torn blouse and trying to avoid the very amorous advances of not only the first but also the second soldier, Duncan did the only thing he could think of. He kicked the first in the crotch and punched the second hard on the nose, just as he was leaning down to reach under Duncan's dress. The two men collapsed amid the cheers and shouts of laughter from the inebriated audience. The light was minimal, so it was not entirely clear to the audience what was really going on, but the comical way the two soldiers tumbled to the floor having been beaten by a good looking blonde woman defending her honor was great entertainment for all.

Duncan didn't wait to see what would happen next. He hurled himself off the stage and dived into the darkness beyond. Stumbling and gasping, he eventually found the stairs and his way back to the women's living chamber. He tumbled into Leilah's alcove, where he sat panting and thought about his predicament while he rubbed his knuckles. He glowered. At least he had knocked a couple of Frenchies down, he consoled himself. "Hah! Take that!" he muttered, reliving the moment, but soon he began to worry about what might be going on below. The noise coming from the theater was very loud as the confused audience clamored for more and the equally bewildered staff of the house tried to appease the two wounded soldiers and placate the drunken and destructive audience.

An hour later, Duncan heard female voices at the door, which opened and Leilah entered alone. She said something to another outside, then closed the door. Turning she noticed the disconsolate Duncan still seated on the bed.

"Ah, you are there, Dunkin! I am glad you are safe, for that means I am safe too." She smiled at the confused boy. "It seems that you are an 'ero for saving Fatima," she said with a dimple. "But they are saying that a woman attacked two of the French soldiers down in the area of the theater. You were not there, were you?" She asked with a frown. "You came back 'ere, did you not? My, but those soldiers are so violent! They break all the furniture! Danush is furious!"

"Hero?" he queried, even more confused. "Er, yes, been here all the time." He tried to look innocent.

Leilah was not paying much attention. "Fatima told us all about it. She said you are so brave. She still is not aware that you are not a woman." Leilah chuckled mischievously.

"Impossible!" Duncan said with a tentative grin.

She began to laugh. "No indeed, she did not hear what we said, she was crying so hard, nor did the other girls let her into the secret. She thinks that a strong blonde girl came to her aid and knocked down the Frenchman. She is very impressed." Leilah gave him an arch look from under her brows as she smiled.

He snorted and rubbed his knuckle. She noticed and took his hand in hers. "You know it was a brave thing to do? The man was drunk and would have been brutal, even dangerous. We know of him. 'e is very bad to the girls."

Then she noticed his disheveled appearance. "Dunkin, what happened to you? Your blouse it is torn."

He tried desperately to change the subject. "What did you do with him?" he asked. "You didn't have him killed, did you?"

Leilah shook her head. "No, but he would deserve it. Not all are like him, but he is bad. The two big men, Ibrahim and Mahomet, will carry him out and leave him in a street far from 'ere. He will wake up with a big headache." She smiled and pressed his hand. "I shall repair this, your blouse too. You have been clumsy, no? I do this for you, do not go away."

She came back with a hot damp cloth and some salve, which she applied tenderly to his superficial wound. It felt very good to have her fussing over him. He sighed and she looked up.

"You like it that I care for you?" she asked him. Her tone was soft.

"Er... yes, I most certainly do, Leilah. You are very kind." Duncan was rapidly falling for this slip of a girl whom he hardly knew.

'So now take off the blouse and the dress. I will sew it back." He complied, but when he handed her the blouse she appeared to hesitate for a moment, then she said, "I do not have work to do tonight. Danush told me I must look after you. I mean ... yes, I must look after you. He said that. You must sleep here tonight." She shook her head and frowned, as though making a decision while looking straight at him.

Duncan could feel his whole body getting very warm and his face going red underneath the flaking make-up.

"Um ...er, what d'you mean, Leilah?" he stammered.

She looked directly at him with her huge gray eyes and said firmly, "You will not be like a woman for tonight, Monsieur Dunkin. But... first we shall take off the make-up. You understand?"

"Er, yes, yes Leilah, I think I do," he whispered, his heart beating a furious tattoo against his ribcage.

CHAPTER 27

CUTTING OUT

The day after the citadel fell Sir Sidney Smith was alerted to the arrival of a French boat flying a white flag of truce making its way towards the *Tigre* .

He met the two green jacketed cavalry officers who arrived on deck with full honors. After the salutes and bow the officers introduced themselves as Captain Henri Landes of General Murat's brigade and Captain Adelard.

Captain Landes spoke."I have the honor of bringing letters to you Sir Sidney Smith from General Bonaparte." he said and produced some packets with a flourish.

"I am equally honored to make your acquaintance," Sir Sidney responded with a bow. "Please. Will you come to my cabin where we may talk in more comfort?"

The officer cast a sharp eye about him as t hough assessing the state of the ship and murmured something to his colleague who remained on deck, Captain Landes then followed Sir Sidney as he led the way below.

Sir Sidney offered his guest a sherry and then while Captain Landes sat quietly opposite him he read the letter.

When he was finished he remarked. "I have to congratulate his Excellency upon a great victory."

The captain inclined his head. "The fortunes of war Sir. You are familiar with how fickle that can be..." his tone was dray.

200

"He mentions here about prisoner exchanges . Alas we have no French prisoners here in my squadron so I am regretfully unable to assist in that matter." Sir Sidney stated. The embarrassment of the slaughter of the garrison in Abukir still fresh in his mind.

"It was just in case , you understand Sir Sidney?' Captain Landes said. "We do not wish our own people to end up in a Turkish dungeon if we can do anything to avoid it."

"Do you have any British prisoners?" Sir Sidney enquired. He was wondering if the boy Graham might have been captured along with captain Williams perhaps.

"There are a few merchant seamen in Alexandria whom we might release. I would have to investigate further."

"The other item we wished to discuss was the evacuation of the sick and wounded. Your ships are blockading the city of Alexandria. General Bonaparte asks that in the interests of humanity you might allow vessels carrying these people to depart for France."

Sir Sidney thought about it for a moment but then he said . "Yes that can be arranged. I reserve the right to inspect them of course. How long before you will have the ships prepared?"

"A matter of two weeks, Sir. We have men in Damietta and in Cairo who would have to be transported to Alexandria and from there to available ships. We would keep you informed of all the details."

Sir Sidney nodded but he then stood up and said, "I wonder. Do you have any news of France these days?"

Captain Landes stared at him then shook his head with a rueful smile.

"No Sir Sidney. Your blockade is very effective. We are starved of news."

"Then as a parting gesture of good will I would like you to have some of our news papers. They are old, several weeks I'm afraid ,but they would perhaps help."

"Your courtesy is deeply appreciated, Sir Sidney." Captain Lades bowed.

Captain Lades and Adelard clambered down to the boat which was to take them back to the French army clutching a bundle of old British newspapers.

Sir Sidney watched him go then turned to Lieutenant Bowles. "I hope I have managed to sow some alarm and despondency in the mind of General Bonaparte with those papers."

"They will hardly cheer him up despite his victory here, what with all the chaos going on inFrance in his absence I suspect, Sir." Lt Bowles remarked with a grin.

"If the newspapers are to be believed and are up to date he has some serious problems ahead of him despite the good fortune he had here. His country is facing not a few disasters thanks to the ineptitude of their revolutionary council." Sir Sidney returned.

The stench of the dead on the peninsula of Abukir was widespread and noxious. Even for the iron-nerved British this was too much. Sir Sidney ordered his ships to haul in anchor and they left the sea of the dead behind, sailing around the peninsula to resume the blockade of Alexandria.

The small flotilla of British ships appeared outside the New Harbor just after dawn of the next day. It announced itself with a light bombardment, which was returned with gusto by the alert French defenders. Sir Sydney, frustrated by the debacle at Abukir, wanted to let the garrison know that even if the Turks had been crushed the British still had teeth.

Alexandria woke with somewhat of a hangover, at least in certain districts. One being the Greek quarter which was never seriously inhibited about the use of wine and wherein was situated the Garden of Paradise. Neither the Greeks nor the French garrison paid much attention to the Islamic rules of no alcohol and nor for that matter did the Arab traders who smuggled it in on the backs of camels from places like Cairo or the very few merchant ships which evaded the blockade.

Today, however, the city awoke to find that its gates were once more closed and bolted; the bulk of the French army was on the move south and the British warships were blocking the harbor entrance. Some reinforcements had been retained in the city to boost the garrison. The Infantrie being among them. Thus the day started off badly and the city of Alexandria gave a collective groan of resignation. The British were back and determined, it seemed, to be a nuisance.

Sir Sidney for his part was planning a raid. In his stuffy main cabin he had gathered his senior officers, including the captains of his two capital ships. Captain Miller of the *Theseus* and Captain Troubridge of the Colloden had been rowed over, as had Captain Drummond of the HMS Bulldog, a bomb ketch, and Captain Oswald of the HMS Perseus, the other bomb ketch in the small squadron. The morning air had been full of the whistle of the bosun's pipes as one captain after another had come aboard to the accompaniment of shouted commands and Marines stamping to attention and presenting arms.

The remaining officers were the two Marines, Colonel Douglas and Major Bromley, and ship's officers Lieutenants Canes and Bowles.

"Gentlemen," said Sir Sidney, as he sipped his sherry, which was rapidly becoming depleted, and watched his officers, "I intend to burn some ships tonight."

There were murmurs of approval from the gathering. "Are we going to send in fire ships, Sir?" someone asked.

"If we had them as with the Toulon incident then I would but we have none available so we will go in and make our own," Sidney continued. "Boney might have given the Turks a black eye, but we are still in the match and I intend to demonstrate this. I want to destroy or badly damage the war ships he still has in the harbor and prevent any thoughts of sorties from taking hold in his mind."

"As we know it today there are two ships of the line inside the harbor and quite a few smaller ships," Lieutenant Canes said. "By the way, Sir, we have not yet heard from Captain Williams."

"Have we heard anything at all about our lost midshipman, Mr Graham?" Sir Sidney enquired.

"Nothing, nothing at all I'm afraid, Sir," Lt Bowles responded.

Sir Sidney frowned. "It's a little unusual for Williams to not be in touch. But he's a very resourceful man and I can only hope he is not in any danger. I am also sure that had he been captured the French would have taken pleasure in telling me that they had discovered a spy. No I think he must be safe...for the moment. But Mr Graham, where on earth could he be?"

Midshipman Graham jerked awake to the distant boom of cannon. He listened to the closer boom as the harbor defenses replied with their own salvo. He was by this time out of bed and fumbling with his clothing.

Leilah turned over languidly in the bed and opened her eyes. "What you doing? Where you going, Dunkin?" she asked sleepily. Then she realized what he was doing and scrambled out of bed herself, quite forgetting her nakedness.

"No! No! You cannot leave, Dunkin. Not until Master Danush gives the permission," she cried, holding onto his arm.

"But that is gun fire! The British are here and I have to leave!" Duncan exclaimed, but his eyes wandered to where they shouldn't and he sounded regretful.

"Have you so soon forgotten the danger, and the danger we will be in if you are seen?" she demanded, well aware of the effect she was having on him. She slipped gracefully back into the bed and crooked a finger at him. "Come to me, my lover. I am not yet ready to let you go," she purred.

Duncan groaned. "All right, Leilah." He dipped his head in resignation and sat on the edge of the bed with a rueful grin. "But I've had enough of this. I want to get back to my ship."

Leilah pouted. "You want to leave me? Just like that? Did I displease you, Dunkin?" she cooed.

He grinned ruefully and shook his head. "No, Leilah, it was memorable. But... I cannot stay here for much longer. I shall go mad!"

By this time the other girls had woken up to the ominous sound of guns and were gathering around the two of them. Their fearful chattering and little wails of anxiety were interrupted by the arrival of Kaylah, who walked in unannounced and shouted at them to all be quiet. The voices subsided and the girls turned their attention to him, then all at the same time they began to ask him what was going on, despite his attempts to calm them.

Finally he managed to call over to Duncan and Leilah, "You, Jasmine, get dressed quickly and come with me. The English wants to talk to you."

Almost an hour later Duncan, in the form of a veiled Jasmine, accompanied Kaylah and Leilah to the room overlooking the garden. There Williams and Danush were seated on cushions enjoying a coffee while they waited.

Williams opened his eyes wide with surprise when Duncan came in with the other two. Alongside Leilah the auburn-haired "woman" looked a little stocky, but otherwise it was an excellent facsimile of a woman.

"Ah, there you are, Graham," he said, trying to keep a straight face as the boy minced into the room. "We've been waiting for you. There is some news."

"Good morning, Sirs," Duncan said to them in his normal voice, speaking French. "What news is that, Sir?" he enquired of Williams.

"Sit with us and we can discuss this, Mister Graham," Danush said with a smile of welcome, and he waved the others away. They tittered and departed, leaving the two men and Graham alone.

"Just as we hoped the fleet has arrived."

"I heard the guns, Sir."

"While you have been idling about in this den of iniquity, and no doubt dipping your wick in places where you shouldn't, I've been checking the harbor," Williams said in English, but then reverted to French for the benefit of Danush.

"I found to my surprise that there are actually some English prisoners working down at the harbor."

Duncan blinked his kohl-darkened eyes with surprise.

"Yes, but more—or just as—importantly, I have located a vessel that might very well suit our needs." Williams went on to explain that not far from the eastern entrance to the harbor there was a ketch that he thought could be handled by a very small crew.

"Would you be able to sail a boat like that if we can get our hands on it?" Williams asked him.

Duncan nodded. "Yes, Sir. I certainly could. It would be hard going for two men, but if we had some help we would be able to do it."

"Then listen carefully, Duncan, because this is what we are going to do."

Monsieur Le Guennet, the city Chief of Police, was seated at his desk waving a light woven fan in front of him. It served to keep the ever-persistent flies away and to provide some relief from the overwhelming heat that had grown in proportion to the thunder clouds gathering in the west. He was concentrating on the night report, which was out of the ordinary.

One of the garrison officers had been assaulted and left unconscious in the street, where he had been found by one of the night patrols. This was not that unusual other than that officers didn't usually fall drunk to the ground every night. More often than not it was the other ranks, but what was unusual was the excuse the officer gave for being there.

"Sergeant!" he called.

The door opened and Sergeant Fournier poked his head in. He looked as hot as his boss. "Oui, Mon Capitaine?" he enquired.

"This Captain Kermaret. What's his story? Sounds like he was just too drunk to do anything but lie around in the street."

Sergeant Fournier grinned. "He claimed that a woman struck him while he was at the Garden of Paradise and that was the last thing he could remember, Sir."

Monsieur Le Guennet looked incredulous. "I wouldn't have confessed to that even on my deathbed. Would you, Sergeant?"

The sergeant laughed and shook his head. "No, Sir, indeed I would not, but he was insistent so we took a statement. He had a huge bruise on his jaw. The surgeon pronounced it might even have been broken, which gives some credence to the story. But a woman, for goodness sake?" he shook his head again. "That was a powerful blow. It might even have been delivered with a club."

Le Guennet nodded thoughtfully. "Now that I could believe. Was he robbed?"

"No, Sir. He had not been robbed," the sergeant responded.

"That's very unusual indeed. The mystery deepens. He said it happened at the Garden of Paradise?"

"Well, that is the last thing he remembers, Sir."

Le Guennet got to his feet. I think we will pay the Garden a little visit later on. Right now I want some lunch and a rest. This heat is oppressive," he told his sergeant.

How I hate it here, he thought to himself. His work was to ensure that the volatile inhabitants of the city kept the peace and he was quite ruthless about it. Executions without trial were the order of the day.

Madame Guillotine was kept busy lopping heads off rebellious fellaheen who never seemed to learn that the French were here to provide law and order, whereas before they had been at the mercy of the whims of their rotten Turkish masters who had done whatever they pleased.

He sighed. The Garden of Paradise was owned and run by a Persian man named Danush, as he remembered. Le Guennet was not quite sure where his loyalties lay. The man put on good entertainment: rumor was that the belly dancer at the brothel was incredible. A visit might well be worthwhile, Le Guennet decided. Blonde or no blonde.

CHAPTER 28

AN UNWELCOME VISIT

It was late afternoon and the house was very quiet. The entire city slumbered in the oppressive heat. Duncan was back in the girls' room and had dragged his bundle out from Leilah's cubicle, where he had stashed it the day before. He unwrapped the clothes and other items, exposing his sword and the pistol.

Seated on the bed, he began to clean the pistol and the sword. Leilah returned about an hour later and regarded the weapons with distaste. "Kaylah told me that you will leave soon, maybe today," she said as she joined him. He looked at her and saw that her gray eyes looked sad. Her pretty mouth was pulled down at the corners.

""I have to go back to the ship, Leilah. I have no place here."

"I know," she said, but there were tears in her eyes.

"What is the matter, you look sad," he asked her and took her hand. It was small and delicate within his large paw.

"I have not made love to a man who has not paid me first before. It was... strange. I wanted to and now you are leaving me behind to go off to war," she said in a tone that sounded wistful. But then her eyes flared. "Do you men always have to go to war? Do you like war?" she demanded, still holding his hand.

"Noo, but there is nothing else a younger son can do where I come from," he told her. "I had a choice to become a minister, which I simply could not do. I like a scrap too much, so it was to join the army or the navy. I chose the latter because I've always liked the sea."

"Is it like this city, where you come from, Dunkin?" she asked innocently.

He smiled. "Er... no. It's a good deal wetter and damned sight colder in winter. Even the sea can freeze at times."

She gave a shudder. "I could not live in a place like that. I like to be warm," she stated firmly.

"Well, there's a bunch of hairy Scots would agree wi' ye about that," he assured her. "All the same, it's my home."

They talked the afternoon away and only noticed that the sun was setting when the call to prayers began. After the hush of prayers Duncan noticed that activity in the house had picked up. He felt a tingle of anticipation as he contemplated what they might be doing later that night. All the same he also felt a twinge of regret at his impending departure from Leilah, who he realized had somehow managed to get under his skin.

He remembered the fumbled kisses of his youth at home in Scotland, the semi-willing girls who considered the son of a small clan laird a catch, but nothing had prepared him for the delights he had experienced with Leilah.

Dusk drew in and she left him with some food, some nan and flavored meat slices, because she said the entertainment downstairs was about to commence and the girls had to be on hand. She had rolled her eyes at this but then gave him a tender kiss. "I 'ope you are 'ere when I get back, my Scottish man," she told him. He ate the food, but he was too excited to eat very much even though it was very good, much better than anything he had eaten on board ship. The thought of that alone made him fantasize that perhaps he could stay here and fight the French as a spy, rather like Captain Williams. He dismissed the fantasy and moodily contemplated the parting to come.

He guessed it was now about eight o'clock; it was quite dark outside. Captain Williams had not yet appeared, which made Duncan worry. Had something happened? God forbid but he might have been discovered and even now be on the torture rack. He grew anxious. However, the evening appeared to be progressing in a normal manner, so he resigned himself to his fate and dozed.

Kaylah shook him awake. "Come now, Duncan," he said; there was urgency in his tone. "There is danger, you must leave at once!"

Duncan struggled awake and wiped his eyes. "What? What is it?" he demanded.

"The police, they are here in large numbers. Danush said that he thinks there is something going on and it is too dangerous for you to remain," Kaylah said, sounding very frightened.

"Where is Captain Williams?" Duncan responded, feeling a knot growing in his stomach.

"I'm here, Graham," Williams said from the door. "Danush said that there is a bad feel to the presence of the Chief of Police. He is watching the belly dancer, but as soon as her performance is over Danush fears that they will turn the house over."

"But why?" Duncan asked as he began to take off his dress.

"The officer you struck last night registered a complaint, and the Police Chief is a nasty man to have coming after you. No time for that! Grab your clothes and other things and come with me!" he snapped.

Duncan needed no further bidding. He snatched up his weapons, the small bundle of clothes, and then on impulse a light hooded cloak that he saw hanging on a hook by the door, then he and ran after Williams, who was hurrying after Kaylah. They sped down the back stairs into the darkness of the back garden. Duncan could hear the shouts and cheers of the soldiers as they were entertained by the fabulous Fatima.

"Come on," Williams called in a loud whisper as they raced across the garden. "The police will be back here any moment."

Kaylah thrust back the long iron bolts and opened the door a crack, peered outside, then signaled them urgently with his hand to go through. He closed the door in their faces and they could hear the patter of his departing feet on the other side, leaving them in silence.

"Well, that's that. We're on our own now," Williams commented in the darkness.

"Are you all right, Graham?" he enquired of his companion.

"Yes, Sir. I'm fine. Just wish I could put on my uniform."

"No time for that, I'm afraid. We have to get to the harbor before the prisoners are taken back to the citadel," Williams said, and led the way at a brisk pace towards the main street called the Road of Thirty Strada. "Remember this place?" he asked of Graham as they exited onto the avenue from the street that led to the Garden of Paradise. Duncan grunted acknowledgement.

"We will follow it for most of its path and then turn right for the harbor. Not many people out now, but it fills up as the evening progresses. Our aim is to be on the pier by around nine tonight. That will be a little before the prisoners are taken back to their cells."

He continued talking as they moved along the street at a good pace, heading for the dense forest of masts and spars that indicated the location of the harbor. Other than an occasional glance from other pedestrians no one paid either of them much attention. Duncan was very glad he had taken the cloak. It hid his features and the wig from inquisitive eyes.

Then they saw a patrol of French soldiers marching towards them. Even in the darkness they could see that the the soldiers wore green jackets and white cross belts as opposed to the standard blue with white cross belts that were worn by the garrison. Duncan hesitated; these men looked like the soldiers they had passed on the road to Alexandria who had been on their way towards the lake.

"Those are the Carabiniere d'Infantrie," Williams remarked casually, as though taking mental notes. "They would normally be out at the peninsula. Must be coming in to sample the flesh pots of the city."

Duncan didn't say anything but tried to cover his face as the soldiers marched by. The man in front, an NCO with a huge mustache, seemed familiar to Duncan. As they came closer the NCO noticed them and his eyes strayed to Duncan. They widened briefly, but the men continued marching, though not without ribald comments about women as they passed.

"I have the boat picked out and can guide us all there if we are successful in getting the prisoners freed. There are only two guards," Williams continued, as though he had not noticed anything. "God, I hope they have the keys to the chains," he added fervently.

They had just arrived at the beginning of the pier and Williams was pointing out the working laborers about a hundred paces beyond when the night lit up and the guns began to roar.

The wharf extended in a horseshoe form with the entrance somewhat to the east. The huge batteries that guarded the harbor were firing on a ship that had crept up to within range and was now bombarding one of them. The long flames of the cannon and the deafening booms filled the night.

Duncan felt a thrill of excitement. His eyes scanned everywhere trying to find the longboats that would surely have sneaked into the harbor to attack the anchored French war ships.

"Seems to me that Sir Sidney is taking his revenge for the mess at Abukir!" Williams exclaimed.

"We'd be fools if we didn't take advantage of this distraction," he added. "Come on, Graham. The last time I saw the prisoners they were about three quarters of the way around the pier, close to that end battery, which appears to be rather busy right now."

Cursing his dress that hampered him as he ran, Duncan gathered up the skirt and chased after Williams, who was pelting down the quayside, dodging in and out of the piles of bales, boxes and mountains of sacks that were strewn all over the area. The darkness was one moment lit up by the roar of a broadside from the English ship and then the earsplitting boom of one of the harbor batteries returning fire.

"Those have to be even bigger than the ship's thirty-fivers," Duncan muttered to himself, as they pounded along the pavement.

They were among the few who were going in this direction. Most of the laborers and other people who worked at the warehouses and on the merchant ships were fleeing in the opposite direction. Some were silently running for their lives while others were wailing with fear, wringing their hands as they contemplated the damage the attack was going to do to their livelihoods. There were several languages being shouted back and forth: French, Greek, and of course streams of Arabic interspersed with calls to Allah for help.

The incessant boom of guns and the fire work displayed by the guns and bombs made the harbor resemble the fiery gates to a hell. The filthy dark waters glittered with the flashes, while the seagulls, now thoroughly disturbed, took to the air screaming their indignation and fear, adding their chorus to the din of battle.

"There!" Williams called back in a low tense voice. "Coming towards us. Do you see them?"

Duncan crouched with him behind some huge cotton bales and peered forward. He saw a group of people half-running, half-shuffling, coming rapidly towards them shepherded by two guards who were yelling at them. He could just make out what was being said.

"Hurry, you Goddam bastards. You are not going to be free, not today. Hurry or we will shoot you!" the lead guard called back at the group of chained men scurrying along behind him. Duncan could now see that the men were chained together by the ankles and to enable them to move each man carried the loose chain from the leg of the man in front of him. In the bad light he could not tell the condition of the men, but it sufficed that Williams had said that they were British prisoners.

"We'll wait until they are going past and then take the rear sentry. I'll do that. The moment I do, you run for the other one and knock him down. Got that, Graham?" Williams demanded in an urgent whisper. The midshipman nodded, his mouth dry.

The the prisoners and their guards were jogging towards them. From his vantage point Duncan could now see the prisoners occasionally lit up by the flash of the guns or an explosion. They didn't look to be in very good condition.

The chain gang shambled by the two men hiding in the darkness of the bales without a sideways glance in their direction. As the last man, the sentry, passed, Williams slapped Graham on the shoulder. "Go!" he snapped, and he himself ran out to hammer the butt of his pistol onto the back of the guard's head. The man fell forward unconscious, dropping his musket as he did so. With impressive reflexes, Williams caught the musket in midair and at the same time grabbed the falling man and eased him to the ground.

The prisoners trotted on, unaware of what had just happened. Moments later they beheld the extraordinary sight of a woman running past them, skirts flying, wig askew, clutching a pistol in her right hand and a sword in her left. The guard at the front of the gang must have sensed that something was amiss because he began to turn and caught sight of the white-faced, wildly grimacing Valkyrie flying at him. He gaped and shouted "Merde!" with surprise and fear in his voice, cocked his musket and raised it to shoot, but by this time Duncan had reached him. Instinctively the boy thrust his sword forward and felt it go in deep.

In his death throws the sentry pulled the trigger and the gun went off with a jet of flame from the muzzle and a loud bang. The sentry groaned and fell back onto the ground. Duncan had to heave hard to release his sword. He felt cold. It was the first time he had ever killed a man in this manner.

"Bollocks!" he exclaimed, feeling ill. But it was too late to do anything about that. He turned towards the prisoners, who shrank away, looking stunned.

"Damn, what happened up there?" Williams called urgently. Then he noticed the sentry on the ground and swore. "Damme! Never mind. See if you can find the keys!" he called again. Then he turned to the prisoners and herded them in a clinking, rattling huddle into the darkness. "Shut up and listen," he called out. "Which one had the keys?"

The front one!" someone called out.

"No, the back one, stupid. Didn't yer hear them jangling all the time? Drove me mad." Within a moment they were all talking at once.

"Shut up, men. We are not out of trouble yet, so listen and pay attention. I am Captain Williams and this is Midshipman Graham. You must get out of these chains and then do as I say."

All eyes turned to stare at Graham, still clutching his bloody sword and the pistol, looking like some menacing female revolutionary from Naples.

"Bloody 'ell. 'e frightened the fockin' life out of me," one commented.

"Still does!" another quipped.

"Looks like me wife; always did scare the shit out of me," another added. This was greeted with guffaws from the others. It eased the tension but Graham was mortified. He simply had to get out of these clothes.

"Quiet," Williams snapped at them, but he was relieved. Morale still seemed to be high. "Mr. Graham, go and get the keys and you lot get those bodies out of sight," he commanded the prisoners.

While Graham dived to the task, Williams told rescued prisoners what he had in mind.

The keys were found and one by one the men were released from their shackles. Most of them promptly sat on the ground to rub their sore ankles, but the ongoing battle worried Williams.

"Time is of the essence here, lads," he told them. "Two of you pick up the muskets and find some powder and ball for the one discharged, then reload it. Who is the senior one among you?" he demanded.

"Me, Sorr." One stepped forward and Williams recognized the petty officer from before. "Name, Petty Officer?" he demanded without preamble.

"Hotchkins, Sorr."

"Get the men together, Hotchkins, and follow us. We have a ship to catch." Williams darted off along the pier, causing the men to chase after him with Graham bringing up the rear. As Duncan ran he glanced back towards the gates several hundred paces behind them, and gasped. A large group of dark figures were emerging from under the old archway. There was no doubt that they were soldiers; they were armed and coming their way. Williams paused and looked back.

"The gun shot must have alerted the guards," Duncan called.

In fact the gun shots had alerted the guards, but it was more than that. Sergeant Émile had continued to march his men in the one direction for a few minutes, but then he'd halted them. He stood, his brows contracted in thought.

"What is it, Sergeant?" Hugo called out. "Why are we halted?"

Just at that moment they heard the musket going off on the pier. "About turn!" Émile shouted.

"Knew I had smelled a rat!" He exclaimed to his puzzled men. "That 'woman' was not a woman!"

"Now I know the desert got to him," muttered one of the men as they changed direction with a smart pivot.

"Not just him!" another replied. "I was sooo looking forward to jumping a real live girl tonight! Now I, too, will go mad."

But Émile had seen that face before. "It was the boy at the beach. I never forget a face, and that face, that woman, was the same face!" he called to his bewildered men. "Double march and prime muskets!" he shouted, and they headed for the entrance to the harbor, which was now in an uproar.

His men mentally shrugged. The Roast Beef were here making a damned nuisance of themselves; where else would they go? Their sergeant might indeed have gone mad but he was at least leading them in the right direction for a fight.

They arrived on the pier to see, about two hundred paces away on their right, some prisoners running down the quay towards a collection of small boats, and leading them was a woman in flowing skirts brandishing a sword. They swarmed aboard a small ship even as Émile pointed and shouted.

"I thought so! Hurry, men, those are the prisoners and they are trying to escape!"

"Looks like they have taken down a couple of our people, the bastards!" Hugo called out, not that the men needed any more incentive. They pounded along the otherwise deserted pier, chasing after the fugitives.

CHAPTER 29

AMBUSH AND ESCAPE.

Chief of Police Le Guennet was seated at a table near the front of the entertainment room, his eyes riveted on Fatima as she performed for the second night. Like every other man in the room, Le Guennet was mesmerized by the seductive dance. His men sat or stood nearby, their eyes bulging and their mouths gaping at the vision, and they applauded enthusiastically along with everyone else when she disappeared.

Le Guennet shook his head to dispel the erotic thoughts racing through his head and remembered why he was here in this brothel. He stood up abruptly and headed for the doorway at the back of the room, calling for his men to join him. A servant moved to intercept him but another man said something and the servant stood back.

Danush stood before the policeman and smiled. "Good evening, Monsieur Le Guennet. May I be of assistance?" he enquired politely.

"You certainly may," the Chief of Police told him rudely. "I am conducting a search of these premises at this moment."

"May I ask why?" Danush asked, looking composed but wearing an expression of concern. Le Guennet's men were already moving around, asking for papers from the civilian visitors and the servants who worked the tables.

"I am looking for someone. We received a report that last night one of the officers of the Grand Army was assaulted and humiliated." Le Guennet made his tone sound menacing, but it didn't seem to faze the Persian.

"Perhaps you could remind me as to whom that officer might have been, Sir," Danush asked.

"His name is Captain Kermaret and he was grievously injured. He claims it was here, in this, this brothel that he was attacked."

"That is an appalling thing to hear, Sir. Does he remember who attacked him, Sir? I shall turn the men over to you immediately."

"Well, er, he said it was a woman." Le Guennet was watching for any sign of amusement or contempt from the Persian. Nothing, just a bland face appearing to be very concerned.

Finally Danush said in a very low voice. "A woman, you say, Sir? I can only say how sorry I am that a woman from my respectable establishment could have done such a thing."

Le Guennet was uncomfortable. He was embarrassed and doubted he would have come at all, other than he had wanted to see the belly dancer. A crash from the kitchens and raised voices as the servants protested the intrusion from the rough police caused them both to turn their heads in that direction.

"Stop that, back there!" Le Guennet bellowed. "No breaking things." He turned back to Danush and said, "It is my turn to apologize, Monsieur. Some of my men are a little enthusiastic a times."

"I quite understand, Sir. Was there any identification offered by the victim?"

"We are looking for a blonde woman who might be able to help us with our enquiries."

"A blonde woman? I fear your search will be in vain, Chief of Police. I have no blonde girls here. I wish I did, it would be good for business, but alas I do not! This is very embarrassing for everyone I am sure," he offered. His tone was nothing if not solicitous.

"Perhaps you would like to come upstairs and we can discuss this further? I do believe that the girls are upstairs at this time, and the beautiful Fatima will be there. Perhaps they can shed some light on the subject?"

Le Guennet needed no further persuasion. The chance to see, even to speak to the vision he had seen on the stage was very enticing. His resolve to investigate this 'blonde woman' seeped away as they mounted the stairs.

Danush ushered him into a room filled with young women in various states of undress, amongst whom was the ravishing Fatima. He had eyes for no one else, but Le Guennet decided to at least check to see if there was a blonde woman among the other girls.

There was not a sign of a blonde anywhere, so he resigned himself to the fact that the officer had been too drunk to know what had happened and that it was time to leave.

Danush bowed slightly. "Perhaps, oh Chief of Police, you might wish to avail yourself of the services of ..."

He didn't get any further. The building shook slightly as they all heard the sound of the guns coming from the direction of the harbor.

Le Guennet shook his head with frustration, but duty was duty. He ground out, "Another time, perhaps. I bid you good night." Then he rushed down the stairs to collect his men and head for the harbor to confront this far more pressing irritation. The Goddams were becoming a serious pain in the rear.

Behind him, Danush took a deep quiet breath and nodded to the girls. "It seems that the British have a fine sense of timing," he commented.

"There's nothing for it now, lads," Williams called back to the huddled men. "See that ketch over there? We have to take her and get her out of here or we are all dead." He began to run hard towards the gang plank of the boat in question.

Out in the harbor the battle had become more lively. The English ship of war had driven past the batteries, which were still being pounded from out to sea by the bomb ships *HMS Bulldog* and the *HMS Perseus*, with *HMS Tigre* providing supporting fire. While they were preoccupying the batteries, boats from the *Tigre* and the *Theseus* were being rowed stealthily in among the cluster of shipping.

Lt Bowles was charged with setting fire to as many ships as possible and creating a further distraction that would allow the *Theseus* to get close enough to attack one of the French men-of-war. *Theseus* was to cause enough damage to disable the ship permanently if possible, or at least cause extensive and costly damage.

The boats succeeded in getting amongst the merchant ships, and men swarmed aboard one of the larger vessels carrying flammable items to enable a good fire. The crews of the merchantmen were for the most part ashore, having left only a couple of watchmen on each ship, who now abandoned their vessels with alacrity. They splashed into the water yelling the alarm, but it was too late.

"Get the fires going, men. We need to make sure it's big enough to distract the war ships from the *Theseus*." Lt Bowles called out.

The men went to work, pouring liquid tar everywhere and tossing flammable cotton waste steeped in turpentine into all the corners, and before long a fire started in the hold. To their delight they found barrels of tar, cases of liquor, and cotton bales aplenty to assist with a good burn.

As soon as the fire was well started on one merchantman, Lt Bowles and his second officer Midshipman Standforth led the men back down into the longboat and made towards another cluster of ships. By now, however, the alarm had been raised that there were English in the harbor, and before the crewmen could board they came under fire.

The shooting was sporadic but accurate enough to cause injuries and one death in *Tigre's* other longboat. The calls of distress from the commander of that boat, Lt Merryweather, alerted Bowles to their peril. They were by now in between two large ships, and had been spotted by the ships' lookouts. Voices were raised in cries of alarm and orders given, followed by the ominous sound of guns being run out.

"Row, men!" Standforth yelled to the crew. "Row for your very lives!" His words were almost lost as one of the cannon was run out from the ship on their port side and fired almost immediately. The flash blinded the men and the noise deafened them, but to their astonishment the ball howled overhead and smashed into the side of the merchantman on the other side of the racing longboat.

"Kerist!" muttered one of the crew, and pulled even harder.

"Must have been too excited to aim, or inexperienced," Lt Bowles muttered as they skimmed out of reach of the ship's guns. However, they were not out of trouble yet.

HMS Theseus was now close enough to the smaller of the French war ships, La Muiron, and loosed off a broadside at almost point-blank range. The French ship was unprepared for the assault, with most of the crew on shore leave, and the reply was sporadic.

"They are lacking a full crew!" Standforth cried exultantly. "Pound them, *Theseus*!" he squeaked, as his voice broke. Meanwhile, the longboat and the following two boats found themselves heading to a place where they would be in a cross fire. Take us behind the *Theseus*!" Lt Bowles shouted to Bosun's Mate Chauncey, who promptly hauled the tiller over just as a shot splashed into the water nearby, drenching everyone with the column of water it tossed high into the air. Where the shot had come from nobody knew, but it would be suicide to row between the two battle ships which were now trying to destroy one another.

The noise of the guns and the hollow banging sound of shot hammering into the sides of the ships was deafening, but on the other side of the *Theseus* it was both darker and more calm. For a moment Lt Bowles thought of asking for a lift but then his eye was caught by some other activity on shore.

By now the longboat was a few hundred yards from the entrance to the harbor where the bomb ketches were still busy. Flashes accompanied by booms and flaming debris were flung high into the night air as bombs landed in and around the forts.

Standforth cocked his head; he could have sworn he heard a voice he knew. He become aware of activity on the pier. "Look, Sir! Over there! Seems to be a fight going on. By that small vessel." He pointed.

The could hear musket fire from the pier and saw figures running towards a ketch. Is that a woman I see running along the pier?" Lt Bowles asked looking puzzled. But then some soldiers turned their attention towards the boat and bullets splashed into the water nearby.

"Bugger! Pull away! Nothing to do with us! Their boat veered away from the new danger. Lt Bowles peered at the darkened pier, now more than sixty paces away. Row, boys, or we'll be trapped." His voice was almost drowned out by yet another broadside from the *Theseus* which was turning about, using its furiously rowing boats and an anchor to bring its bows round towards the harbor entrance.

"Looks like we created a goodly burn over there, Sorr," Chauncey remarked with satisfaction as he stared at the raging fire consuming the merchantmen. Then he focused on getting the boat to the entrance of the harbor and out to the relative safety of the open sea. They could be destroyed any moment by just one ball from the forts if they were noticed. Thankfully the bomb ketches were keeping the forts busy and distracted. The flares and rockets lit up the sky in a display of pyrotechnics that would have otherwise been a spectacle to admire. Hopefully a couple of small boats would attract no attention.

"I could swear I heard Graham's voice earlier, and just now I am just as sure I saw a woman leading that pack of men!" Standforth muttered out loud as he continued to stare back over his shoulder at the turmoil within the boundaries of the harbor. He shook his young head. "Too many bangs for one night," he reflected. "Wonder what on earth was going on?"

Duncan, still clad as a woman, had overtaken and passed Williams, who had tripped on a rope lying across the pier and had tumbled to the ground. The released sailors swept Williams up and chased after the manic-looking creature in the flapping skirts who now led them in a wild screaming charge up to the ketch, along the gangplank and onto the deck of the small ship.

Duncan jumped down onto the deck just in time to surprise a crewman emerging from below carrying a short sword. The shock of seeing this wild female apparition, screaming like a banshee as it landed on his deck brandishing a sword and a pistol, was a horror he was unprepared for.

"Ah, Mon Dieu! Merde, une couchemar!" he exclaimed, but his hesitation cost him his life. Duncan did not hesitate. His shout of, "Bollocks!" was drowned out by the loud bang of his pistol. His victim fell back down the hatchway without a another sound.

By this time the rest of the men had pounded onto the deck and were rummaging about looking for weapons, anything to use on the crew of the ketch if they were brave enough to fight. Belaying pins and pikes were ready to hand and the men snatched them up.

"'Cast off from those bitts! Dump the gangplank and cut the ropes if you have to," Duncan shouted, automatically taking charge.

"Aye aye, Sorr," Master Hotchkins responded, bellowed an order that the men nearest him ran to comply.

"Hurry, I can see soldiers along the quay and they're coming this way," Williams called, as he tentatively opened the doorway that led down below. He leapt away as a ball smashed into the side of the doorframe, followed by some swearing in French.

"Bastards want a fight it seems," he said, as he sidled back towards the doorway. "You take care of the sailing, Graham. I'll keep their heads down." He fired his pistol into the darkness below him.

Duncan was frantically trying to reload his pistol, acutely aware that they were very limited with regard to weaponry.

Master Hotchkins was also aware of the danger. "You two men," he called to the sailors with the muskets, "get into the afterdeck and keep the Froggy heads down when they come within range. Don't waste your ammunition or you'll answer to me!"

He turned to Duncan who had finished his re-loading and said, "Orders, Sir?" The expression on his face was wooden.

Duncan took note of the wind and said, "Sails up, quick as you can, all of them, including the jibs. We have an offshore wind but not for long. There's a storm coming in from the southwest."

Within minutes the main sail and the huge lugsail on the aftermast were being hauled up the masts. The sails flapped, caught the wind and bellied, and at last they were in motion. Some sailors had found long poles lying on deck and used these to push the vessel away from the pier. It seemed to Graham as though everything on board was going in slow motion, while the soldiers who were running towards them were moving far too fast. He had no appetite for a clash with those long bayonets, but the green-clad soldiers would shortly be swarming over the side of the boat if he couldn't delay them.

He stood on the afterdeck, hanging onto the huge tiller bar, with Hotchkins standing nearby. The two men with the muskets were crouched at the stern board with their guns cradled firmly sighting at the French.

Gauging the distance and the risk of allowing the enemy to get any closer he made a decision. "Fire now," he ordered.

There was a short pause as the men aimed, then the muskets were fired within seconds of each other. The balls ploughed into the ranks of the soldiers, who scattered for cover, leaving one of their number lying on the stones.

Duncan sighed with relief. It had arrested their headlong charge. "Good shooting, men. Reload as fast as you can and give them another. Goddam, I wish we had access to the powder for those two pop guns," he muttered, as he looked at the two small cannons on either side of the ship. By this time the soldiers had recovered. There were shouted commands and they fired a volley at the ship. Bullets zipped overhead, punching holes in the recently hoisted sail, while several smashed into the transom, sending splinters to hum through the air. Hotchkins gasped, staggered sideways and then fell on one knee to the deck clutching his arm.

"Hit, Sorr," he groaned.

Duncan shouted to one of the men who were working the sails. "Get over here and help Hotchkins, he's hit. Hang on. We'll get you taken care of," he reassured the fallen man although he had no idea as to how to help him.

Hotchkins nodded his head, wincing at he pain. He was bleeding heavily. A sailor ran up and immediately set about binding off the arm. "Don't fret, Hotchy. I've got yer," he said. "'e'll be awl right, Sorr."

More balls hummed by, snapping through the sails or thudding into the hull. The two musketeers fired and frantically reloaded, trying to keep the enemy at bay. Duncan looked about desperately, but there was nothing they could do to speed the ship's passage. He wished the wind would pick up. The light breeze coming offshore was driving them steadily towards the entrance. It was slow going, but at least the small vessel was well clear of the pier.

He noticed something else. The hatch near to where Hotchkins and the sailor were situated opened a crack. A face appeared that peered fearfully out at them. Duncan shouted a warning and then in French, "Rendez-vous. Surrender or I will shoot."

The man regarded him with wide eyes. "Please. Do not shoot," he called back.

"Come on out, all of you, now!" Duncan shouted, pointing his pistol at the fearful sailor. He ducked as a stray ball whipped close overhead. "Bugger that," he muttered, "We should be out of range by now!"

The man lifted the hatch and climbed out, followed by another.

"Only two of you?" Duncan demanded.

"Oui. There are only two of us. Some swine shot our comrade and everyone else is ashore."

"Ye'd better not be lyin'," Duncan snapped in English, as he covered the two apprehensive-looking men with his pistol.

All three ducked as another round slammed into the mast nearby. "Those infantry men have a rifled musket. I hope they kill this crazy woman," one of the men muttered to his companion.

"They'll kill us too if we don't take cover!" the other told him. "Are you really a woman?" he demanded of Duncan. "If so you are very ugly."

"No! I'm an officer in the British Navy!" he snapped back.

The two men snickered with disbelief. "So the British dress up like the women to go to battle these days? Ooer, I am so terrified!" the bolder one said. He sported a massive mustache and sneered, quavering his hands with imaginary fear. "If you came for me you would trip over your skirts and I would pique you in the titties!" he laughed at his own wit.

"Ye fockin' will be terrified if I have to let go of this bar to deal with ye. I'll cut yer damned balls off!" Duncan snarled. His Scottish accent always became thicker when annoyed. They of course could not understand him, but the tone of his voice and the ferocious glare silenced them.

"You two just shut up!" Duncan growled at them in French. He brandished the pistol while clinging to the tiller with his left hand.

"Keep your heads down, men, we are almost out of range," he called to the sailors, who needed no persuasion.

Williams hurried over ignoring the flying balls. "So they've surrendered, have they?" He nodded with satisfaction at the two prisoners.

"Just you two men?" he demanded aggressively in French. "Put your hands in the air where I can see them."

They held their hands high in the air with a look of wooden resignation on their faces. To their surprise Williams pointed overboard. "I hope you can swim. Go!" he said sharply.

With surprised and wary backward glances the two men took him at his word and clambered over the side to drop into the water and began to paddle towards the pier, which was now about a hundred paces away.

The spy slapped his hands together as though washing them. "That's one less problem to worry about," he stated.

The two swimmers were dragged out of the stinking harbor water by the Infantrie soldiers on the pier.

"Who are those men? Are they the English?" Sergeant Émile asked the two bedraggled crewmen when they were safely sitting in a puddle of water on the edge of the pier, looking out at the departing ketch.

"All my possessions! Those bastards took everything I own!" exclaimed one of the men, wringing his hands.

"I asked you a question!" Émile snapped.

"Yes, they are the fucking Goddams." the other man sighed, running his fingers through his sodden hair.

"One of them a woman?" Émile demanded.

"No, yes. Er, no, she... he is an officer in the British navy," they told him. "At least, that is what he told us."

The men around the two crewmen gaped. "So now they dress up as women to fight? I have never been so insulted!" Phillip exclaimed, pretending to be mortally offended, and joined in the laughter.

Émile slapped his thigh with the flat of his hand. "I thought so!" he turned to his men. "I told you, didn't I? You all thought I was soft in the head! I never forget a face. That damned boy we saw on the beach was disguised, but it takes more than a disguise like that to fool Émile, eh?" He sounded delighted with himself.

"Well, now they are not our concern, Sergeant. The batteries should be able to deal with them. I hope they blow them out of the water, and that young bastard with them. We have to get Claude to a surgeon as soon as we can," Hugo told him.

Sergeant Émile nodded. "You are right. Come on, men. Merde to those Roast beef, we have other work to do. You two come along with me. I'm taking you to the Chief of Police to make a statement," he ordered the two disconsolate crewmen.

Having disposed of the prisoners Captain Williams looked Duncan over critically.

"Really can't have you looking like this when we get to the *Tigre*, young man. Better get changed into something more um... appropriate. I'll keep us on course. Between those two forts, I presume?" he chuckled, waving at the distant firing. "Off you go."

Duncan needed no further persuasion. With a sharp glance up at the two sails to see if they were tight, he ran the length of the deck, retrieved his bundle where he had dropped it on his arrival, and went below. He almost tripped over the body of the man he had shot, glanced down but then sped on. He located the after-cabin and climbed out of the dress and blouse, kicked off the slippers and threw the wig into a corner with a thankful growl of relief.

It took only a minute to scramble into his knee length breeches, don his shirt and jacket and put on his shoes. His stockings were torn and useless, so he left them on the floor and belted on his sword and scabbard. He looked around quickly for any other weapons but could only find a cutlass lying on a bench near the after-windows.

He snatched that up, stuffed it into his belt to give to one of the sailors, and then looked for a mirror. The face he saw resembled something from a nightmare. A mess of smeared lip paint, sweat runnels, and kohl streaked the pale face covered in powder. There was no time to do anything but to rub his face vigorously with a linen napkin and hope for the best. The boat began to rock more than before, which indicated to him that they were approaching the entrance to the harbor. It would not be long before they were under the guns of the fort; he had to hurry.

His next task was to find some powder and shot. He found a lantern that was still alight and walked along the lower deck, ducking under the low beams as he went, holding his pistol before him just in case. Just about midships he found the tiny powder room and, taking care to leave the lantern just outside the small chamber, he let himself in. A few minutes later he poked his head over the combing of the forward hatch and shouted to the men standing there.

"Give me a hand here!"

Men rushed to help him bring up some small canvas bags and some six-pound shot.

"Load the guns, men," he commanded.

"I hope you are not going to do with those guns what I suspect you are, young fella," Williams said, as Duncan joined him and took over the helm. The boy checked their position carefully and made a small adjustment of their course to take them right down the middle of the harbor opening before answering.

"If we are to run past the guns of the fort I want to at the very least shoot back, even if it is merely a gesture, Sir."

Williams clapped him on the shoulder and laughed. "Good man! You seem to be in your element now, Midshipman. By the way, have you looked back recently?" he enquired. "I think we have company. It's welcome company this time."

Duncan glanced over his shoulder to see the huge bulk of HMS *Theseus* bearing down on them with all sails set. Despite its much larger size the ship could put on much more sail, and this was driving the vessel rapidly down upon their tail.

"They don't know who we are!" Duncan cried. "They're only half a cable away!"

"Damme. I didn't think of that," Williams said in alarm. "They could run us down!"

The musketeers were standing now and pointing back at the huge vessel as they too saw the danger coming up behind the ketch.

"Tighten the sails!" Duncan yelled to the crewmen who rushed to comply. He could feel the vessel heel just a little and their speed increased fractionally, but it would not be long before they were not only exposed to the guns from the fort but were right in the path of the behemoth bearing down on them. Just as he was thinking this a gun boomed from the port side fort and a column of water as tall as a house rose from the sea twenty yards off their port bow.

"Bugger, now we're for it!" Duncan exclaimed. "First things first. Sir, please get hold of some linen sheets which I saw in the main cabin. There are a couple there. We have to show the white flag to the ship behind us."

Seeing the sense in this, Captain Williams rushed off to carry out the request. While he was gone there was another boom of a huge gun as the battery on the starboard side opened up. This time the huge ball smacked through the foresail with such force that it almost tore the sail off the mast. Duncan and all the crew flinched. Things were going to get very bad very soon.

He decided that he needed to take the initiative. "Come and hold the tiller," he called to one of the musketeers.

He then ran along the deck to one of the little guns. "Is it loaded?" he asked.

"Yes, Sorr," the men replied. He looked incredulous."Yer not goin' ter shoot back, are yer, Sorr?"

"I damned well am!" the Scot replied. "I'll no go down without a fight."

This declamation, uttered in his Scottish burr, elicited first a chuckle and then laughter from the men around him. "He's right, lads!" one of them exclaimed. The other scarecrows nodded their agreement.

Duncan bent over the small cannon and then hammered a wedge under the front, which caused the muzzle to point up at a sharp angle.

"Stand back!" he yelled, and pulled the lanyard.

The gun bellowed and a long flame shot out of the muzzle. The little gun leapt back against its restraining ropes. He nodded with satisfaction. "I hope it hits something," he muttered and ran to the other gun. "Reload that gun!" he shouted, pointing back to the first one. The men laughed and ran to do his bidding.

Again he hammered a wedge and snapped the lanyard. The satisfying boom of the cannon helped to alleviate some of his own fears. The crew jumped to reload both guns.

Captain Williams came running back on deck with his arms full of linen. "Don't they ever wash this stuff?" he exclaimed, wrinkling his nose at the stinking linen.

Despite everything the fleet could throw at them the batteries were still functional, and the danger of being destroyed by a direct hit was very real. At the same time, they still ran the risk of being being run down or fired upon by the *Theseus* if they were mistaken for a French ship fleeing the battle. Williams and the crew members tied the sheets to the stern flagpole in the faint hope that someone on the battle ship behind them would notice and take evasive action.

For long minutes they waited with bated breath, but the French gunners manning the batteries could now see not just one but two vessels attempting to leave the harbor area. This had to be a priceless target for them. They opened up with all their guns, throwing everything they had at the two ships. At this point the English war ship was in the middle of the entrance while the ketch was on its way out, and the distance between them was a mere third of a cable.

HMS Theseus fired both broadsides at almost the same time. The ripple of flashes followed by the roar of 32-pounders was so unexpected and deafening that Duncan thought his eardrums had been destroyed. His ears ringing, he forced himself to regained his senses and focus on their exit. He was still unsure as to whether the war ship had noticed his little vessel in its path. Then the guns of the forts replied with a salvo of their own.

The men on the ketch only just heard the approaching ball as it made a rocketing sound through the air, and all they could do was to cringe and hope. The monster ball smashed through the deck cabin, obliterating half of it in a screeching explosion of flying splinters, and passed on out the other side taking a good six feet of transom with it. The vessel shook like a leaf and heeled badly. Duncan had spun away from the lethal splinters, some of them longer than his arm, and grabbed at the tiller bar to hold it steady. He was dizzy with shock. His glance went to the two sailors at his feet to see if they were still there. Hotchkins was still lying where he had been placed, but where the other sailor had once been there was nothing. No evidence was left that he had ever existed.

Shocked and struggling to retain his composure, Duncan croaked, "Report casualties! Damage?"

"Davies! 'e's gone, Sorr," Hotchkins called from his prone position.

"Poor bugger. He was so happy to be goin' home," someone said in the darkness.

One of the sailors peered over the side. "It smashed the transom away, Sorr. But no damage that I can tell below the water line."

"Hold on, men! We are almost out of danger," Duncan shouted, trying to sound optimistic.

"Another blow like that and this vessel will be a mess of driftwood," commented Williams. His normal calm appeared somewhat shaken as he staggered to Duncan's side. "At least *Theseus* is taking some of the heat from us."

Indeed, the English battle ship was taking fire but appeared to be delivering as good as it received. Another broadside roared, the bright tongues of flame from the guns seeming to reach out towards the batteries. Then as the ketch moved out of range into the darkness of the open sea Duncan could make out a slight change of course by the vessel behind them. Sure enough, the huge war ship was drawing by and men were leaning over its starboard bows, holding up lanterns and calling down to them.

"Surrender or we will blow you out of the water!" someone called in really bad French.

"We most certainly will not! We are British!" Captain Williams bellowed back. "Captain Williams at your service, and Midshipman Graham commanding this vessel."

There was a surprised pause. Then a bullhorn called down, "Lieutenant Spaulding here, Sir. On behalf of Captain Miller who is indisposed, wounded, we welcome you back. We had thought you dead."

Williams chuckled then shouted back. "No fear of that, Lieutenant. I hope the captain will recover. What orders?"

"Take up station behind us and er,... do try to keep up, Sir!"

"Cheeky monkey!" Williams chuckled. "D'you think we can, Graham?"

Duncan glanced up a the holed sail. the ball had cut an almost perfect sphere in the material half way up the sail. "In a full wind we would probably even have the edge on them, Sir. But there is a storm coming, so I hope we can all get far enough from land to avoid any more problems. We will be fine, but we need help for Master Hotchkins here."

"I'll be all right, Sorr," the Master replied. "Could do with some water though."

"We all could," Captain Williams stated, "but I did find something else below that might raise our own spirits. I'll fetch it right away." He strode off and disappeared below decks, to return with a large jug of water and two bottles of something indeterminate.

"Water for our patient, but all of us will take a swig of this Eau de Vie. Two bottles; one made, from what I can tell, from cherries, and the other plums! Imagine that! Inventive people, those French." He laughed and began to dole out cups to the eager men.

CHAPTER 30

A STORM

They exited the harbor in grand spirits. The crew, having drunk the powerful concoctions without having eaten anything, felt it more than the officers and slowly slid into a half torpor around the base of the mast. Duncan sipped his second mug of Eau de Vie with relish while the captain waved the empty bottle that had contained plum brandy.

"Pity about that. I was just beginning to enjoy it," he said, then tossed it overboard. "Go back... go back to the place where they made you! " he chanted.

Duncan found that he was having difficulty focussing on the lantern of the great ship ahead of them. For some reason there were more than one, then he fuzzily realized that indeed there were, for the stern windows of the ship were a blaze of light. Even so, the the short bowsprit of the ketch was moving about more than it should be. He hung onto the tiller with all his might. "Goddam, it must be that French stuff," he muttered, as he staggered over to peer at the dark pit of the on deck compass.

He was just beginning to make out the North pointing needle by the flame and light of the city behind them when they ran into a force from another quarter.

A sliver of warm wind flowed over the boat.

"That's a sly wind, Sorr," Hotchkins called, sounding alarmed. "There's much worse behind it. Might need to get the sails down."

Duncan sensed rather than saw the squall on their port side that was bearing down on them, but it was already too late. A gust of hot wind, carrying with it grains of sand picked up from the desert, struck the sails without warning and drove the ketch over so hard that men were tossed into the scuppers, which were momentarily level with the sea. Duncan only prevented himself from being catapulted over the side by throwing himself over the steering bar. He clutched at the pole for dear life and skidded sideways, hanging on desperately while trying not to alter their course.

His feet landed on something solid and he managed to regain his position with an effort. At that moment Captain Williams lost his hold on the side of the cabin because, weakened by shot, it broke off in his grip, and he tumbled across the deck towards the sea. With an exclamation Duncan shot out a hand and seized the captain by his collar and prevented him from sliding into the dark waters below.

"Bugger!" he exclaimed, as the full weight of the captain tugged at his arm, almost dislocating his shoulder. He hung on grimly.

"Goddam!" Captain Williams shouted as he struggled to get back on his feet. 'It's all right, Graham, you can let go now, I have a hold. By God, that was close!" His voice was almost lost in the keening wind. "I think you saved my worthless life, Graham. Thank you!"

Captain Williams edged closer to Graham at the tiller. "I doubt if you would have been able to stop and pick me up if I'd gone over. Well done, lad. I owe you one."

Duncan grunted acknowledgement. "We have a bad one coming in, Sir. Take hold of something solid and tie yourself off with a rope. You too, Hotchkins." The two men complied with alacrity. Williams helped Hotchkins, then gave Duncan a length of rope. "Do the same for yourself, lad," he advised.

The ketch heeled and groaned at the violent treatment it was receiving from the wind; the sails were snapping and in one case tearing, while pieces of the shattered cabin window fell inward to crash into the open well of the cabin below. All this had passed within a few moments, but during this time Duncan sobered up very quickly as he realized the peril they were now facing.

"Get the sails down! Now, now!" he yelled at the tumble of men, who had begun to pick themselves up from lying or kneeling in the water that had come over the side. No one could see very well, but it was vital that the sails come down or they were finished. The boat was now so far over that the deck canted at an angle of more than 45 degrees with the starboard transom under water. At least the water pouring over the side and splashing them cleared their heads enough for them to wake up and deal with this new threat. But if this continued they would be tipped right over.

Those who could ran to do Duncan's bidding and struggled desperately with the now heavily flapping sails. The wildly swinging blocks that had broken free could smash a head in, loose ropes whipping about at head height could strike without warning. These hazards were barely visible in the gloom and became a serious menace as the men fought to bring the sails off the mast.

Abruptly and with an unearthly shriek the squall was upon them, but this time it was cold. Duncan had heard of storms in the Mediterranean which sprang up from almost nowhere; his senses had been telling him it was coming, but he was ill prepared for how violent it became in such a short space of time.

The rain came in a roar that lashed at the boat and its small crew of struggling men, drenching them from head to foot in seconds. Duncan was soaked and numb with cold to the point where his teeth were chattering. The comforting drink was a thing of the past and he scowled fiercely trying to clear the remaining cobwebs from his mind.

The lamps of the ship ahead of them swayed up and down for a while, but then were extinguished. It left Duncan feeling very alone and with the uncomfortable thought that they might run into the stern of the massive ship of war, which now presented itself as an obstacle to be avoided at all costs. He was unsure of where the ketch was positioned with respect to the coast but knew he must find a way to keep moving in a northerly direction or they would surely founder on the peninsular of Abukir—one of the last places on earth that he wanted to revisit.

He looked down at the dark shape of Hotchkins, still lying near the broken cabin structure. "You should get below," he called to the Master, who shook his sodden head. "No, Sorr, I want to be on deck if we founder."

Duncan agreed with him. They didn't even have a small rowing boat on the ketch. The French crew must have taken it to shore when the ship was in the harbor. He glanced forward and saw that the crew had finally managed to take down the main sail but were still struggling with the after mast. The canvas lay in a untidy bundle at the base of the mast. He felt the tension go out of the steering bar as the boat lost way and began to drift. They urgently needed some kind of means to keep them down wind and not broach to, which would be a disaster. He prayed that his heading was still good, or they would soon be back on the coast of Egypt and either dead or prisoners.

As if sensing his concern the Master waved at him to attract his attention. "You should try to get a small sail onto the foremast, Sorr," he called. "That will keep our bows down wind."

"I am not sure of our heading!" Duncan peered at the simple compass housing located near to the Master. There was a compass within, but it was too dark to see where the needle pointed. With their corkscrewing action due to the agitated sea it was spinning back and forth. "I think we are headed north enough to avoid the cape. But the storm is coming from the South west and will drive us towards the cape."

He didn't add that it would be very close and the collision, if it happened, would happen without any warning. One moment they would be tossing on the sea and the next shattered on the ugly black teeth of the shore.

"We can't turn into this one without being overturned. We have to run with it until it passes," the Master shouted.

Duncan barely heard him but nodded reluctant agreement. He was running blind now without even the elusive lantern of the larger ship to guide him. He had no appetite for a turn in this darkness. There were no stars to see by, as the storm clouds obscured even the sliver of the moon. He shook the rain from his hair and eyes, then had to bellow several times to get the attention of the men crouching in the waist of the boat, but finally they heard and ran to comply with the command to raise a small sail. The willing men managed to haul a short, wildly flapping sail half way up the foresail and secure it.

Suddenly the gusts of wind and rain abated, leaving an ominous calm and little wind to fill the rigged jib sail. The ship was wallowing, but making some headway. The men on deck were uncharacteristically silent, sending apprehensive glances towards the southwest where even in the darkness they could feel the monstrous black cloud bank moving relentlessly towards them. During the calm Duncan shouted at the men to keep them busy, shouting at them to double lash down everything. They complied willingly enough. They had to avoid being driven onto the shore of the cape, but inexorably the wind continued to thwart his efforts. He tried to steer them a few points more to port, which would take in a more northerly direction, but stopped when it became clear that he was running across the sea and there was a real danger of waves tipping them over again. With a resigned curse he allowed the boat to fall off a couple of points until they were again being carried by the waves.

Then he had an idea. Just as he did so the rain and wind came back. Leaving the captain huddled over the tiller, Duncan scrambled towards the men. "Help me get this over the stern!" he called out, indicating the sail on the deck. "Sheet anchor! We need a sheet anchor!"

Several of the men understood and joined him hauling the wet and heavy sail along the deck, pausing from time to time to hang onto anything they could as the waves poured onto the deck, lashing their faces with spume.

Using all their strength against the wind and rain and the drag of the soaking canvas, they arrived at the tiller area. The men bound ropes through the eyes of the sail and when they were done they called to Duncan, "Ready, Sorr."

Without a word he helped them to push the mass of canvas over the stern and watched it fan out in the increasingly turbulent waters behind the ketch. When it was about twenty yards behind Duncan held his hand up. "That's far enough. Make it fast." They fastened the end ropes to cleats on either side of the stern deck so that the sail was spread out flat on the sea. A slow but sure response to the drag of the canvas resulted. The small sail on the foremast took them down wind while the drag of the sail kept them from surfing the wild waves. They had slowed their headlong race for the shoreline and with luck might be able to pass to the north without incident. Duncan wished there was more brandy.

Captain Williams swore, then shouted, "Its damned cold with all this rain. I'll go and see if there are any oil coats below. This is miserable!" he disappeared down the stern hatch.

"Bring some more of that Eau de whatever, Sir!" Duncan called after him. The captain laughed and shouted back, "If I can find some."

Captain Williams surfaced on deck with some smelly jackets. "Here take this," he called, shoving one of the stiff coats at Graham, who thankfully took it and shrugged into the stinking covering. He realized that he was shivering from the cold. "Here this might help." Williams pushed a bottle of something into his hand. Duncan took a swig and felt the warm glow of strong alcohol suffuse his body. "Ah, God, but that's nice stuff, Sir." he gasped as he took another swig.

Williams gently took back the bottle and said, "Can't have our captain and navigator too drunk to steer now, can we, Graham? You're doing well, lad." He laughed and took a swig of his own before handing the bottle over to Hotchkins, who had been looking longingly at the bottle as its contents began to disappear. "Thank 'e, Sorr. Thank 'e very much," he said, and he took a healthy swig.

"Well now we are all drunk and in the middle of a shit storm. Who gives a damn?' Williams shouted into the wind.

There was a flash of lightning about a mile away, followed almost immediately by a rolling crash of thunder almost overhead. The lightning lit up the agitated sea all around them and very briefly the *Theseus*, which was now many cables to their north. Duncan felt relieved that they were not nosing into its stern, but the sea had risen and the ketch was now pitching and rolling uncomfortably. Assuming that the Master of the *Theseus* knew what he was about and could see own compass, Duncan altered course to follow in the path of the ship as best he could.

At times they would appear to be heading down into a deep watery valley and he would brace himself to prevent falling forward, but then the wave would pass under them, surfing the light ketch for a while in a welter of foam and water pouring over the transom on both sides, and then their bow would be pointing up into the air at another impossible angle while he hung on to the steering bar for dear life trying desperately to prevent the bows from falling off and presenting the vessel sideways to another oncoming monster. The drag of the sheet anchor was helping greatly, that much he could tell, but in the darkness there was not much to indicate how close to the shore they might be.

Abruptly a blast of cold air struck the ship. The sail filled with a cracking sound and Duncan could have sworn the mast bent a little. The blast of wind almost knocked him and Captain Williams off their feet, causing them to clutch at anything that came to hand just to remain upright.

A high, keening sound rose as the wind howled through the rigging, followed by another wall of rain. It washed over the men on the deck of the ship in torrents, lashing at exposed skin, soaking them to the bone. A flash of lightning nearby startled them all, and it was followed almost immediately by a clap of thunder that deafened the men on the afterdeck and made them cower.

Men were lifted off their feet as the squall hammered at the ship and forced it to heel over to port. The crew hung onto anything they could to prevent themselves from being washed overboard. Some used rope to tie themselves to the mast or the transom.

The ripping, tearing sounds of thunder bellowing overhead made men duck, and the bolts of lightning lit up the racing waves. Each time Duncan tried to take advantage of the momentary light to search for the *Theseus* or a dark strip of land ahead of them which would spell disaster. So far he had seen neither, which was reassuring. At least they were being driven out to sea, which was possibly the safest place to be at this time.

The ketch righted itself and continued, but now they were being buffeted by waves that marched in serried ranks up from the southwest. The entire sky was lit up continuously now as the lightning increased in intensity. Even the air around them smelled of something unpleasant, almost as though it were burned.

The storm hit the struggling ketch with a force that made the entire vessel shudder like a bell struck by a monstrous hammer. Slashing rain and lightning hissed into the sea around them, followed almost immediately by numbing crashes of thunder that shook the air and made their bones vibrate. The ship shuddered and yawed, then began to rise and fall with the waves. Captain Williams joined Duncan with his struggle to maintain course, but they were thrown about as they struggled with the beam and tried to keep the ketch from yawing, falling off into a valley and then being rolled over by a following wave.

The wind screamed and howled as though a thousand demons were at work, their one intent to sink the vessel and claim all the lives on board. The waves had in the shortest space of time gone from a couple of paces high to mountains of foaming water that formed deep valleys and tall hills all around the struggling vessel. At times Duncan could barely breathe, the air around him was so full of water, he was very glad of the skin of the jacket, which repelled most of the rain. Hotchkins and Captain Williams both wore the same, but the rest of the unfortunate crew were in miserable condition and had very little protection from the rain and the water that continuously slopped over the sides.

The ketch would nose into a wall of water that would bury the bowsprit and then pour over the bows and along the main deck in a foaming rush, and then very slowly the forward part of the ship would begin to rise. Water poured off the decks in torrents as they climbed out of the valley between breakers, so that they seemed to be pointing at the sky for one moment; and then they would crest the wave to descend sickeningly into yet another deep valley of water, pushed from behind by the foaming crest of the wave they had just run over.

The spume and spray from the waves joined the torrential rain which washed over the decks, stinging faces with such force that men cowered trying to cover themselves with any cloth to hand.

As the ketch rolled from side to side it would take on the sea, and the men on the waist deck would be up to their waists in water, in danger of being swept away; then the ship would begin to roll in the other direction. Anything that was not lashed down properly was taken overboard, and Duncan, watching this happen, was filled with dread. There had to be a lot of water pouring into the open cabin space.

He was unaware of the passing of time until he noticed a dim light in the east as the boat crested a wave. Dawn was coming, and to the relief of his numbed and exhausted senses he saw that the storm was passing to the north, leaving their tiny boat bobbing in an angry sea. As the light in the east slowly increased he began to notice more details. There was land to their south: a long, low, dark strip. He pointed towards it and nudged the captain, who had a death grip on the tiller but was almost asleep with exhaustion.

"Sir, I think that is Abukir," he shouted over the still keening wind. "We cleared it, but I don't know how!"

Williams shook his head and stared. "If you say so, Graham. I'm just glad to be alive at this moment." He gave Duncan a tired grin.

Duncan glanced forward towards the bows which were still twisting up and down with spray flying back over the miserable men crouched near the main mast. "She's low in the water!" he exclaimed.

Then he saw something that made his blood run cold. A quarter of a mile ahead there was a flurry of activity on the surface of the water. Peering forward he was horrified to see a body floating face down in the water, then another, and then a group of bodies. The corpses were half-naked, the rags of their clothing hanging off and swaying in the water, and they were being attacked by large fish that churned up the sea all around the indifferent dead.

"Ah God, help us!" he cried out involuntarily. "Captain, look over there!" Williams lifted his head and stared to where Duncan was pointing. The bodies and their accompanying carrion eaters were going to drift right by the ketch off the starboard bow by about fifty yards.

"Dear God! It's some of the Turkish dead from the battle! The current has taken them all this way out. Poor devils," Williams exclaimed, sounding just as appalled as Duncan. As he said this a large dark fin, Duncan assumed it belonged to a shark, slid past the ketch heading in the direction of the activity. Duncan found himself staring into its eye as it passed: black and dead and menacing. It joined the throng of other creatures feasting with a flurry of spray and agitated water. Duncan shuddered.

By now the rest of the crew members had noticed and were exclaiming and pointing. One even crossed himself. Then followed the cries of disgust as the wind changed direction slightly and brought the full stink of rotting flesh to their shocked senses. Slowly, the dead drifted by, and the men on the ketch, still covering their noses and mouths, thankfully turned away. There was a long silence as people digested the horror of what they had just witnessed.

"I heard thousands and thousands were killed on that day," Hotchkins said.

"It was a monumental slaughter, Mr Hotchkins," Captain Williams replied. "I have rarely witnesses such a thing. So many of them fled into the sea to escape the French, you see. These are but a few of those who drowned."

It seemed to Duncan that somehow the ghosts of Abukir had reached out yet again to disturb his peace of mind. He shook his head at the vivid memories of the panic, the terror in their distorted faces, and the slaughter he had witnessed. He would be haunted by those memories for a very long time to come.

Hotchkins glanced up from his huddled position in the lee of the cabin. "I can hear water sloshing about below, Sorr," he said. There was urgency in his tone. "We are fillin' up fast. The hole in our side let most of it in."

Duncan bellowed at the men in the waist of the vessel. "Bailers! We need bailers. Now!"

Several of the men heard him and scrambled to their feet, swaying with the erratic motion of the boat. "Get below, men. Do what you can, or we go to the bottom!" Duncan shouted.

Before long, buckets full of sea water were being passed rapidly up through the broken cabin to the men on deck to be dumped overboard.

Duncan searched the horizon for any other vessels and thought he saw a sail to the north. He shouted and pointed and another couple of men noticed. "Its a sail!" one shouted. "But ah've no idea what kind of vessel. Ship 'o war, perhaps?"

"Lets hope to God it's the *Theseus* and not a Frenchie," Williams remarked, "or we are all on our way back to the grand city of Alexandria."

The large vessel was visible on the horizon, with only its top sails set to allow it to ride out the storm. It was difficult for Duncan to tell whether its crew had noticed them but he changed course just enough to take the ketch towards the vessel. There was little choice now. He could not sail counter to the sea, which could still sink them in an unguarded moment, in the hope that a lookout might see them and come to investigate. The wind had abated somewhat but it was still too strong for them to raise another sail. Meanwhile the bailing continued at a frantic pace, for the ketch was wallowing in the water instead of floating high.

"We can dispense with the sea anchor now," Duncan said, and ordered two of the crew to cut the lines. The sail drifted off, looking like some great pale sea creature that had been driven to the surface by the agitated seas. The ketch began to move forward with a marked increase in speed.

"Still too early to get a larger sail up," Duncan said out loud.

"Her seams up in the bow area must have opened in the storm, Sorr. We can't drive her too hard, as that will bring in more water," Hotchkins remarked, as he scrambled painfully to his feet and observed the way the vessel rode in the sea.

"She would have taken on a lot of water through that hole," Captain Williams observed.

"Aye, and I hope that is all we have to worry about, Sorr," Hotchkins responded. "But I have a nasty feeling it ain't all that's wrong."

Duncan agreed with him. The bailing was not making a great difference, despite the energetic activity with the leather buckets. Then one of the men inside the cabin shouted and another relayed the request to Duncan.

"Sir, you are needed by the men in the cabin, Sir," he called over to the men at the tiller.

Duncan left the tiller with Captain Williams and Hotchkins and went to peer over the edge of the shattered wall of the cabin. Down in the well were three men up to their thighs in sloshing water. One looked up at him with a gaunt, exhausted look on his face. "She has started her seams somewhere up forward near the bow, Sir," the man said. "Fast as we fill the buckets more water comes in. We began with water at our knees but now it's almost a foot higher. Don't seem to matter how much we take out."

Duncan felt a tight feeling in his guts. They were sinking and he had no idea whether the ship on the horizon had even noticed them.

"Is there any way to get to the forward hold and stave it off with some plugs?" Duncan asked.

"Jonesy here took a dive to 'ave a look, Sorr. Couldn't get below the first deck. There's too much stuff floating about that could kill a man. Water's comin' up from several places and we can't get to the source of the leaks."

"Bugger and damnation and blast the Devil's balls to pieces!" Duncan muttered. He hadn't meant the men to hear him, but some did and despite their anxiety they snickered with amusement.

"Ye'r right, Sorr. Fock the Devil for doin' this te us," one of the men with an Irish accent stated. He got a nudge from his mate. "Yer don't swear in front of an orficer, Paddy," he admonished him sotto voice.

"Sorry, Sorr. Forgot me place," the unrepentant Paddy grinned.

Duncan took a deep breath.

"Do everything you can, men. If it gets too bad then get out of there."

"Aye aye, Sir," they responded in unison.

Duncan went back to the tiller and answered the mute question in Captain William's eyes. "We are sinking, Sir, and won't be able to make land at this rate." Duncan said in a low tone. His voice was tight with anger.

"We need to get their attention." Hotchkins jerked his thumb at the distant ship.

"I doubt if we have a single charge of powder that isn't soaked," Duncan said. On deck the tiny guns would be useless and half full of water, while below everything was submerged.

"Could we not rig a flag of some sort and get it onto the main mast?" Williams said, looking up at the swaying pole.

"Good idea, Sir. Its better than nothing and we don't have much in the way of options," Duncan responded. "Get the men to rig a line and we'll haul a sheet up to the top of the main mast, Hotchkins."

"Aye aye, Sorr."

"We need someone to get up to the top and hook a line to the block up there to use for the sheet," Duncan remarked. "I'll go."

"Much as you might want to, Midshipman, I am going to overrule you. You are in charge of this vessel and as such will not be risking your neck. One of the other men can get up there and carry out the task," Captain Williams told him in a firm tone that brooked no dissent.

Duncan opened his mouth to object, but by this time one of the crew men was already half way up the narrow stays, taking with him a line. He nearly ran up the wildly corkscrewing pole with the agility of a monkey and tied of the line before calling down. One of the large sheets was tied off quickly by the men on deck and the sailor at the top hauled it up, where it flapped wildly, almost dislodging him from his precarious perch while he tied it off. The ragged sheet then streamed out in the wind.

For long minutes every man on deck stared towards the ship in the distance. It remained a small, dark silhouette with a single white smudge at its top that appeared and disappeared at irregular intervals as the waves carried the ketch up and down.

Out of the corner of his eye Duncan noted with some despair that the men who had formerly been in the cabin were being helped out by their mates. The bedraggled and soaked men stood on the deck looking very dispirited. The one who had spoken to him before looked over to Duncan and shook his head. Duncan's heart sank. He could feel the whole vessel becoming more sluggish as the minutes went by. If no help arrived soon they would all be swimming.

Then one of the men with sharper eyes gave a shout. "It's making more sail. I can see there is more sail being set! God save us! There, 'is main and 'is topsails is on, and now 'is mizzen."

"Is it changing course for us?" called Hotchkins.

"Not sure, Sir." called back the same man. But then he pointed. "Dear Lord, I do believe it's coming about! It's comin' towards us!"

The ragged, soaked, and chilled men cheered and slapped each other on the back at the news. "Lord bless us, Sorr, but we might be all right!" Hotchkins said with a happy grin.

"Still some way off, though." Duncan observed. "It's going to be a close call." He glanced at the bow of the ketch, which didn't rise from a wave as fast as it used to. The water poured back over the fore hatch and streamed past the men on the deck. He thought he felt a shudder as the ship tried to right itself and only managed to so so very slowly.

"Bollocks," he said under his breath.

"What are you muttering about, Graham? Ye look peeved," Captain Williams asked. His eyes were red-rimmed and he looked haggard. "Can't swim, eh? Neither can any of those other gentlemen, I dare say. I've no desire to feed that bunch of sharks we just passed, either."

"Noo, while I don't like the idea of swimming, Sir," Graham replied giving a rueful shake of his head, "It's no that. My first command and it sinks beneath my bluddy feet!" he shook his head in disgust. "I just wanted to sail this vessel into Larnaca and claim some prize money, Sir," Duncan growled. "I could do with some."

Williams slapped his thigh and gave a bark of hoarse laughter. "Well I never. Listen, you young cockerel. There will be other opportunities for that, and don't forget that you saved some lives here. By the way, I will be very willing to teach you something about fencing, should the opportunity present itself."

"Fencing, Sir?"

"Oh yes, Graham. I have little doubt as to what was going on in the bushes back there on the beach. Very clumsy, from what I could tell. Those kind of things need to be finished within a minute, not all over the place. That's when the wrong person gets hurt." He chuckled. "I've a shrewd idea who it was you were scrapping with, too."

Duncan gaped but there was no time to respond, because another yell called their attention to the arrival of the ship, which, with main and top sails set, was descending upon their little craft at great speed.

The men on the ketch cheered as the war ship, *HMS Theseus*, itself hove to half a cable away and rapidly lowered a boat.

"Not before time either," Captain Williams remarked. "My feet were about to get wet!"

Duncan could now hear the water in the cabin below sloshing about, and when he went to peer over the wall it was a mere three feet from the upper deck. The boat was wallowing very low in the water, and if the waves had not been reduced to a choppy sea they would have been swamped and doubtless under water by now. As it was, he waited with mixed emotions as the long boat approached.

They were hailed by the officer in the bow. "Ahoy there! Are you Captain Williams and crew? We saw the flag."

"Yes, we damned well are, and get us off this thing, it's going down!" Captain Williams bellowed back with some asperity.

"Aye aye, Sir," called back the officer.

They were able to step easily across from the ketch to the longboat, which accommodated all of the men. Hotchkins was gently assisted aboard by his mates. He winced with pain at one point, then looked up at Captain Williams and Duncan, who were the last to leave the stricken vessel, and said, "We would still be rotting in a Froggie prison but for you, Sirs. Please accept our 'eartfelt thanks." The men around him chorused their agreement.

"Mum's the word about how this young man achieved it, eh?" Williams said, tapping his nose. The scruffy bunch of ex prisoners, huddled in the waist of the longboat, laughed and nodded their heads. "Mum's the word, Sorr." That received some puzzled looks from the lieutenant and his bosun, but no further questions were asked.

Without without further ceremony they were rowed across the intervening gap between the two vessels. Duncan sat in brooding silence near to Captain Williams and the officer, Lt Harrison, who was eager to know what had happened. While they talked Duncan glumly contemplated his first command as it wallowed lower and lower, giving off hissing sounds as though it resented being abandoned. It was under water with only its mast showing by the time they arrived at the side of the huge war ship.

After seeing Hotchkins up the side, the remainder of the bedraggled group followed Captain Williams up the ladder to the main deck, where they were greeted by Lt Spaulding, who knew the captain and welcomed him warmly.

"Sir Sidney Smith will be delighted that you made it, Sir. Although I imagine you could have wished the circumstances to be somewhat less, er... arduous? Looks like we were just in time, eh?" He chuckled, looking critically at their scarecrow appearance. "I dare say you would like to clean up, Sir. Please avail yourself of my cabin. The Captain's steward will find some clean clothes for you."

Captain Williams gave him a tired smile and gestured towards the disconsolate midshipman at his side, who gave a half bow. "I, we all owe it to Midshipman Graham here; it was he who steered us through the storm and enabled our escape."

"Mr. Graham? I had heard that you were missing." Spaulding gave Duncan a quizzical look, then turned to Williams with a look of enquiry on his face.

"Been with me all the time and has conducted himself with honor and courage and ... at all times with dignity." Captain Williams stated firmly.

Duncan turned his head towards the captain just in time to catch a very slight lowering of his right eyelid.

THE END

AUTHOR'S NOTE

The French invasion of Egypt was a hugely ambitious campaign but one that promised Napoleon enormous rewards, for himself but also France. His determination to build France an empire and to even take India from the British brought about a truly remarkable series of events that in their way matched the conquests of Rome in an earlier time. Napoleon was a superb leader with equally capable generals to assist him in this campaign.

While he conquered Egypt relatively easily with his highly disciplined army he had not taken into consideration that the British would side with the Turks and thwart his attempt to take Acre, a milestone which he simply could not bypass on his way to taking Constantinople itself. It might have been better for him and his army if they had stayed in Egypt and explored the Upper Nile, where there were treasures beyond imagining waiting for his Savants to discover.

Sir Sydney Smith is the 'other' great British admiral (actually he was a Commodore at Abukir) of the period who used his ships at the siege of Acre as mobile heavy artillery, hence preventing history from taking a totally different course from that which eventually occurred.

It reflects upon the brilliance of Napoleon and his remarkable, hardened army of Infantrie, Grenadiers and cavalry that, thwarted though they might have been, and exhausted from their awful retreat across the Sinai desert, nonetheless these same men could recover sufficiently to force march from Cairo and conclusively defeat a vast army of Turks who had landed on Abukir with the aid of Sir Sidney's ships.

This particular battle does not reflect too well upon Sir Sidney, because had he investigated the area around Abukir he would have found out quickly enough that there was no place for his ships to be deployed usefully. There is little doubt that had he been able to bring his big ships with their guns to bear then Abukir might have gone to the Turks. As it was it disintegrated into a spectacular rout which was the end of any further attempts by the combined British and Turkish forces to take back Egypt. The story of Abukir is rendered as faithfully as possible as a factual account of an historic event. Naturally enough there are many accounts of this battle, but I have tried to reproduce the essence of what actually happened with some quotes from officers who were actually there at the time.

Sir Sidney really was made a member of the order of the Templars by the archbishop of Nicosia. That is a matter of record and I have described it as it as such. Deservedly so, because he and he alone, with a very small squadron of ships, kept the east end of the Mediterranean clear of French ships and Napoleon from his vast ambitions.

I have taken some license with the interaction between Sir Sidney and the Pasha and his officers, but for the most part there was room for Midshipman Graham as one of the many junior officers on the British war ships at that battle. He is a figment of my imagination, as is Captain Williams, although Sir Sydney did have spies in his employ who spoke several languages, including Arabic. Graham was put there to bring a more personal and lighter side to the whole, and I hope that he succeeded. We might not be done with this young scamp as yet.

James Boschert

James Boschert grew up in the then colony of Malaya in the early fifties. He learned first-hand about terrorism while there as the Communist insurgency was in full swing. His school was burnt down and the family, while traveling, narrowly survived an ambush, saved by a Gurkha patrol, which drove off the insurgents.

He went on to join the British army serving in remote places like Borneo and Oman. Later he spent five years in Iran before the revolution, where he played polo with the Iranian Army, developed a passion for the remote Assassin castles found in the high mountains to the North, and learned to understand and speak the Farsi language.

Escaping Iran during the revolution, he went on to become an engineer and now lives in Arizona on a small ranch with his family and animals.

IF YOU ENJOYED THIS BOOK

Please write a review.
This is important to the author and helps to get the word out to others.
Visit

PENMORE PRESS
www.penmorepress.com

All Penmore Press books are available directly through our website, amazon.com, Barnes and Noble and Nook, Sony Reader, Apple iTunes, Kobo books and via leading bookshops across the United States, Canada, the UK, Australia and Europe.

Force 12 in German Bight

by
James Boschert

Considering that oil and gas have been flowing from under the North Sea for the best part of half a century, it is perhaps surprising that more writers have not taken the uncompromising conditions that are experienced in this area – which extends from the north of Scotland to the coasts of Norway and Germany – for the setting of a novel. James Boschert's latest redresses the balance.

The book takes its title from the name of an area regularly referred to in the legendary BBC Shipping Forecast, one which experiences some of the worst weather conditions around the British Isles. It is a fast-paced story which smacks of authenticity in every line. A world of hard men, hard liquor, hard drugs and cold-blooded murder. The reality of the setting and the characters, ex-military men from both sides of the Atlantic, crooked wheeler-dealers, and Danish detectives, male and female, are all in on the action.

This is not story telling akin to a latter day Bulldog Drummond, nor a James Bond, but simply a snortingly good yarn which will jangle the nerve ends, fill your nose with the smell of salt and diesel oil, your ears with the deafening sound of machinery aboard a monster pipe-dredging ship and, above all, make you remember never to underestimate the power of the sea.

–Roger Paine, former Commander, Royal Navy .

PENMORE PRESS
www.penmorepress.com

OTHER TALON BOOKS BY JAMES BOSCHERT

ASSASSINS OF ALAMUT
BY
JAMES BOSCHERT

An Epic Novel of Persia and Palestine in the Time of the Crusades

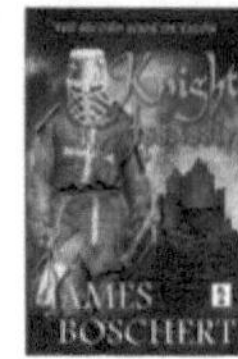

Knight Assassin

The second book of Talon

by

James Boschert

Assassination

in

Al Qahira

James Boschert

GREEK FIRE
BY
JAMES BOSCHERT

A Falcon

Flies

by

James Boschert

The fifth book of Talon

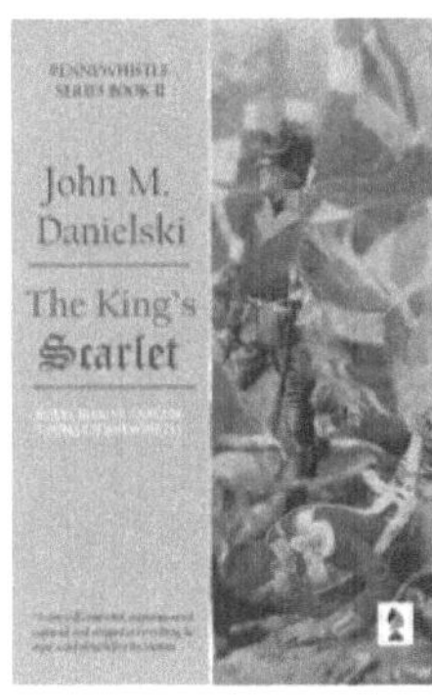

KING'S SCARLET

BY

JOHN DANIELSKI

Chivalry comes naturally to Royal Marine captain Thomas Pennywhistle, but in the savage Peninsular War, it's a luxury he can ill afford. Trapped behind enemy lines with vital dispatches for Lord Wellington, Pennywhistle violates orders when he saves a beautiful stranger, setting off a sequence of events that jeopardize his mission. The French launch a massive manhunt to capture him. His Spanish allies prove less than reliable. The woman he rescued has an agenda of her own that might help him along, if it doesn't get them all killed.

A time will come when, outmaneuvered, captured, and stripped of everything, he must stand alone before his enemies. But Pennywhistle is a hard man to kill and too bloody obstinate to concede defeat.

PENMORE PRESS
www.penmorepress.com

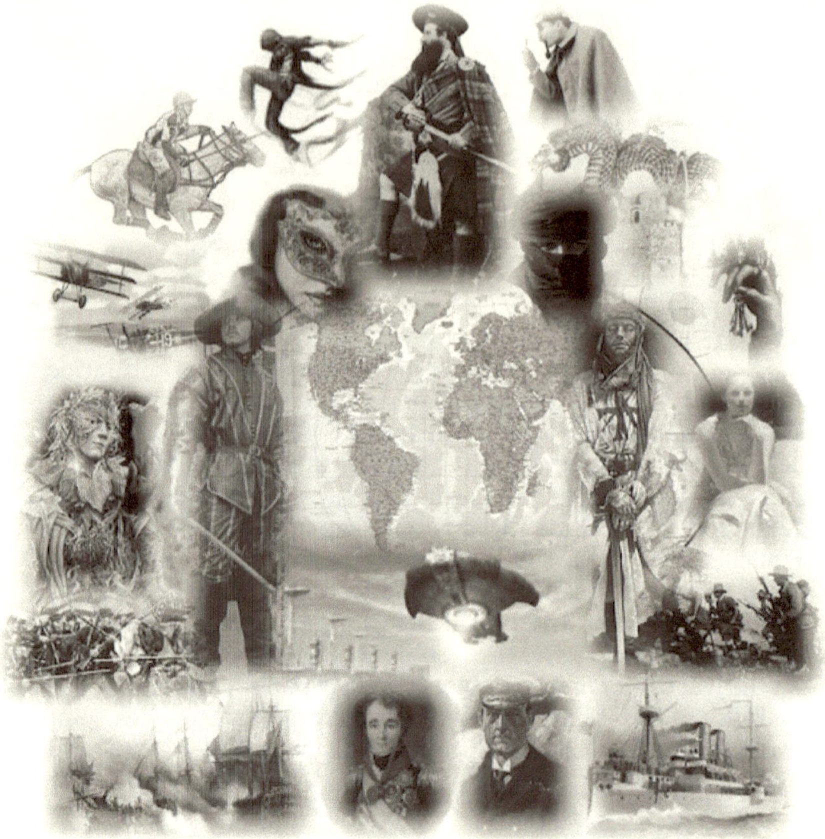

Penmore Press

Challenging, Intriguing, Adventurous, Historical and Imaginative

www.penmorepress.com